QUIET BLOOM

STONEBOUND
BOOK 2

N.B. CROSS

NIMBUS BOOKS

For my family,
who remind me that love survives the quiet seasons too.

PROLOGUE

The stones shift beneath their feet, wet shale clicking like teeth. He keeps his fingers laced through hers, both their palms damp from the fog that rolls in thick off the water. The beach stretches gray in both directions, narrowing where the tide pushes close to the cliff face.

She pulls her jacket tighter with her free hand. The fabric is already heavy with moisture, beading on the nylon surface. They've been walking for twenty minutes, maybe more. Time feels different here at dusk, when the horizon dissolves into nothing and the gulls have gone quiet.

"Watch the driftwood," he says, guiding her around a bleached log half-buried in stones. The wood looks like bone in this light, smooth and pale. More pieces scatter across the tide line, some massive as fallen trees, others small enough to pocket. His grandmother used to collect the interesting ones, arrange them on her mantel like artifacts. But these seem different somehow. Too uniform in their weathering. Too deliberately placed.

The fog presses closer. It clings to their clothes, their hair, leaves salt on their lips. The air tastes metallic. Behind them, Marrowick's lights blur to suggestions through the haze.

Ahead, the beach curves toward the point where ships used to wreck, though he can't see that far now.

"Look." She stops walking, tugs his hand.

The tidepool sits just beyond the reach of the waves, caught in a depression of rock. At first, he thinks it's just the usual trapped water, the surface slick with algae film. But there's light beneath. Pale and cold, pulsing with a rhythm that doesn't match the sea.

They step closer. The smell hits them both at once, not quite rot, not quite earth. Something between. Sour but oddly sweet, like fruit left too long in the sun. She covers her nose with her sleeve, but he breathes it in, curious despite himself.

The mushrooms cluster along the pool's edge, sprouting from cracks in the stone. They're nothing like the ones that grow in the woods behind town. These are translucent, almost crystalline, with caps that catch and hold the dying light. Beneath the water, more bloom in delicate formations. They pulse together, a slow heartbeat of luminescence.

"What is...what is that?" She whispers. Her voice sounds too loud in the stillness. Even the waves seem quieter here, as if the water itself holds its breath.

He crouches beside the pool. Up close, the fungi look even stranger. Veins run through the caps, dark threads that branch and split like blood vessels. The stalks are thick, fleshy. When a drop of condensation rolls off one cap, it leaves a trail that glows briefly before fading.

"Don't," she says, but there's no real conviction in it. She's crouching too now, drawn by the same fascination that pulls at him.

"They're beautiful." The words come out without thought. It's true, though. There's something hypnotic about the way they pulse, the way the light moves through them. Like watching fire, or clouds. Pattern without pattern.

She laughs, nervous and quiet. "Beautiful and probably toxic."

"Probably." He shifts his weight, stones grinding beneath his knees. The fog has thickened enough that he can barely see ten feet in any direction. Just them, the pool, the strange garden beneath its surface. "Dare you to touch one."

"You first."

It's an old game between them, this pushing at boundaries. Usually over small things like sneaking into the abandoned mill, staying out past curfew, stealing kisses in her father's workshop. But this feels different. Heavier somehow.

He extends his hand toward the water. His fingers hover an inch above the surface. The glow intensifies, as if responding to his proximity. She grabs his other arm, not to stop him but to steady herself, or maybe him. Her grip is tight enough to hurt.

The water is perfectly still. No ripples, despite the wind that pushes at their backs. No movement except the slow pulse of light from below. He can see his reflection, distorted and pale, and beneath it, the mushrooms reaching upward like hands.

"Do you hear that?" she whispers.

He listens. There's no sound except his own breathing, her breathing, the distant suggestion of waves. But she's right. There's something else. Not a sound exactly, but a vibration. It moves through the rocks, through his bones, sets his teeth on edge.

His fingertips break the surface.

The water is warm. Too warm for any tidepool this far north. It feels thick, viscous, like oil but lighter. The mushrooms pulse faster, their light spreading outward in rings. And beneath them, deep in the pool where the rock should be, something moves.

Not the lazy drift of seaweed or the scuttle of crabs. This movement has purpose, intelligence. Tendrils rise through the murk, pale as the mushrooms above, reaching toward his hand. They stop just short of his fingers, swaying with that same deliberate rhythm.

She pulls at his arm. "Something's wrong."

He knows she's right. Every instinct tells him to pull back, to run, to get as far from this place as possible. But he can't move. The tendrils are beautiful too, in their awful way. They dance just beneath his fingers, waiting.

The fog closes in completely. The beach, the cliffs, even the driftwood disappears. There's only the pool, the light, the warm water that seems to pulse with its own heartbeat. Her hand on his arm is the only thing that feels real, solid, safe.

But even that won't last long.

The warmth spreads up his arm, but her grip tightens, fingernails digging crescents into his skin. Between their clasped hands, something pushes upward, white as chalk, thick as his thumb.

The stalk breaks through their interlocked fingers with the wet sound of splitting fruit. It rises fast, too fast, forcing their hands apart with a strength that shouldn't exist in something that looks so delicate. She stumbles backward. He tries to pull his other hand from the water but can't. The tendrils have wrapped around his wrist, not tight, not painful, just there. Holding.

The stalk keeps growing. Two feet, three feet, swaying slightly though there's no wind. At its tip, a bulb swells, translucent skin stretching thin. He can see structures inside that look like chambers and vessels, things that pulse with their own circulation. The smell intensifies. Sweet rot, copper pennies, earth after rain.

She reaches for him, then stops. Her eyes are wide, reflecting the pool's glow. The bulb splits.

Not violently. It opens like a flower, four perfect segments peeling back to reveal a cavity lined with what looks like velvet. Pale velvet that breathes. Then the spores come.

They lift in a cloud, each particle catching the light like

dust in a sunbeam. But these don't drift aimlessly. They rise with purpose, spreading outward in a perfect sphere. The fog seems to welcome them, drawing them in, mixing them with its own moisture until the air itself glows faintly.

He tries to hold his breath. She turns her head away. But the spores are already there, already in their noses, their mouths, coating their tongues with a taste like old metal. His lungs burn. He has to breathe. Has to.

The first inhale brings them deep inside. They settle in his chest, spreading warmth that isn't warmth, comfort that isn't comfort. His vision shifts. Colors drain away except for the pool's light, which burns brighter, more beautiful than before. His pupils dilate until his eyes are mostly black.

She makes a sound. Not quite a word, not quite a gasp. Her mouth opens and closes like she's trying to speak, but nothing comes. Her hand rises to her throat, fingers pressing against vocal cords that won't respond. He tries to say her name. His lips move. His tongue moves. But the sound that emerges is wrong, hollow, like wind through empty rooms.

The tendrils release his wrist.

He doesn't run. Doesn't even step back. His body isn't his anymore, not entirely. He watches his own hand reach toward her, watches her hand reach back, but they're movements are perverse. Jerky. Like marionettes with tangled strings.

She takes a step forward. Her foot catches on a stone, but she doesn't stumble. The movement just... adjusts. Compensates. Her leg bends at an angle that should hurt, but her face stays blank, serene. Another step. Another. Each one bringing her closer to the pool.

He wants to grab her, pull her back, but his arms won't obey. They hang at his sides, fingers twitching with small, purposeless movements. All he can do is watch as she steps into the water.

It rises to her ankles, her calves. The mushrooms pulse faster, brighter, welcoming. The tendrils that held him before rise again, but now there are dozens of them, hundreds, a garden of pale fingers reaching up from depths that shouldn't exist in a tidepool. They wrap around her legs with delicate precision. Not violent. Almost tender.

She doesn't struggle. Her face is calm, empty, eyes reflecting nothing but light. The tendrils climb higher. Her thighs, her waist. They're pulling her down, but slowly, gently, like a mother putting a child to bed.

His own feet are moving now. Not toward her but parallel, to another part of the pool he hadn't noticed before. It's deeper here. The water darker despite the glow. Things move beneath the surface. Not tendrils but something else. Something larger.

The roots find his ankles first. They push up through the gaps between stones, thin at first, then thickening as they climb. His jeans tear. The roots don't. They spiral around his calves, his knees, holding him in place as more emerge. These wrap his wrists, his forearms. One circles his throat, not choking, just present. A collar of living wood.

She's waist-deep now. Her jacket floats around her like wings. The tendrils have reached her chest, her shoulders. They cradle her head, fingers in her hair, against her cheeks. Her eyes close. Her mouth opens slightly, and spores drift from between her lips, adding to the cloud that surrounds them both.

The fog is so thick now he can barely see her. Just the suggestion of her shape, the glow of the pool, the persistent pulse of the mushrooms. His own vision is failing. Not darkness but something else. A different kind of seeing. He perceives the network with connections running beneath the beach, through the stones, into the sea. The pool is just one node. There are others. Many others.

The roots pull him down. His knees hit water. It's still warm, still thick, but now it feels right. Like coming home.

Like something he's been missing without knowing it. He can't remember the girl's name now, can't remember his own.

The fog swallows everything. The beach, the stones, their bodies. Only the sound remains. Not waves. Not wind. Something deeper. A heartbeat that isn't a heartbeat. A breath that isn't breathing.

Then even that fades, leaving only the tide's return and the cries of gulls that won't come close, won't land, won't feed on what the sea has taken.

The pool sits empty again, its surface still as glass. The mushrooms pulse slower now, satisfied. Beneath the water, new growths begin to form. Pale and patient. Waiting.

CHAPTER
ONE

The swamp mist threads between the cedars like something alive, and Vincent watches it from his bedroom window, one palm flat against the cold glass. His fingers drum a rhythm he doesn't recognize like nervous energy with nowhere to go. Outside, Duswood breathes its familiar rot-sweet air, the smell that's lived in his clothes since birth.

The suitcase waits on Vincent's bed like an accusation. He packed it last night with more care than usual, folding each shirt with precise corners, rolling socks into tight balls. As if neatness could make this vacation easier, could transform it into something ordinary.

The clothes stare at him from the suitcase. Too organized. Too ready. He fights the urge to dump them all out, to crawl back into bed and pretend tomorrow isn't coming. But tomorrow always comes. That's one thing he learned from watching his mother count days is that time moves forward whether you're ready or not.

A floorboard creaks in the hallway. He knows that particular sound, the way his mother steps when she's trying to be careful. Everything about her is careful now. Careful movements, careful words, careful hope that she holds like something fragile between cupped palms.

Angela appears in the doorway, and he sees her in profile first and then she pauses, gathering herself before fully entering his space. Her hair needs dyeing again, the roots showing pale against the faded blonde. She's wearing one of her cardigans, the blue one with the missing button she keeps meaning to fix.

"One hundred fifty six," she says under her breath, so quiet he almost misses it. "No, one hundred fifty seven."

One hundred fifty seven days. She doesn't think he knows she counts them, but he does. Every morning, every night. Sometimes in between when things get hard. Her fingers find the edge of her sleeve, worrying the fabric between thumb and forefinger.

"We're leaving tomorrow," she says, louder now, addressing the words to the space between them. Not quite looking at him, not quite looking away.

Vincent turns from the window but keeps his hand on the sill, needing the anchor. "I know."

"Your suitcase…"

"It's packed."

She nods, a small, quick movement. Her eyes drift to the open suitcase, taking in the neat rows of folded clothes. Something flickers across her face that suggests surprise, maybe, or recognition of effort she wasn't expecting.

"This feels forced," Vincent says, the words coming out harder than intended. "The whole thing. Why do we need to go to Marrowick? Why do we need to spend time with his family?"

Angela's hand moves from her sleeve to her collar, adjusting something that doesn't need adjusting. "It's not… forced isn't the right word."

"Then what is?"

She looks at him directly for the first time, and he sees the work it takes. The recovery isn't just about not drinking. It's about looking people in the eye again, about believing she deserves to take up space in a room.

"Important," she says. "It's important to me, Vincent. Elias and I..." She trails off, searching for words that won't sound like betrayal to either of them. "We're trying to build something. And that means knowing each other's..." She stops again, her fingers back at her sleeve.

"Each other's what?"

"Contexts," she finishes, the word sounding borrowed, like something Elias might have said. "The places that made us who we are."

Vincent wants to tell her that even a short time away from Duswood feels like they're risking the fragile peace they've fought for. But the words stick in his throat, too hard to say without sounding foolish.

A presence shifts in the doorway behind Angela, and Vincent knows without looking that it's Mira. She appears without announcement, as usual, filling spaces with a quiet that feels intentional rather than empty. Angela glances back, a quick, nervous motion, then steps aside to let Mira through.

Mira enters wearing one of her thrifted sweaters, the red one with holes at the elbows that she refuses to mend. Her hair is tied back today, exposing the pale curve of her neck. She looks between them, taking in the tension that hangs in the air like humidity before a storm.

Vincent searches her face for support, for agreement that this trip is a mistake, that they should stay where things make sense even when they don't. But Mira only shrugs, the movement barely disturbing the fabric of her sweater. Neither agreement nor disagreement. Just acceptance of what is.

"The fog will be different there," she says, which isn't really an answer to anything but feels like one anyway.

Angela nods as if this makes perfect sense, her hand

finally still at her side. "We should leave by nine. We might be able to get to North Dakota tomorrow."

She retreats from the doorway with that same careful gait, counting something under her breath that could be steps, maybe, or heartbeats, or the seconds until tomorrow becomes today. Vincent listens to her footsteps fade down the hall, the soft click of her bedroom door closing.

Mira stays, moving to stand beside him at the window. Together they watch the mist curl through the cedars, shape and reshape itself into suggestions of meaning that dissolve before they can be named.

————

The path down to the tracks is one Vincent's feet know by heart. Each loose stone and broken rail tie burned into muscle memory. He walks it now with hands shoved deep in his pockets, shoulders hunched against the evening chill that drapes everything in Duswood like heavy cloth. The pines lean close here, their trunks forming a corridor that turns the pale light green and restless.

He smells the steel long before he hears it: that sharp tang of rails warming in the late afternoon air. Some folks hate it, but to Vincent it's as familiar as breathing. It's the town's heartbeat, the rhythm by which he measures everything else.

Jayce is already there, perched on a rotten wooden tie that bridges the two tracks. His back is to Vincent, broad shoulders framed in a worn denim jacket, but of course he heard Vincent coming. Jayce always hears everything. It's a habit they sharpened early on, back when every sound could mean trouble.

"Look who made parole," Jayce says without turning.

Vincent slides onto the tie beside him, a few inches of space left between. Close enough that his shoulder could brush Jayce's if either wanted more comfort. Far enough that they both keep the pretense of just two guys on the tracks.

"Figured I'd at least say goodbye."

Jayce snorts. "Goodbye makes it sound like you're dead." His voice tries for lightness but fails; Vincent can hear it in the slight tremor, the way he frowns down the rail.

Vincent watches a breath of steam curl off his friend's jacket. "Mom needs me to go with," he says. "This trip with Elias…she's convinced it'll change things."

"Your mom's glad, I get that." Jayce turns finally, eyes steady on Vincent. "But two weeks is a long time. You're going to miss Duswood. Duswood will miss you."

They both grin, but there's more in Jayce's look than teasing. He notices details: the new threadbare cuff on Vincent's jacket, the way his boots are scuffed in the same spot, the loose knot in his tie-back of hair.

"Someone's got to keep an eye on this place," Jayce says, hand drifting to his side as if to reassure himself. "Make sure no one goes crazy."

Vincent watches a fire fly drift by, its yellow-green pulse briefly illuminating the air between them before disappearing into the darkness beyond the tracks. "I'll be back before school starts," he promises.

"Yeah." Jayce's gaze flicks down the track, where it disappears into mist and early light. "School starts in two weeks."

They ease into silence, listening to a bird's call that echoes like someone clearing their throat. Vincent thinks about all the nights they spent here, lying on these ties, talking about futures that felt as far off as the horizon.

"You ever think of leaving for good?" Vincent asks softly. "Not just town, but… everything?"

Jayce laughs, but it's hollow. "Where would I go?

Duswood's in my blood. I've got roots here." He gestures at the horizon. "If I'm gone, what's gonna keep Duswood from drifting off the map?"

They both know the answer doesn't lie in jokes. It's in the space between words, in the way Jayce's shoulders tense when a cold wind breezes through his jacket. It's in Vincent's chest, tight with something similar to excitement, fear, loyalty, guilt, all tangled.

"My mom's counting on this," Vincent says. "She wants to try something new. For us… and her sobriety."

Jayce nods slowly, as if weighing that. "She's right," he says. "But don't get too soft out west. City folks don't understand places like this, or the people who grow up here."

Vincent stands, and Jayce does the same. For a moment they face each other, two friends shaped by swamp air and late-night dares, knowing the same things in the same way.

"Call me if you need anything," Jayce says, pressing his shoulder into Vincent's hard enough to leave a bruise. His grip lingers the check enough that Vincent knows he's real, he's here, he'll be okay.

"I will."

Jayce steps back onto the ballast, already heading down the embankment toward home. "Don't disappear," he calls over his shoulder.

"I won't," Vincent answers.

He watches Jayce's silhouette shrink between the pines, swallowed by evening mist. The rails solid under his boots, and Vincent feels the pull of them almost like a voice that's steady, insistent, familiar. But he turns toward the path home, toward packed bags and his mother's hope.

The tang of steel and pine clings to his clothes. He knows it'll linger long after he's gone or maybe forever. Maybe that's the point: carrying this place with you, even when you're in a car heading west, toward new promises and unknown roads ahead.

Angela sets each plate with the kind of precision that comes from counting; four plates, four forks, four knives, everything in its place like a ritual against chaos. Her hands don't shake anymore, not like they used to, but Vincent sees the effort in her movements, the deliberate care that makes each gesture a small victory. She's using the good plates, the ones that usually live in the cabinet above the refrigerator, gathering dust.

Elias stands in the kitchen doorway like he's not sure he's allowed to enter. His pressed clothes make him look like a gap in the room, an absence rather than a presence. Everything about him is pressed and proper, his crisp collar, clean cuffs, and shoes that reflect the overhead light. He looks like he's perpetually dressed for an appointment, which Vincent supposes makes sense, given his profession.

"Can I help with anything?" Elias asks, his voice formal, words carefully pronounced.

"No, I've...I've got it," Angela says, adjusting a fork that doesn't need adjusting. "Almost ready."

The kitchen fills with the smell of roasted chicken and something else that might be rosemary, maybe, an herb Angela never used to cook with. New recipes for a new life. Vincent takes his usual seat, and Mira slides in beside him, her presence immediately softening the sharp edges of his discomfort.

Dinner is a study in careful navigation. The scrape of forks against plates sounds too loud, each clink of glass against wood a small percussion in the silence. Elias cuts his chicken into precise, even pieces, chewing thoroughly before swallowing. He eats like someone who understands the mechanics of consumption but takes no pleasure in it.

"The drive tomorrow should take approximately nine hours," Elias says, his voice filling the quiet with unnecessary information. "We will need to stop a few times for fuel and food."

"That's good," Angela says quickly, too quickly. "Good to know."

Vincent watches his mother's eyes dart to Elias after every sentence, checking his reaction, gauging whether she's said the right thing. Her hand hovers near her water glass, fingers tapping a nervous rhythm against the table. It's painful to watch, this careful dance of two damaged people trying to find a way to fit together.

"The weather should be clear," Elias continues, as if weather is a safe topic, neutral ground where nothing can go wrong. "Though Marrowick tends toward rain this time of year. Expect that when we get closer to the coast."

"Vincent likes rain," Angela offers, glancing at her son with something like hope.

Vincent doesn't respond. He does like rain, but not the way she means it, not as small talk to smooth over awkwardness. He likes the way rain in Duswood smells like earth and green and decay, the way it makes the swamp rise and breathe. Marrowick rain will be different, salt-touched and foreign.

Mira eats in her characteristic quiet, cutting her food into small, deliberate bites. She doesn't fill the silences or try to ease the tension. She simply exists within it, unperturbed, like someone watching a play they've seen before.

"Your daughter seems..." Angela starts, then stops, searching for the right word to describe Mira.

"Composed," Elias finishes. "Yes. She has always been that way. Even as a child."

It's the most human thing Vincent's heard him say, a glimpse of father beneath the clinical mask. But the moment passes quickly, Elias returning to his chicken in its bite-sized pieces.

After dinner, after the careful clearing of plates and Angela's insistence that she'll handle the dishes alone, Vincent knows, marking another sober evening completed. He finds Mira on the porch. She's sitting on the top step, arms wrapped around her knees, looking out at the cedars that crowd the yard's edge.

"It will be different there," she says without preamble, repeating her earlier words but with new weight.

Vincent sits beside her, their knees almost touching. "Different how?"

She tilts her head, considering. "The sadness is older. Wore into the stones. Here it's still sharp, still cutting. There it's smooth. Polished."

He doesn't ask how she knows this. Mira knows things the way some people know weather patterns or bird migrations. Instinctively, bodily, without need for explanation.

"Are you worried?" he asks.

"No." She turns to look at him, her dark eyes steady. "Are you?"

"I don't know."

"That's honest."

They sit in comfortable silence, watching the mist begin its evening rise from the swamp, creeping between the trees like something searching. Tomorrow feels both too close and impossibly far away.

———

Morning arrives gray and damp, the kind of Duswood dawn that makes everything feel underwater. Vincent loads his suitcase into the trunk of Elias's pristine sedan, the car looking lost in their driveway, too clean for a place where everything is touched by moss and moisture.

Angela checks everything twice: the locked front door, the windows, the mail she's asked the neighbor to collect. She counts under her breath, and Vincent catches fragments: "Keys, wallet, phone. Another day tomorrow." Her sobriety and her preparations tangled together in a litany of careful control.

"Do you have everything?" she asks Vincent for the third time.

"Yeah, Mom."

She nods, pulling her cardigan tighter despite the morning's warmth. "Good. That's good."

Elias starts the car with barely a sound, the engine purring like something well-maintained and foreign to Duswood's usual symphony of struggling motors and rust. Vincent takes the back seat, Mira sliding in beside him. Angela sits in front, her hands folded in her lap, fingers intertwined so tight her knuckles go white.

As they pull away from the house, Vincent turns to watch through the rain-spotted rear window. Duswood recedes slowly, leaving behind their house with its peeling paint and crooked mailbox, then the street with its familiar cracks and puddles, then the cedar trees that mark the town's edge. The swamp mist rises behind them, curling up from the dark spaces between trees like fingers, like a hand waving goodbye or reaching out to pull them back.

He watches until they round the bend and Duswood disappears, swallowed by green and gray and distance. The smell of it lingers in his clothes, in his hair, a reminder that some places never really let you go. They just allow you to stretch the tether, to test how far you can run before it snaps you back.

The car moves west, toward Marrowick and its promised different sadness, its polished stones and salt-touched rain. Vincent settles into his seat, feeling the pull of home already, that ache of separation that tells him he'll return. He always returns. Duswood makes sure of that.

CHAPTER
TWO

The coast road curves like a wound through gray rock and grayer sky, and Vincent watches rain race down the window in rivulets that branch and merge and branch again. Each droplet finds its own path down the glass, some fast, some slow, some joining together before the wiper blade sweeps them away. The car feels smaller with every mile, the air inside thick with recycled breath and the chemical smell of Elias's air freshener trying to mask something older, damper.

"Look at those waves," Angela says, her voice pitched too bright, too eager. "They're so much bigger than I expected. Different from Lake Michigan back home."

Her fingers tap against her knee. Three taps, pause, three taps. Vincent recognizes the pattern. She's counting something, maybe heartbeats, maybe seconds, maybe the days since her last drink. One hundred sixty now, if she's still keeping track the way she was yesterday. Her other hand grips the door handle, knuckles pale.

"The Pacific is more volatile than the Great Lakes," Elias says, his voice flat as medical dictation. "Different weather patterns. Different geology."

Vincent catches his mother's quick glance toward Elias, the way she searches his face for approval or interest or anything beyond that clinical distance. She finds nothing. Elias holds the wheel in a death grip at ten and two, just like driver's ed, but with his arms locked, elbows sharp, neck stiff as a board. He doesn't so much steer as impose his will upon the sedan, knifing down the slick curves with a calm that's almost menacing. Every bend of the highway is a challenge, and he answers each with a subtle lean, accelerator feathered, never overcorrecting, never hesitating. He takes the next swerve faster than Vincent's stomach can process, and in the tight silence that follows, Vincent imagines the tires skimming the edge of the asphalt, the world one mistake from spinning out.

No one in the car speaks. Angela's tapping has stopped, replaced by the faint rasp of her thumb rubbing the upholstery raw. Mira looks through her reflection in the rear passenger window, watching the cliffs flash gold and gunmetal as the headlights slice through mist. Sometimes, when the car banks left, her shoulder pins against Vincent's, but she doesn't move away and he doesn't ask her to. Her hair smells like rain and rosemary, not like the saccharine shampoo from the Walgreens back in Illinois, but something wild grown in the cracks of a salt-bleached town.

A road sign whips by, unreadable in the gloom. Marrowick: 7 miles. For a moment, Vincent thinks about asking how much longer, but the words die before reaching his throat. Elias's attention is so total, so consuming, that to interrupt would feel like tapping a surgeon on the shoulder mid-incision. Instead, Vincent watches Elias's face reflected in the windshield with his jaw clenched, eyes cold, as if daring the coastline to throw its worst at them.

The windshield wipers beat their steady rhythm. Back and forth. Back and forth. The sound fills the spaces between words, between breaths. Rain hammers the roof in waves, sometimes gentle, sometimes violent, as if the sky can't decide how angry it wants to be.

"There's a lighthouse," Elias announces, lifting one finger from the wheel to point. "Built in 1892. Still operational, though automated now."

Vincent looks at the lighthouse while keeping one eye on the road as if that would help Elias stay on it. The lighthouse stands on a promontory of black rock, its white tower barely visible through the rain and mist. It looks lonely. It looks like it's been lonely for a very long time. Not like the water tower back in Duswood, which at least has the company of cedars and telephone wires. This lighthouse has nothing but stone and salt and endless gray water.

"It's beautiful," Angela says quickly. Too quickly. Her fingers tap faster now. Four taps, pause, four taps.

Beside Vincent, Mira shifts slightly, her first movement in twenty minutes. She's been watching everything with that particular stillness she has, the way she can make herself into a piece of furniture or a shadow when she wants to disappear. Her reflection in the window overlaps with the rain, making her face fracture into a dozen incomplete versions.

"The fog here tastes different," she says, so quiet Vincent almost misses it.

Angela turns in her seat, that nervous smile flickering. "What do you mean, honey?"

Mira doesn't answer right away. She rarely does. Words come to her like birds to a feeder, cautious and selective. "Salt," she finally says. "And something else. Something old."

The car passes a rusted sign: MARROWICK - 3 MILES. The letters are barely legible, eaten away by years of salt air and neglect. Vincent feels something tighten in his chest. Three miles from this new place that's supposed to mean something, supposed to change something. Three miles from his mother's fresh start with this man who speaks in facts instead of feelings.

"There's the old pier," Elias says, pointing again with that same mechanical gesture. "Used to be the main fishing dock before the new harbor was built. Abandoned now."

Vincent sees it through the rain, a skeleton of rotted pilings stretching into the churning water. Some of the posts still standing, others collapsed into the waves like broken teeth. Seabirds huddle on what remains, dark shapes against the gray.

The salt smell grows stronger, seeping through the car's vents despite Elias's attempt to keep the outside world at bay. It's nothing like the swamp smell of Duswood, that mixture of mud and green and decay that Vincent knows like his own skin. This smell is sharper, cleaner, but somehow more threatening. Like it wants to scour everything down to bone.

Angela's hand moves from the door handle to her collar, adjusting the cardigan that doesn't need adjusting. "We should be there soon," she says to no one in particular. "Elias, your sister knows we're coming today?"

"I informed her of our estimated arrival time," Elias replies. "Between two and three o'clock, accounting for weather conditions."

The way he says it, like he's reading from a report. Vincent wonders if Elias talks to his patients this way, if he describes cavities and root canals with the same detached precision. No wonder Mira grew up the way she did, learning to speak in riddles and metaphors as if regular words might turn clinical in her mouth.

The rain intensifies, and Elias adjusts the wiper speed. The rhythm changes, faster now, more urgent. Through the water streaming down his window, Vincent catches glimpses of the town approaching. Low buildings hunched against the weather, their shapes indistinct and unwelcoming. A few boats in what must be the new harbor, bobbing like toys in the rough water.

"One sixty," Angela whispers, so soft only Vincent hears it. Her counting again. Her lifeline.

Mira's hand finds Vincent's on the seat between them. Not holding, just touching. A reminder that he's not alone in this strange car heading toward this strange place. Her fingers are cold, but the contact grounds him, keeps him from floating away into the gray nothing outside.

The windshield wipers beat on. The rain drums harder. Marrowick draws closer with each mile, and Vincent feels the weight of it pressing against the windows, trying to get in.

The shape comes from nowhere, or from fog, which amounts to the same thing. One moment the road ahead is empty except for rain and mist, the next a deer lurches into the headlight beams. Elias's foot slams the brake pedal. The car slides on wet asphalt, tires screaming a high note that cuts through the drum of rain. Vincent's seatbelt locks hard against his chest. Angela's hands fly to the dashboard. The car stops just feet from the animal, close enough that Vincent can see every terrible detail.

The deer stands in the cones of light like something pulled from a fever dream. Its antlers, what should be clean bone, are covered in pale growths. White and petal-like, they cluster along each tine, opening and closing with a rhythm that has nothing to do with wind or rain. More of these blooms spread down the animal's flank, pushing through the fur in patches that look soft and horrible at once. Like flowers growing from meat.

"Oh my heavens," Angela breathes, the words barely sound.

The deer doesn't run. It should run. Any normal animal would bolt back into the forest, startled by the car and the lights and the noise. But this one stays, swaying slightly, its legs planted wide as if the ground might suddenly tilt. Its mouth hangs open, tongue visible, and Vincent can see more of those white growths inside its throat. Smaller ones, but moving with the same awful pulse.

Rain continues to hammer the roof. The wipers sweep back and forth, back and forth, clearing the windshield only to have it immediately obscured again. But through each clear moment, Vincent sees more. The way the deer's ribs show through its hide, not from starvation but from something else. The skin looks thin, stretched, like whatever's underneath has been hollowed out and replaced.

The animal takes a step forward, then staggers. Its front legs buckle. It catches itself, but the movement releases something into the air. Puffs of white that drift from the fungal blooms, too light to be rain, too solid to be fog. Spores. They float through the headlight beams, beautiful and terrible, dispersing into the darkness beyond. Pressed down by the rain.

"Don't open the windows," Elias says, his voice maintaining that same clinical tone even now. "Keep the air circulation on internal."

His hand moves to the climate control, adjusting settings with steady fingers. No panic. No revision. Just practical response to observable phenomena. Vincent wants to scream at him, to demand some human reaction to this abomination standing in their headlights.

The deer thrashes suddenly, violently, as if something inside is trying to escape. Its head whips side to side, antlers heavy with those pale blooms, and more spores release with each movement. They coat the wet asphalt, stick to the car's hood, gather in the grooves of the windshield where the wipers can't reach.

"That's not normal," Mira whispers, leaning forward between the front seats.

The understatement of it, the quiet certainty in her voice, makes Vincent turn to her in surprise. Because of course it's not normal. Nothing about this is normal. The way the deer's eyes have gone dull and glassy, reflecting the headlights like dirty marble. The way its breathing sounds wet and heavy, audible even through the closed windows and the rain.

Another thrash, weaker this time. The deer's back legs give out. It falls to its knees on the wet road, a position that looks almost like prayer. Its head droops forward, antlers scraping the asphalt. The white blooms pulse faster now, opening and closing like mouths gasping for air that will never come.

Vincent's knuckles are white on the seatbelt latch. He can feel his pulse in his throat, in his temples, in the tips of his fingers. Every instinct tells him to run, to get out of the car and run, but run where? Into the forest where more of these things might be waiting? Into the rain that carries those drifting spores?

Angela's hands tremble in her lap. She's stopped counting, stopped tapping, stopped everything except staring at the dying animal in their headlights. Her breath comes in short bursts that fog the passenger window. Vincent can see her fighting not to look away, forcing herself to witness this even as every part of her wants to close her eyes.

The deer collapses fully now, onto its side. The impact sends up another cloud of spores, thicker this time, like smoke from a snuffed candle. Its body seems to deflate, the skin sinking inward as if whatever was holding it up from inside has suddenly vanished. The ribcage caves. The stomach hollows. Even the legs seem to shrink, muscle and bone compressing into something smaller, emptier.

"It's being consumed," Elias observes, as if narrating for a medical journal. "From the inside out."

Vincent turns to look at Mira, needing to see someone else's horror, someone else's human response to this nightmare. But Mira just watches, her dark eyes taking in every detail, filing it away in that strange catalog she keeps in her head.

The deer gives one final shudder. Then nothing. It lies on the road like a deflated balloon covered in fur and those terrible white blooms that continue to pulse even after the animal has stopped moving. Still releasing spores. Still spreading whatever this is into the rain and the wind and the world.

Silence fills the car except for the rain and the wipers and Angela's ragged breathing. They sit frozen, all four of them, watching the corpse in the road. Waiting for it to move again. Waiting for something worse to emerge from the fog.

"We should go," Vincent says, his voice cracking on the words.

Elias nods once, shifts the car into reverse, backs up slowly. Then forward, steering carefully around the deer's body. The headlights sweep away from it, leaving it in darkness behind them. But Vincent turns to watch through the rear window as they drive away, and he can still see those white blooms pulsing in the red glow of the taillights. Still alive. Still feeding on something that should have been beyond their reach.

The car continues toward Marrowick, and no one speaks. The wipers beat their rhythm. The rain drums on. And Vincent knows, with a certainty that sits cold in his stomach, that whatever killed that deer is already here. Already in Marrowick. Already waiting.

Aunt Clare's house sits at the end of a gravel drive, weathered gray shingles dark with rain. The wraparound porch sags slightly on one side, and Vincent notices how the whole structure leans into the wind as if it's been doing so for decades. Rain gutters overflow in steady streams. A wind chime made of shells and driftwood clatters against a post, the sound both welcoming and lonely.

Clare appears at the door before Elias can knock, as if she's been watching from a window. She looks like a softer version of Elias, the same sharp features gentled by time and different choices. Her auburn hair, streaked with gray, is pinned back in a practical style. She wears a simple blue dress with a cardigan that might be hand-knitted, and when she smiles, it reaches her eyes in a way Elias's smiles never do.

"You made it," she says, pulling Elias into a hug he doesn't quite return. "I was starting to worry with this weather."

She releases him and turns to Angela, taking both her hands. "You must be Angela. I'm so glad to finally meet you." The warmth in her voice sounds genuine, unforced. Angela's shoulders relax slightly, her first real ease since they left Duswood.

Behind Clare, two figures hover in the doorway. The girl, Emily, practically vibrates with barely contained energy. She has her mother's coloring but something wilder in her expression, freckles scattered across her nose like stars. The boy, Ryan, leans against the doorframe with studied casualness, dark hair falling into his eyes. He watches them with the kind of assessment teenagers perfect, measuring whether these visitors are worth his interest.

"Come in, come in," Clare says, ushering them through the door. "You must be soaked through. Emily, help with the bags. Ryan, stop lurking and be useful."

The house interior wraps around them like a blanket that's been stored too long. The smell hits Vincent first: dried herbs hanging in bunches from the kitchen ceiling, their leaves brittle and aromatic. Wood smoke from a fire that must have been burning earlier, the ghost of it still clinging to furniture and walls. Underneath it all, that particular mustiness of old books and older faith.

Crucifixes mark the walls like punctuation. Not ostentatious, not overwhelming, but present. A simple wooden cross above the doorway. A more ornate silver one in the hallway. The shadows they cast in the lamplight stretch long and thin.

Emily appears at Mira's side immediately, eyes bright with curiosity. "Mira! When's the last time we saw each other? 10

years? What's Michigan like? That's so far! Is it really flat? Do you have lakes? Of course you have lakes, that's literally what it's famous for, but like, can you swim in them?"

The questions tumble out without pause for answers. Mira regards her with that particular stillness, not unfriendly but clearly overwhelmed by the sudden attention. Emily doesn't seem to notice or mind, continuing her cheerful interrogation as they move deeper into the house.

Ryan sizes up Vincent with a look that's part challenge, part amusement. "So you're the Duswood crew," he says, the words carrying a smirk. "Don't worry, we don't bite. Well, not hard."

He grabs Vincent's suitcase without being asked again, hefting it with easy strength. There's something in his movements, a restlessness that Vincent recognizes. The way kids move when they're trapped somewhere too small for their ambitions.

Clare leads them upstairs, the old wood creaking under their weight. "The house has its quirks," she says, touching the bannister with familiar affection. "The hot water takes a minute to warm up. The radiator in the back bedroom clanks at night, but you get used to it. And sometimes the power flickers in storms, but we have candles."

She shows Angela and Elias to one room, Vincent and Mira to another. The room is simple but clean: a single bed with a quilt that looks handmade, a dresser with a mirror that needs resilvering, a window that faces the street. A small crucifix hangs above the bed, Jesus's face worn smooth by years of touch or time.

"Dinner will be ready by six," Clare says. "Nothing fancy, just soup and bread, but it'll warm you up." She pauses at the door, studying Vincent with eyes that see more than they should. "You look tired. Rest if you need to."

After she leaves, Vincent sits on the edge of the bed. The mattress squeaks. Through the window, he can see the rain still falling, turning the street into a river of black water. Somewhere in this house, Emily's voice carries on, bright and persistent. Ryan's lower tones respond occasionally. Adult voices murmur from the room next door.

Dinner passes in a blur of Clare's gentle hospitality, Emily's endless questions, Ryan's sardonic observations. The soup is good, thick with vegetables and herbs from Clare's garden. The bread is homemade, dense and filling. Clare says grace before they eat, her words practiced and smooth, and Vincent sees his mother bow her head automatically, fingers finding each other under the table.

Later, much later, Vincent lies in the strange bed listening to the rain against the window. Across the room, Mira's breathing has settled into the slow rhythm of sleep, her form a dark island beneath the quilt of her twin bed. The radiator clanks, just as Clare warned. The house settles around him with sounds he doesn't recognize, different from the settling of his house in Duswood. Everything here creaks in a different key.

He can't stop seeing the deer.

The image plays behind his eyelids every time he closes them. Those white blooms pulsing on the antlers. The way the animal's body deflated, hollowed out from inside. The spores drifting through the headlight beams like snow that burns instead of melts.

What kind of thing does that? What kind of fungus, or disease makes an animal into an empty shell? And if it can do that to a deer, what else can it hollow out? What else can it consume from the inside?

The rain intensifies, drumming harder against the glass. Vincent pulls the quilt up to his chin, but he can't get warm. The crucifix above the bed catches streetlight from outside, the figure of Jesus appearing and disappearing as clouds pass over.

Somewhere in the walls, pipes gurgle. The house breathes

around him, alien and alive. He thinks about Duswood, about his own bed, about the familiar rot-sweet smell of the swamp. That seems impossibly far away now, separated by more than miles. Separated by that moment on the road, that deer in the headlights, that abhorrent thing that announced itself with spores and dim glassy eyes.

Vincent turns onto his side, facing the wall. The wallpaper has a pattern of small flowers, barely visible in the darkness. They could be roses, maybe, or something else. In this light, they look like those fungal blooms, white and pulsing, growing from within the walls.

He closes his eyes tight and tries not to think about what might be growing in the darkness outside, in the rain and the fog, feeding on things that should be beyond its reach.

CHAPTER
THREE

The smell of bacon pulls Vincent from sleep, ordinary and foreign at once, as if the world has forgotten what happened on the road last night. He lies still, listening to the sounds filtering up through the floorboards. Pans clattering. Water running. Voices murmuring in tones too soft to make out words. The radiator gives its promised clank, then falls silent. Through the window, rain continues its steady percussion against glass, neither harder nor softer than when he finally fell asleep.

Mira's bed is already empty, the quilt pulled tight and smooth as if she was never there at all. Vincent dresses quickly in yesterday's clothes, not ready to unpack yet, not ready to admit this place might be more than a brief interruption.

The stairs creak under his weight, each step announcing his descent. The kitchen spreads before him like a stage set for domestic comfort. Clare stands at the stove, her movements sure and practiced, flipping bacon with one hand while stirring something in a pot with the other. Steam rises around her, catching the overhead light. She hums something low and rhythmic, might be a hymn, might be nothing.

Angela hovers near the counter, slicing bread with careful precision. Her knife moves in steady strokes, and Vincent catches her lips moving. "One sixty-one," she whispers between slices. Another day counted, added to her tally like a prayer or a shield. Her hair is pulled back, and in the morning light filtering through the rain-streaked window, she looks younger. Almost like she used to, before.

"Morning, Vincent," Clare says without turning, as if she has eyes in the back of her head. Maybe all mothers develop that skill. "Hope you slept well. The radiator didn't keep you up?"

"No, it was fine." The lie comes easy. No point mentioning the hours spent seeing white blooms behind his eyelids.

Clare glances over her shoulder, and something in her expression suggests she knows anyway. But she only smiles, turning back to her cooking. "Coffee's ready if you want it. Mugs are in the cabinet above the sink."

Elias sits at the table, a mug cradled between his palms. But there's something different about him here, in his sister's kitchen. His shoulders have lost their rigid set. When Clare passes behind his chair, she touches his shoulder briefly, and he doesn't stiffen the way he does when Angela touches him.

"Remember when Mom used to make Sunday breakfast like this?" Clare asks him, her voice warm with memory. "Every week, no matter what."

"She never let us help," Elias says, and there's something almost fond in his tone. "Said we'd just make a mess."

"You would have." Clare laughs, a sound that fills the kitchen. "You tried to help once and and we had eggshells in our pancakes."

Vincent tries to imagine Elias young enough to lack the coordination he has now and can't quite manage it. But the ghost of a smile touches the man's lips, so brief Vincent might have imagined it.

Emily bursts through the doorway like weather, all energy

and movement. Her hair is still damp from a shower, and she's wearing a sweater that might have been her mother's once, too big in the shoulders. She spots Mira at the table and immediately claims the chair beside her.

"So what's it really like being homeschooled?" Emily leans in close, too close, her elbow nearly knocking over Mira's glass of water. "Do you miss having other kids around? I mean, I guess you have Vincent, but that's not the same as having, like, a whole class. Do you have to follow a real schedule or can you just learn whatever?"

Mira regards her with that particular stillness, the way she has of becoming very still when overwhelmed. "It's quiet," she says finally.

"Quiet?" Emily's face scrunches. "That's it? Just quiet?"

"Most things are."

Emily opens her mouth for another question, but Ryan shuffles in, saving Mira from further interrogation. He's wearing the same clothes as yesterday, or maybe all his clothes look the same. Dark jeans, dark hoodie, dark expression. His hair falls into his eyes, and he doesn't bother pushing it back.

Ryan drops into a chair across from Vincent, his gaze measuring. "So your town's called Duswood." He says it like an accusation.

"Yeah."

"Those little trees you've got there, those aren't real woods." Ryan's mouth quirks into something that's not quite a smile. "The forests here will eat you alive if you're not careful. Get turned around out there, might never find your way back."

"Ryan." Clare's voice carries a warning.

"What? Just making conversation." He leans back in his chair, balancing on two legs. "Figured Dusboy here should know what it's like out there."

Vincent feels heat rise in his chest but keeps his voice level. "I can handle woods." He says as he glances at Mira.

"Sure you can." Ryan lets the chair legs drop back to the floor with a thump. "We'll see."

Clare sets plates in front of them, each one loaded with more food than any person could reasonably eat. Bacon, eggs, thick slices of the bread Angela cut, some kind of hash browns that smell of rosemary. She's still talking as she serves, her voice filling the spaces between raindrops.

"This house has been in our family for three generations," she's saying. "My grandmother came here from Ireland, worked in the cannery before it closed." She pauses, spatula in hand. "The town was different then. More alive. The mill still ran, the boats still went out every morning. Now..." She doesn't finish, but her gaze drifts toward the window, toward something beyond the rain.

Vincent takes a bite of eggs.

Clare's words fade into the rhythm of forks against plates, the comfortable sounds of a family breakfast. Emily finishes first, pushing her plate away with dramatic satisfaction.

"We should go to the cove," she announces, looking between Vincent and Mira. "Show you what a real beach looks like. Not like your lakes."

Ryan snorts. "It's raining."

"It's always raining." Emily stands, already moving toward the door. "That's what jackets are for. Come on, before the tide gets too high."

Clare pauses in clearing plates, her hand hovering over Emily's abandoned fork. "Be careful on the path. It gets slick when it's wet like this." She glances at the window where rain streams down in steady rivers. "And don't go near the point. The rocks are unstable there."

"We know, Mom." Emily's voice carries that particular teenage exasperation, love and annoyance wound together. "I've only lived here my whole life."

Vincent catches his mother's quick glance, the way her fingers tap against her thigh. Three taps, pause, three taps. She wants to say something, maybe tell him to be careful too, but she holds back. This new version of her, the one hundred sixty-one days sober version, seems afraid of seeming afraid.

They layer themselves in borrowed rain gear from the closet by the door. The jackets smell of salt and age, vinyl cracking at the elbows. Emily's is bright yellow, making her look like a beacon against the gray morning. Ryan doesn't bother with rain gear, just pulls his hood up and shoves his hands deeper into his pockets.

The path starts behind Clare's house, marked by a wooden sign so weathered the words have worn away. Emily leads them between dripping ferns and salal bushes, their leaves heavy with water that dumps onto their shoulders when disturbed. The ground beneath their feet is more mud than earth, sucking at their boots with each step.

"Watch the root," Emily calls back, hopping over a twisted cedar root that crosses the path like a barrier. "It's slippery."

Vincent's foot skids on the wet bark, and he catches himself against a tree trunk. The bark comes away under his palm, soft with rot. Ryan watches from behind, that smirk playing at his lips.

"Careful there, Dusboy. Wouldn't want you to break something on your first day."

The path drops sharply, switching back and forth down the hillside. Through gaps in the trees, Vincent catches glimpses of gray water stretching to a gray horizon. No line between sea and sky, just variations of the same color bleeding into each other. The sound grows louder with each turn, waves against stone, constant and hollow.

They emerge from the trees onto a beach that looks nothing like the photos in travel magazines of beautiful destinations. No sun-soaked sand, no gentle waves. Ashen Cove spreads before them in shades of gray and black. The beach is stones and shale, slick with rain and sea spray. Driftwood piles along the high tide line, massive logs bleached white as bone, twisted into shapes that don't quite make sense.

The smell hits Vincent hard. Salt, yes, but underneath it something else. Rot, but not the familiar swamp rot of Duswood. This is sharper, marine decay, things that died in salt water and washed ashore to decompose in rain. His stomach turns slightly.

Emily skips ahead, her yellow jacket the only color in the landscape. She moves across the slick rocks with practiced ease, pointing at various spots with the enthusiasm of a tour guide who loves her subject.

"That's where I found the sand dollar," she says, crouching beside a cluster of rocks. "Perfect, not a single crack. And over there, see that log? Sometimes seals rest on it at low tide."

She picks through the stones, occasionally holding one up to examine before tossing it back. Her voice carries over the wave sound, bright and persistent. "The best shells come in after storms. The waves dredge them up from deeper water. Once I found a piece of glass so smooth it looked like ice."

Mira moves slowly along the tide line, stopping frequently to examine things Vincent can't quite make out. Strands of kelp maybe, or patterns in the stone. She has that particular focus she gets sometimes, when the world narrows to whatever has caught her attention.

Ryan kicks at a piece of driftwood, sending it skittering across the stones. "Boring beach," he says, loud enough for Emily to hear. "Nothing but rocks and dead things."

"You have no poetry in your soul," Emily shoots back, not looking up from her searching.

"Poetry's for people with nothing better to do."

Vincent walks between them, feeling the weight of the gray sky pressing down. The waves roll in with mechanical regularity, each one reaching slightly different points on the beach, leaving foam that looks too white against the dark stones. Something about this place sets his nerves on edge. The way the driftwood logs lie at angles that seem deliberately arranged. The way the fog clings to the water's surface, never quite lifting.

He can't shake the feeling of being observed. Not by Ryan, whose attention has shifted to throwing stones at a partially submerged log. Not by Emily, who's now explaining to no one in particular about the different types of barnacles. Something else watches from the fog, from the tree line, from somewhere he can't quite identify.

A sound from Mira makes him turn. She's crouched beside a cluster of rocks where the shale has cracked, creating a narrow crevice. Her hand hovers above something, fingers spread but not touching.

"This wasn't here before," she says, her voice barely audible over the waves.

Vincent moves closer, Ryan and Emily converging from their separate wanderings. In the crack, something white pulses with a rhythm that has nothing to do with the waves. Pale and soft-looking, like the blooms on the deer's antlers but smaller, more delicate. It spreads along the crevice in a line, each bloom opening and closing like tiny mouths breathing.

"Don't touch it," Vincent says, remembering the spores, the way they drifted through the headlight beams.

Mira's hand remains suspended, trembling slightly. "It's growing from the stone," she whispers. "How does something grow from stone?"

Emily leans in, her earlier enthusiasm dimming. "I've never seen anything like that here. And I know this whole beach."

Ryan's smirk has faded entirely. He takes a step back, then another. "We should go. Tide's coming in anyway."

As if responding to his words, a larger wave crashes against the rocks, sending spray over all of them. The salt water touches the fungal bloom, and it reacts, pulsing faster, releasing a small cloud of white that the wind catches immediately, dispersing it along the beach.

The fog chooses that moment to thicken, rolling in from the sea like a living wall. It swallows the horizon first, then the water, then the far ends of the beach. Within moments, they can barely see ten feet in any direction. The temperature drops, or maybe it just feels that way, the moisture in the air pulling heat from their skin.

"We need to go," Emily says, her voice smaller now, scared. "The path gets dangerous when you can't see."

They turn back toward the trees, but in the fog, everything looks different. The driftwood logs could be any logs. The rocks could be any rocks. Even the sound of the waves seems to come from all directions at once, disorienting, making it impossible to tell which way leads to safety and which to deeper water.

Vincent reaches for Mira's hand, finds it cold and damp. Emily's yellow jacket becomes their beacon, the only point of reference in a world suddenly made of gray nothing. Ryan brings up the rear, for once without comment, his breathing audible in the strange quiet that fog brings.

Behind them, Vincent imagines he can still hear that fungal bloom pulsing, breathing, growing from stone that should give it no purchase. Growing like the things on the deer. Growing like something that doesn't need normal rules to spread.

The fog presses closer, and they climb.

———

The sound that wakes Vincent has no name. Not quite footsteps, not quite breathing, not quite the settling of old wood. It exists in the spaces between familiar noises, perverse in a way that pulls him from sleep without fully waking him. He lies still, eyes closed, listening.

The rain has stopped. That's the first thing he notices, the absence of that constant percussion that's been the backdrop to everything since they arrived. Without it, the house seems louder. Every creak carries. Every shift of weight translates through the bones of the building.

There it is again. A soft sound, like fabric against wood. Like someone moving very slowly, very carefully, trying not to be heard.

Vincent opens his eyes. The room is dark, darker than his room in Duswood ever gets. The dusk-to-dawn light in the yard is either out or very dim, no moon through the clouds. Just variations of black and the faint suggestion of the window, slightly less dark than the walls. The crucifix above his bed is invisible, but he feels it there, that weight of watching even in darkness.

Across the room, Mira's breathing continues steady and deep. He can just make out the shape of her under the quilt, a darkness against darkness. She hasn't stirred.

The sound comes again, clearer now. From the hallway beyond their door. Movement, deliberate and strange. Not Clare checking on them, her footsteps would be more purposeful. Not Ryan sneaking to the bathroom, he wouldn't bother being quiet.

Vincent sits up slowly, the bed frame creaking despite his care. His bare feet find the cold floor, shocking him more fully awake. He stands, waits for his eyes to adjust, then moves toward the door. His hand finds the doorknob, worn smooth by generations of hands. It turns without sound.

The hallway stretches before him, lit only by what might be moonglow through a window at the far end. Or maybe not moonlight. Maybe just the darkness being less dark there. His eyes struggle to make sense of the shapes, the walls seeming to breathe in his peripheral vision.

A figure stands halfway down the hall.

Vincent's heart stops, restarts, pounds so hard he's certain it must be audible. The figure faces away from him, toward the wall. White nightgown. Dark hair hanging loose. Standing perfectly, impossibly still.

"Mira?" His whisper barely disturbs the air.

She doesn't turn. Doesn't acknowledge him at all. Just stands there, facing the wall like she's reading something written on it that only she can see. Her feet are bare, and even in the darkness, he can see they're not quite touching the floor. Not floating, exactly, but not fully connected either.

Vincent moves closer, each step careful on the old boards. Some creak anyway, betraying him, but Mira doesn't react. As he gets nearer, he sees more details that don't make sense. Her hair moves slightly, as if in a breeze that doesn't exist. Her nightgown ripples at the hem, that same impossible movement.

"Mira, what are you doing?"

Nothing. No response at all. She could be a statue except for that subtle movement of hair and fabric. He reaches out, hesitates, then touches her shoulder.

His hand passes through.

Not like she's not there. She's there, he can see her, but his hand moves through her shoulder like she's made of cold mist. The sensation sends ice up his arm, a feeling that makes him jerk back.

But the motion makes him turn slightly, and through the open doorway of their room, he sees Mira's bed. Sees Mira in it. Still under the quilt, still breathing steadily, definitely still there. Solid. Real.

Vincent looks between them. The Mira in the hall, facing the wall, translucent to his touch. The Mira in bed, sleeping normally. Two Miras. Two versions of the same person in different places, which shouldn't be possible, can't be possible, but here it is happening in front of him.

His mind tries to rationalize. A dream. He's dreaming. Or hallucinating. The stress of the trip, the deer on the road, the fungus on the beach. His brain creating impossibilities to process the fear.

But the floor under his feet feels real. The cold air on his skin feels real. The rapid beating of his heart feels terribly, undeniably real.

He backs toward the room, keeping his eyes on the hallway Mira. She hasn't moved, still facing that wall, still surrounded by that subtle motion of hair and cloth. He reaches the doorway, steps inside, moves to the bed where the other Mira sleeps.

His hand hovers over her shoulder. What if she's not real either? What if touching her makes her dissolve too? What if he's alone in this house with things that only look like people?

He touches her shoulder. Solid. Warm through the nightgown. Real.

Her eyes open immediately, alert in a way that suggests she wasn't deeply asleep. "What's wrong?" Her voice is thick but aware.

"You're in the hallway," Vincent says, the words not making sense even as he says them. "But you're also here. You're in two places."

Mira sits up, the quilt falling away. She looks at him, then at the doorway. "What do you mean?"

"Look." He turns toward the hall, but the figure is gone. The hallway is empty, just shadows and that distant not-quite-moonlight. "She was there. You were there. Standing by the wall."

Mira swings her legs out of bed, stands, moves to the doorway. She examines the hallway with that careful attention she brings to everything. "I don't remember getting up," she says slowly. "I was dreaming, but not about walking."

"You didn't get up. You were here the whole time. But you were also there." Vincent points to the spot where the other Mira stood. "I touched you. Her. My hand went through."

They stand together in the doorway, looking at the empty hallway. The house settles around them, making those sounds that old houses make. Sounds that could be footsteps, could be breathing, could be nothing at all.

"Wait," Mira says. She moves to where Vincent pointed, crouches, touches the floor.

Her fingers come away damp.

Not wet like water. Damp like morning dew, like condensation, like the moisture that collects on windows when warm air meets cold glass. She examines her fingers in the dim light, then touches the floor again. The dampness extends in two small patches, roughly the size and shape of bare feet.

"Something was here," she says.

Vincent crouches beside her, touches the floor himself. The wood is definitely damp, cooler than the surrounding boards. The moisture has no smell, no color when he examines his fingers. Just wetness where wetness shouldn't be.

"Was it you?" he asks. "Some part of you?"

Mira doesn't answer immediately. She stands, looks at the wall where the other version of her had been facing. There's nothing special about it, just old wallpaper with that flower pattern, barely visible in the darkness. But she stares at it as if reading something there.

"I don't know," she finally says. "I don't remember."

They return to their room, but neither goes back to bed immediately. They sit on Vincent's bed, backs against the wall, watching the doorway. Listening to the house breathe around them. The damp spots in the hallway will be dry by morning, Vincent knows. There will be no evidence except their memory, and memories are fragile things in houses like this, in towns like Marrowick.

"Has this happened before?" Vincent asks.

Mira pulls her knees to her chest, wraps her arms around

them. "Not like this. Not that I remember. But sometimes I dream of being in two places. Sometimes I wake up and feel like I've been somewhere else."

The crucifix above the bed catches some stray light, the figure of Jesus appearing for a moment before disappearing back into shadow. Vincent thinks about Clare's faith, her certainty that God watches over everything. He wonders what she would make of Mira appearing in two places at once. Miracle or haunting. Divine or trickery.

They sit in silence, waiting for morning, for light to make the impossible seem less possible. But Vincent knows that damp spot on the floor tells a different truth. Something is happening here. Something that has to do with Mira, with this house, with this town that smells of salt and decay.

Something that leaves wet footprints where no feet should be.

CHAPTER
FOUR

Morning comes gray and reluctant, and Vincent feels every hour of lost sleep in his bones as he pulls on his jacket in the front hall of Clare's house. His eyes burn with that particular ache of a night spent watching shadows, waiting for something impossible to happen again. Angela fusses with her purse, checking for her wallet three times while Clare gathers reusable shopping bags with practiced efficiency. The normalcy of it all contrasts against the memory of Mira bilocating, those damp footprints on the hallway floor that dried by dawn, leaving no proof except what lives in Vincent's mind.

"The market closes at three on Sundays," Clare says, pulling on a rain jacket that looks older than Emily. "We should get there before the good fish is gone."

Angela nods, her fingers finding the zipper of her own borrowed jacket, working it up and down in a nervous rhythm. "One sixty-two," she whispers, so quiet only Vincent catches it. Another day added to her count, another small victory measured in hours.

Elias stands by the door like he's waiting for permission to exist in this space. His clothes remain pressed despite the constant dampness, his shoes polished to a shine that seems to mock the weathered floorboards beneath them. When Clare passes, she touches his arm briefly, and something in his face softens for just a moment before returning to its usual careful neutrality.

The drive into Marrowick proper takes only five minutes, but the town reveals itself slowly through the rain-streaked windows. First come the outlying houses, their paint peeling in long strips like diseased skin. Then the gas station with its flickering neon sign, half the letters dark. Then more buildings, pressing closer together as they near what must be the center of town.

Vincent watches it all pass, this place that's supposed to mean something to his mother, to Elias, to their attempt at building whatever fragile thing exists between them. The buildings sag under the weight of constant moisture. Moss grows on rooftops, in gutters, along the edges of sidewalks where foot traffic doesn't discourage it. Everything looks tired, worn down by decades of rain and salt air.

Elias parks near a row of storefronts, their windows fogged with condensation. The moment they step out, the smell hits Vincent again. That sharp tang of salt mixed with something else, something that reminds him of things left too long in water. A gull wheels overhead, its cry harsh and accusing.

"We'll meet back here in two hours," Clare says, already moving toward the market with Angela in tow. His mother glances back once, a quick check that Vincent is okay, before disappearing into the crowd of locals doing their Sunday shopping.

Elias mutters something about needing to walk, to think, and heads off toward where the masts of boats rise above the buildings. He moves with purpose, as if drawn by something only he can sense. Vincent watches him go, this strange man who speaks in facts instead of feelings, who helped make something terrible happen back in Duswood, who now shares breakfasts with his mother.

"Come on," Emily says, grabbing Mira's arm with casual familiarity that makes Mira stiffen slightly. "I'll show you the thriving metropolis of Marrowick."

Ryan snorts. "Thriving. Right."

They walk the main street, Emily pointing out landmarks with the enthusiasm of someone who's never been anywhere else. "That's Henderson's Hardware, they've been here since forever. And the bakery, but it's not as good since Mr. Garcia retired. Oh, and the bookstore, but it's mostly romance novels and fishing guides now."

The sidewalks are slick with more than rain. Some kind of algae grows in the cracks, making each step slightly treacherous. Vincent notices how the locals navigate it without thought, their feet finding the safe spots through long practice. They move slowly, unhurried, as if the rain has seeped into their bones and weighted them down.

"Look at the tourists," Ryan says, loud enough for others to hear. "Taking in our beautiful sights." His voice carries that edge Vincent is starting to recognize, not quite mean but testing, always testing.

"We're not tourists," Vincent says. "We're visiting family."

"Same thing." Ryan kicks at a loose piece of concrete. "You'll go back to your swamp and forget this place exists."

Emily rolls her eyes. "Ignore him. He's cranky because Martha didn't text him back."

"Shut up, Em."

"Martha from the diner? The one who's definitely too old for you? Brah, she's like 20."

Ryan's face darkens, and he shoves his hands deeper into his pockets, hunching against rain that isn't really falling that hard. Emily grins, pleased with herself, and continues her tour.

But Vincent finds himself looking past Emily's enthusiasm, past Ryan's defensive sarcasm, to the details that don't quite fit. The way an old woman crosses the street to avoid walking past them. The way a man stands in a doorway, not going in or out, just standing there with his face turned up to the gray sky. The way the few children he sees stay close to their parents, no running or playing despite it being Sunday morning.

In the window of an antique shop, Vincent sees a display of old photographs. Marrowick through the decades, according to the handwritten sign. But in every photo, the town looks exactly the same. Same buildings, same gray light, same exhausted quality. Only the clothes change, the cars get older or newer, but the town itself seems frozen, unable to decay further or improve.

"There's the diner," Emily announces, pointing ahead. "Best coffee in town, which isn't saying much, but still."

Through the diner's windows, Vincent can see people hunched over their meals, not talking, just eating as in a magazine. Steam fogs the glass from inside, but he can make out enough to see that no one looks happy. No one looks sad either. They just look empty, going through the motions of a Sunday breakfast because that's what people do.

Mira has been quiet through all of this, her dark eyes taking in everything with that particular intensity she has. She stops suddenly, looking at something Vincent can't identify, some pattern or absence that means something only to her.

"What is it?" he asks.

She doesn't answer immediately, still studying whatever has caught her attention. Then, quietly: "The birds avoid certain buildings."

Vincent looks up. She's right. The gulls wheel and cry overhead, but they give certain structures a wide berth, as if invisible barriers keep them away. Those same buildings, Vincent notices, have the darkest windows, the most moss, the deepest sense of abandonment even though some clearly have lights on inside.

"So?" Ryan says. "Birds are stupid."

But Emily has noticed too, her earlier enthusiasm dimming slightly. "That is weird. They usually roost everywhere, even where people don't want them."

They continue walking, but something has shifted. The tour feels less like Emily showing off her hometown and more like a progression through a place where the rules have quietly changed when no one was looking. Where moss grows too thick and birds know to stay away and people move through their routines with the hollow precision of automation.

They pause outside the diner because Emily insists on pointing out the faded mural on its brick wall, something about fishing boats and prosperity that the rain has turned into ghostly vestiges of ambition. Vincent can barely make out the shapes anymore, just blues and grays bleeding together like everything else in Marrowick. The diner's door swings open with a bell's tired chime, and a couple emerges into the gray morning.

At first, they seem ordinary. The man wears a flannel shirt tucked into jeans, the uniform of working men everywhere. The woman has her hair pulled back in a ponytail, her jacket practical rather than fashionable. They could be anybody's parents, anybody's neighbors, anybody at all.

Then something shifts.

"You always do this," the woman says, her voice starting low but sharp. "Every single time."

The man stops walking. His shoulders tense. "Do what, exactly?"

"You know what." Her voice rises, carrying across the street. "Twenty years, Carl. Twenty years of your lies."

People on the sidewalk slow their steps, that universal human instinct to witness drama while pretending not to.

Vincent feels Emily shift beside him, uncomfortable but unable to look away. Ryan actually takes a step forward, like he's watching a show about to start.

"Lies?" Carl's voice cracks with something between rage and disbelief. "You want to talk about lies? What about Tommy's? What about every Tuesday when you said you were at book club?"

The woman's face twists into something ugly. "Don't you dare. Don't you dare bring him into this."

"Why not? He's been in everything else. Our bed, our bank account, our…"

"I hate you." She spits the words like they're poison she needs to get out. "I've hated you for years. The way you chew. The way you breathe. The way you look at me like I owe you something just for existing. I know you've never loved me."

Vincent wants to move, to walk away, to not be witnessing this dissolution of a marriage on a public street. But his feet feel rooted to the damp concrete. Beside him, Mira has gone completely still, that particular stillness that means she's absorbing everything.

Carl steps toward his wife, his hands clenched into fists. "You think you're so much better? You think Tommy wants you for anything more than…"

"Stop." An old man across the street says it loud enough to carry, but neither Carl nor his wife seem to hear.

"…a quick distraction from his real family? You're nothing, Sharon. You've always been nothing."

Sharon's hand comes up like she might slap him, but she doesn't follow through. Instead, she laughs, bitter and broken. "At least I tried to feel something. You're just a shell, Carl. Empty inside. Dead since the day I met you."

The words cut deeper than any physical blow could. Carl's face goes red, then purple, his mouth opening and closing like he's drowning in air. Around them, the people of Marrowick have all turned away now, deliberately not seeing, not hearing. They continue their errands with studied focus, examining shop windows, checking phones, anything to avoid acknowledging what's happening.

Vincent recognizes this particular kind of public blindness. It's what people do when something too raw, too private, spills into shared space. But there's something else in how the locals look away, something practiced, like they've done this before. Like they know what comes next.

And then it stops.

Not gradually, not with any natural conclusion. Sharon's mouth is open, mid-word, something about wasted years, and then nothing. Her face goes slack. The anger drains away like water from a broken cup, leaving nothing behind. Carl's purple rage fades to gray, his clenched fists opening into loose, empty hands.

They stand there for a moment, facing each other but not seeing. Their eyes have gone unfocused, pupils dilated despite the gray light. Then, moving with the same rhythm, they reach for each other's hands.

The grip is wrong. Vincent can see it from ten feet away. Their fingers don't interlace the way couples' hands do, don't squeeze with affection or even habit. They just touch, palm to palm, like two pieces of paper pressed together by acci-dent. No warmth, no pressure, just contact without connection.

They turn and walk away together, their steps synchro-nized but practiced. Left foot, right foot, left foot, right foot. Like they're following a pattern they've memorized but don't understand. They don't speak. They don't look at each other. They just walk, hand in hand, toward wherever people go when they've been emptied out.

Vincent shivers. Not from cold, though the morning air carries that particular dampness that seeps through clothing. This shiver comes from deeper, from the place in his spine that recognizes malevolence even when his brain can't name it. His skin prickles with goosebumps that have nothing to do with temperature.

"Well, that was intense," Emily says, her laugh coming out forced and too high. "Guess someone forgot to drink their coffee this morning." The joke lands flat, dies in the air between them. Even she seems to know it's not funny, but she had to say something, had to try to make the world normal again.

Ryan rolls his eyes with practiced sibling disdain. "Small-town drama. Happens all the time. They'll kiss and make up by dinner." But his voice lacks its usual edge, and he's already walking again, putting distance between himself and where it happened.

Vincent notices that people are returning to normal now, the locals emerging from their deliberate blindness to continue their Sunday routines. They walk through the space where the argument happened like it's just sidewalk again, nothing special, nothing wrong. The old man who tried to intervene stands in his doorway, shaking his head slowly before retreating inside.

Mira hasn't moved. She watches the couple until they turn a corner and disappear, her eyes tracking them with an intensity that makes Vincent nervous. Her head tilts slightly, that bird-like gesture she makes when she's processing something others can't see.

"It's feeding," she whispers, the words so quiet they almost disappear into the sound of distant waves and calling gulls.

Vincent turns to her. "What?"

But she's already walking again, following Emily and Ryan, leaving Vincent to trail behind with that word echoing in his head. Feeding. Like the fungus on the deer, consuming from the inside. Like the blooms on the beach, growing from stone. Like something in Marrowick that takes what makes people human and leaves only the shell behind.

He thinks about Carl and Sharon's empty eyes, their automatic walk, their hands touching without feeling. He thinks about love turned to hate turned to nothing at all. He thinks about what kind of hunger could swallow emotions whole, leaving people to go through the motions of being together while everything that made it matter has been devoured.

———

The living room at Holt House wraps around them with a warmth that feels forced, like a sweater worn in summer. Vincent sits on the couch beside his mother, watching her try to arrange her face into something pleasant while her fingers tap their secret rhythm against her thigh. The fire Clare built earlier has died to embers, but nobody moves to add more wood. They're all just sitting here, pretending today was normal, pretending they didn't see what they saw.

"Marrowick's quite the quiet town," Angela says, her voice pitched too bright, like she's auditioning for the role of someone who's fine. "Not unlike Duswood in some ways. That same small-town feeling where everyone knows everyone."

Vincent catches the quick movement of her other hand to her wrist, fingers finding that spot where she counts heartbeats or seconds or days. One sixty-two, she mouths silently, then covers it with a smile that doesn't last. She's trying so hard to make this work, to prove that this trip, this relationship with Elias, this whole new life she's building one sober day at a time, means something.

Clare moves through the room with practiced efficiency, picking up coffee cups that don't need collecting yet, straightening magazines that were already straight. Her movements have a rhythm to them, almost like prayer, each action deliberate and contained. She pauses at the window to adjust curtains that don't need adjusting, and Vincent notices how her fingers briefly touch the small cross at her throat.

"The weather should clear tomorrow," she says to no one in particular. "Might be nice enough for a proper walk."

Elias sits in the armchair by the window, last month's issue of Marrowick Monthly spread across his lap. He reads with the same meticulousness he brings to everything, eyes moving left to right, top to bottom, absorbing information without seeming to process it as anything more than data. Occasionally he turns a page, the paper crackling in the quiet room.

"We should go to the old Bridgeport Mill," Emily announces from where she's sprawled on the floor, surrounded by what looks like old photo albums she's pulled from somewhere. "It's supposed to be haunted, though that's obviously nonsense, but the building itself is fascinating. All that old machinery just sitting there, rusting away."

Ryan snorts from his corner chair, not looking up from his phone. "Fascinating. Right. Bunch of tetanus waiting to happen."

"You have no appreciation for history."

"I have no appreciation for boring."

"Everything's boring to you unless it involves Martha."

"Shut up, Em."

The familiar rhythm of their bickering fills the room, and for a moment Vincent can almost pretend this is just a normal family evening. Almost forget the couple on the street, their transformation from rage to emptiness. Almost forget Mira's whispered word: feeding.

But Mira herself sits apart from the general conversation, curled in a chair by the bookshelf, studying the spines of old books. She hasn't mentioned what happened in town, hasn't acknowledged it at all, but Vincent knows she's processing it in her own way, filing it alongside all the other strange pieces of this place.

"There's also the coastal path," Emily continues, undeterred by her brother's disinterest. "It goes all the way to

Shepherd's Point, though you can't go all the way anymore since the erosion. But the views are incredible on clear days. You can see for miles."

Clare pauses in her tidying to touch Emily's shoulder gently. "Not too far, though. The paths aren't as stable as they used to be."

"I know, Mom."

The evening wears on with this kind of surface normalcy, everyone playing their parts in the family gathering. Angela asks Clare about her garden, listening with determined interest to descriptions of soil quality and seasonal vegetables. Elias occasionally contributes a fact about coastal agriculture. Emily chatters about school friends, while Ryan interjects with sarcastic commentary that Emily deflects with practiced ease.

Eventually, the evening fragments. Clare announces she needs to prepare for early mass tomorrow, disappearing into the kitchen with an armload of dishes. Angela follows, insisting on helping, her need to be useful almost painful to watch. Elias retreats upstairs with his newspaper, and the cousins drift to their rooms, Emily still talking about tomorrow's possibilities while Ryan maintains his aura of aggressive disinterest.

Now Vincent lies in his bed, watching shadows move across the ceiling as clouds pass over the moon. The radiator gives its periodic clank, the house settles with mysterious creaks, and somewhere in the walls, pipes gurgle with water moving to unknown destinations.

He turns onto his side, then his back, then his other side. The pillow feels too warm, then too cold. The blanket tangles around his legs no matter how he arranges it. Every position feels unforgiving, his body unable to find that sweet spot where sleep becomes possible.

Every time he closes his eyes, he sees them. Carl and Sharon, their faces twisted with rage one moment, empty the next. The transformation plays on loop behind his eyelids, a horror movie he can't turn off. The way their eyes went dead, pupils dilated into black holes that reflected nothing. The way their hands came together without meaning, like magnets clicking into place rather than people choosing to touch.

Vincent sits up, giving up on sleep for now. Through the window, he can see the gravel driveway below, wet and dark with rain. The motion-sensor floodlight on the barn flickers, casting the oak tree and woodpile in alternating light and shadow. The yard feels different at night, not quieter but eerie-quiet, like something holding its breath.

The gulls are crying somewhere over the harbor, their calls carrying on the wind. But even they sound different at night, less like birds and more like warnings, telling anyone who'll listen that Marrowick is not what it seems. That underneath the rain and salt and small-town quiet, something is consuming the town from the inside out, leaving only shapes where people used to be.

Vincent lies back down, pulls the blanket up to his chin, and stares at the ceiling. He knows sleep won't come easily, maybe won't come at all. But he lies there anyway, listening to the rain, watching the shadows, and trying not to think about empty eyes and mechanical hands and the terrible possibility that whatever is feeding here isn't satisfied yet.

The crucifix above his bed catches a stray beam of light, Christ's face appearing momentarily before disappearing back into shadow. Vincent wonders if Clare's faith protects her from seeing what he sees, or if she sees it too and chooses to believe in something stronger. Either way, he envies her certainty, her ability to move through this house, this town, with such determined normalcy.

The rain continues. The radiator clanks. And Vincent lies awake, counting not days sober like his mother, but the hours until dawn, when he can stop pretending to sleep and face whatever new impossibilities Marrowick has to offer.

Morning comes to Holt House through windows fogged with condensation, the light so weak it barely separates itself from the gray outside. Vincent sits at the kitchen table, watching Clare move through her morning routine with the practiced efficiency of someone who's made the same breakfast in the same kitchen for decades. Her hands know where everything lives without looking, fingers finding the handle of the coffee pot, the edge of the bread box, the drawer where spoons nest together like sleeping fish.

The kitchen fills with ordinary sounds. Butter sizzling in the pan. The percolator's rhythmic gurgle. Clare humming something low and tuneless as she works. These sounds should be comforting, domestic, safe. But after yesterday, after watching that couple drain of all feeling in town, Vincent can't shake the sense that even these morning rituals carry hidden weight.

Angela enters first, her movements careful as always, like she's afraid of taking up too much space. She's already dressed, her cardigan buttoned wrong but she doesn't seem to notice. Her lips move in that familiar counting pattern. "One sixty-three," she whispers, adding another day to her tally. She catches Vincent watching and offers a quick smile that doesn't quite land, then busies herself setting out plates with unnecessary precision.

Elias follows, his presence changing the room's temperature somehow, making everything feel more formal. He takes his seat with the same concision he brings to everything, newspaper already tucked under his arm. The way he unfolds it, each crease sharp and deliberate, makes Vincent think of someone performing a ritual they've forgotten the meaning of.

Emily bounds in with her usual energy, hair still damp from a shower, wearing a sweater that might have been from a thrift store, the sleeves rolled up to expose her freckled wrists. "Morning, everyone! Smells amazing, Mom." She slides into her chair with a grace that seems unconscious, reaching immediately for the orange juice pitcher.

Ryan appears last, hood up despite being indoors, shuffling to his seat like movement itself is an imposition. He drops into his chair with a grunt that might be acknowledgment of the morning or might be nothing at all.

Ryan reaches for the coffee pot, then pauses, squinting at his mother. "Thought you had mass this morning."

"Already went." Clare doesn't look up from the eggs she's scrambling, her spatula moving in steady circles. "I went to 6 a.m. Remember? You used to come with me before you started school. You're still welcome to." She casts him a sorrowful, but loving smile. He rolls his eyes.

Clare brings plates to the table. Scrambled eggs, toast, strips of bacon arranged with the kind of care that suggests love expressed through food. She's still humming, the sound mixing with the rain that's started again, a gentle patter against the windows that makes the kitchen feel smaller, warmer, more contained.

"Pass the salt?" Clare asks Emily, her voice casual, reaching across the table.

Something shifts in Emily's face. Not gradually, but all at once, like a mask sliding off to reveal something else underneath. Her eyes, bright with morning energy a moment ago, go hard and flat.

"Get it yourself," Emily says, but the words come out rigid, edged with something sharp and unfamiliar. "You're always asking for things. Salt. Help with dishes. Someone to care about your sad little life in this pathetic house."

The kitchen goes silent except for the rain. Even the percolator seems to pause mid-gurgle. Vincent sees his mother's hand freeze halfway to her coffee cup. Sees Elias's fingers tighten on his newspaper until the edges crumple.

Clare's face doesn't change, not really. She maintains that same pleasant expression, but her hand trembles as she reaches for the salt herself. Just a slight shake, barely visible, but Vincent catches it. "Of course, dear," she says, her voice steady as her hand is not.

"It's suffocating here," Emily continues, and her voice sounds hollow now, like words being pushed through an empty pipe. "The way you hover. The way you pray over everything like God cares about your little problems. The way you pretend Dad's death was some divine plan instead of just another mill accident in a town full of accidents."

The words hang in the air like spores, poisonous and drifting. Clare's other hand finds the edge of the counter, gripping until her knuckles go white. But she doesn't respond, just continues salting her eggs with those trembling fingers, each shake of the shaker too forceful, too much salt falling onto the yellow mound.

Vincent looks at Mira, who hasn't moved since Emily started speaking. She sits perfectly still, her dark eyes fixed on Emily with an intensity that makes Vincent's skin prickle. Her lips press together in a thin line, and her hands rest flat on the table, fingers spread wide like she's trying to feel something through the wood.

The silence stretches. Plates clink against the table as Clare sets the salt down, the sound too loud in the quiet kitchen. Forks scrape against ceramic. The rain intensifies, drumming harder against the glass.

Emily blinks rapidly, like someone waking from a dream. Her face shifts again, the hardness draining away to leave confusion behind. "I..." She looks around the table, taking in everyone's frozen positions, their careful not-looking. "I don't know why I said that." Her voice comes out flat, emotionless, like she's reading from a script she doesn't understand.

"It's just the weather," Clare says quickly, too quickly, her smile pulled tight across her face like a bandage. "Makes us all a bit tense. Rainy season and all." She turns to clear plates that don't need clearing yet, and Vincent sees how her fingers shake visibly now, unable to hide it as she stacks dishes with less than her usual care.

Ryan rolls his eyes, the gesture so normal it feels almost violent in its casualness. "Drama before nine a.m. Great." He goes back to his eggs like nothing happened, but Vincent notices he doesn't look at Emily, doesn't look at his mother.

Angela and Elias exchange glances across the table, the kind of weighted look that says they're both thinking the same thing but won't say it aloud. Angela's hand moves to her collar, adjusting the cardigan that still isn't buttoned right. Elias returns to his newspaper, but his eyes don't move across the words. He's just staring at the same spot, seeing nothing.

Vincent catches Mira's gaze finally, just for a moment. Something passes between them, recognition maybe, or fear. But she looks away immediately, her attention returning to Emily with that same unwavering focus. Watching. Waiting. Like she knows something's inside Emily now, something that speaks cruelty through her mouth and leaves her confused in its wake.

The breakfast continues in this broken rhythm. Forks against plates. Rain against windows. Clare at the sink, washing dishes that could wait, her shoulders rigid with the effort of maintaining normalcy. And Emily, sitting at the table with her eggs growing cold, staring at her hands like she doesn't quite recognize them.

————

The drizzle falls steadily as they leave Holt House behind, each drop so fine it feels more like walking through a cloud than rain. Ryan strides ahead, his shoulders squared against the weather, throwing challenges over his shoulder that the wind tears apart before they fully form.

"Bet you can't keep up, Dusboy," he calls back, his voice carrying that edge of competition that seems to be his default setting. "Out-of-towners always slow on real trails."

Vincent matches his pace without comment, his shoes squelching in the mud that sucks at each step. The path winds between blackberry brambles and salal, everything green and dripping, the air thick with the smell of wet earth and vegetation. Emily skips between puddles, somehow maintaining her energy despite the breakfast scene that should have drained her. She hums something tuneless, jumping from one relatively dry spot to another with practiced ease.

Mira follows at her own pace, deliberate and unhurried. Her black boots splash through puddles Emily avoids, like the water doesn't matter to her. She hasn't spoken since they left the house, but Vincent knows she's processing everything, filing away Emily's behavior alongside all the other wrong things about Marrowick.

The abandoned Bridgeport Mill rises from the landscape like a wound that won't heal. Its corrugated metal walls streak with rust in patterns that look deliberate, almost artistic, if art could be made from decay. The structure hulks against the gray sky, massive and hollow, windows broken into jagged teeth that catch the dim light and throw it back fractured.

"There it is," Ryan announces unnecessarily. "Marrowick's pride and joy. Or it was, back when this place actually made things instead of just rotting."

The smell hits them before they reach the fence. Sour and thick, the scent of sawdust that never properly dried, never properly rotted, just exists in some in-between state of decomposition. It coats the back of Vincent's throat, makes him want to spit but he doesn't, not wanting to give Ryan the satisfaction of seeing him affected.

"Bet you're too scared to get closer," Ryan says, already climbing through a gap in the chain-link fence where someone has cut the wire. "Probably worried about getting your nice clothes dirty."

Vincent follows without hesitation, though something in his chest tightens as he approaches the building. The ground around it is soft, almost spongy, covered in a layer of decomposed wood chips that release their sour smell with each step. Emily dances through behind them, laughing at something only she finds funny.

"It's just an old building," she says, spreading her arms wide as if to embrace the decay. "Nothing scary about rust and rot."

Vincent reaches the outer wall first, drawn by something he can't name. The metal is cold under his palm, colder than the air around it, like it's pulling heat from his hand. He presses harder, and he swears he feels something beneath the surface. A rhythm. Slow and deep. The building expanding and contracting so slightly he might be imagining it.

Except he's not imagining it. The metal moves, just barely, like the ribs of something breathing in sleep.

"What are you doing?" Ryan asks, impatient. "Looking for a way in?"

Vincent doesn't answer, moving along the wall until he finds a gap between two sheets of metal where rust has eaten through the bolts. He leans closer, squinting into the darkness inside. The smell is stronger here, that sour sawdust mixed with something else, something fungal and alive.

His eyes adjust slowly to the dim interior. Massive beams stretch across the space, old wood that should be dry and dead but isn't. Along the beams, in patterns too regular to be natural, pale mushrooms grow. They're white as paper, clustered in groups that expand and contract with their own rhythm, not matching the building's breathing but complementing it somehow.

"What do you see?" Emily pushes past him, pressing her face to the gap. "Oh, gross. Look at all that mold."

"It's not mold," Mira says, her first words since they left the house. She stands a few feet back, her body tense like an animal sensing danger.

"Whatever it is, it's disgusting." Emily reaches through the gap, her fingers stretching toward the nearest cluster of pale blooms. "Probably some kind of wood fungus. We studied them in biology. They break down dead tissue, totally natural."

"Don't..." Vincent starts, but Emily's fingers have already brushed against one of the pale caps.

The reaction is immediate. The mushroom releases a cloud of spores, white and dense, that swirls around Emily's hand like smoke with purpose. The particles catch what little light filters through the broken roof, glowing faintly as they disperse into the air. Emily laughs, waving her hand to clear them, not understanding what she's done.

Mira moves faster than Vincent has ever seen her move. She lunges forward, grabs Emily's wrist, and yanks her back from the wall with enough force that Emily stumbles, nearly falls. The anger on Mira's face is shocking, transforming her usual calm into something fierce and frightening.

"Don't touch it," she snaps, her voice carrying an edge Vincent has never heard before. "Never touch it."

Emily blinks, her face going through that now-familiar transformation from animation to confusion. The laughter dies in her throat. She looks at her hand, where spores still cling to her skin like ash, then at Mira's furious face.

"I'm sorry," Emily says, but the words come out flat, emotionless, like she's apologizing for something she doesn't remember doing. "I just wanted to see what would happen."

Ryan shifts uncomfortably, the bravado draining from his posture. "Maybe we should head back. Mom will worry if we're gone too long." The excuse sounds thin, but no one challenges it.

They retreat from the mill, but Vincent notices how Mira positions herself between Emily and the building, walking backwards for the first few steps as if the structure might follow them. Her hand still grips Emily's wrist, not hard but firm, keeping her moving away from those pale blooms and their drifting spores.

The mill recedes behind them, swallowed by drizzle and distance, but Vincent can still feel it there. Breathing. Waiting. Growing its pale fruit along beams that should be dead but aren't. He thinks about the spores that touched Emily's skin, wonders if they're already working their way inside, already beginning to feed on whatever makes her Emily.

The walk back is quiet except for the rain and their footsteps in the mud. Emily doesn't skip through puddles now, just walks with purpose, her hand still in Mira's grip. Ryan doesn't taunt or challenge, just leads them home with his hood pulled low against more than just the weather.

And Mira watches Emily with that same intense focus from breakfast, like she's trying to see through skin and bone to whatever might be taking root inside.

———

Vincent lies awake in his room, the mattress beneath him feeling both too soft and too hard, his body unable to find that position where consciousness finally releases its grip. The rain taps against the window in an irregular rhythm, sometimes gentle, sometimes insistent, like something trying different combinations to get in. He's kicked the quilt off twice, pulled it back up twice more, but nothing helps. His mind won't stop turning over the day, examining each disturbing moment like evidence of a crime he can't quite name.

The radiator gives its periodic clank, then falls silent. The house settles around him with sounds that might be wood contracting in the dampness or might be something else moving through the walls. Each creak seems deliberate, weighted with meaning he can't decipher. Through the window, the yard light flickers, casting the room in alternating dimness and darker dimness, never quite achieving real darkness or real light.

He can't stop seeing Emily's face at breakfast, the way it transformed when her mother asked for something as simple as salt. That sudden hardness in her eyes, like shutters slamming closed. The words that poured out, cruel and specific, designed to wound in ways only family knows how to wound. And then the confusion after, that blank incomprehension, as if someone else had spoken through her mouth and left her empty when they were done.

Vincent turns onto his side, then his back again. The pillow feels wrong no matter how he arranges it. Too warm where his head has been, too cool when he flips it over. His thoughts shift to Clare's hands, the way they trembled as she continued serving breakfast, pretending nothing had happened. That kind of practiced denial that comes from years of smoothing over difficult truths. But this was different from normal family tension. This was something invasive and external.

The mill haunts him most of all. That sensation under his

palm when he touched the metal wall, the slow expansion and contraction like the building was some massive living thing playing dead. He knows buildings don't breathe. Metal and wood and rust don't have lungs or need air. But he felt it, as surely as he feels his own chest rising and falling now. The mill was breathing, and inside, those pale mushrooms pulsed with their own rhythm, growing from wood that should have been too dead to sustain them.

He sees Emily's fingers reaching through that gap, brushing against the fungus with casual curiosity. The spore cloud that erupted, dense and purposeful, swirling around her hand like it knew exactly where it wanted to go. How she laughed, waving it away, not understanding that she was breathing it in, that it was settling on her skin, finding its way inside through pores and lungs and the spaces between cells.

The memory makes him pull the quilt up to his chin despite not being cold. He thinks about spores, about how they're designed to travel, to find new places to grow. How they only need the smallest foothold to begin transforming whatever they touch into something else. Something that feeds them.

A shape in the corner of the room draws his attention. He's been aware of it peripherally, but now he focuses on it properly. Mira sits in the chair by the window, so still she could be part of the furniture except for the subtle rise and fall of her breathing. She's been there since they came up to bed, but she hasn't moved to her own bed, hasn't changed from her day clothes. Just sits there, watching something through the fogged glass that Vincent can't see.

She hasn't spoken since they returned from the mill. Through dinner, she maintained that intense focus on Emily, watching every gesture, every word, like she was looking for signs of something. Clare tried to draw her into conversation, but Mira only gave minimal responses, her attention never wavering from Emily's face. Even when Emily laughed at something Ryan said, sounding normal, sounding like herself, Mira watched with that particular stillness that means she's seeing more than what's on the surface.

Vincent shifts again, the bed frame creaking. He's about to ask Mira what she's thinking, what she's seeing out there in the darkness, when she speaks. Her voice is low, barely above a whisper, but in the quiet room it carries perfectly.

"It's spreading."

Two words, but they land with the weight of certainty. Not a question, not a theory. A statement of fact as sure as gravity or the tide. Vincent props himself up on one elbow, studying her silhouette against the window's faint light.

"The fungus?" he asks, though he knows that's not all she means.

She doesn't look at him, her eyes fixed on something beyond the fogged glass. Maybe the yard, maybe the distant shadow of the tree line, maybe something only she can perceive with whatever strange sensitivity allows her to be in two places at once.

"It's in her now," Mira continues, still in that whisper. "In Emily. I can see it working, changing things inside her. Taking the connections between thoughts and feelings and eating them. Leaving just the actions without the why."

Vincent thinks about Emily's flat apology, her confusion about her own cruelty. Like the emotion had been consumed, leaving only the mechanical motion of words without meaning behind them. He thinks about the couple in town, their rage transforming to emptiness, their hands joining without feeling.

"Can we stop it?" he asks.

Mira doesn't answer immediately. The rain intensifies against the window, running down in streams that distort the outside world into abstract patterns. When she finally speaks, her voice carries a weight that seems too heavy for someone her age.

"I don't know what it wants. But it's patient. It's been here longer than the town, maybe. Growing in the dark, in the spaces people don't look. And now it's ready for more."

The house creaks around them, a long, low sound that starts in the walls and moves through the floors. Not the settling of old wood but something more deliberate, like joints flexing or bones adjusting position. Vincent strains to hear if it's just the structure responding to temperature and moisture, or if something moves within the walls themselves, spreading through the spaces between beams like those pale mushrooms in the mill.

Outside, the fog presses closer to the windows, so thick now that even the yard light becomes just a suggestion of illumination. Somewhere in that gray nothing, Vincent imagines he can feel the mill breathing, its metal lungs expanding and contracting, releasing more spores into the night air. Spores that will settle on surfaces, find cracks to grow in, discover new things to hollow out and consume.

He lies back down, pulling the quilt up despite knowing sleep won't come. Mira remains at the window, standing guard or bearing witness, he's not sure which. The rain continues its irregular rhythm. The house continues its suspicious creaking. And somewhere in another room, Emily sleeps with spores working their way deeper inside, changing her thought by thought, feeling by feeling, until only the shell remains.

Vincent closes his eyes, but behind his eyelids he sees those pale blooms pulsing, breathing, spreading. Always spreading.

CHAPTER
SIX

The morning light through the kitchen windows has that quality of illumination without warmth, casting everything in shades of gray that make the eggs on Vincent's plate look like something dredged from the sea. He pushes them around with his fork, creating patterns that mean nothing, while the kitchen fills with the sounds of another fractured morning at Holt House. The coffee percolates with its familiar gurgle, bacon pops in the pan, Clare hums something that might be a hymn but comes out more like a dirge.

Vincent watches his mother from the corner of his eye. Angela stands near the doorway, not quite in the kitchen, not quite out of it, existing in that liminal space she's perfected since they arrived. Her lips move in that familiar pattern he knows so well. "One sixty-four," she whispers, the words barely breath. Her finger taps against her wrist, three times, pause, three times. The counting that keeps her tethered to sobriety, each day added like a brick in a wall she's building between herself and the past.

Clare moves through her morning routine with the efficiency of someone who finds comfort in repetition. She flips pancakes without looking, her hands knowing exactly when to turn them. The kitchen should feel warm with all this activity, but something in the air resists comfort. The smell of breakfast mingles with that persistent dampness that seeps into everything here, creating an atmosphere that's both domestic and vaguely threatening.

Emily enters with less energy than usual, her movements sluggish like she's walking through water. She drops into her chair without her typical morning chatter, reaching for the syrup before Clare has even set down the pancakes. Her fingers wrap around the bottle with unnecessary force, knuckles white.

"Could you wait until everyone's served?" Clare asks, her voice gentle, the kind of maternal correction that barely registers as criticism.

The change in Emily's face happens between heartbeats. Her eyes, dull a moment ago, sharpen into something hard and cutting. Her mouth twists into an expression that doesn't belong on a teenager's face, too old, too cruel.

"Always controlling everything," Emily says, her voice carrying an edge that makes everyone in the room freeze. "Every little thing has to be your way. The food, the prayers, the constant hovering. You think your faith makes you better than everyone, but you're just scared. Scared of being alone, scared of admitting Dad's death meant nothing, scared that your precious God doesn't even know you exist. You know what? I don't want your God. I want Dad back."

The words pour out with malicious intent, each one calculated to wound. But Emily's eyes remain somehow separate from what her mouth is saying, like someone else is speaking through her, using her voice but not her intent.

Clare's hand trembles as she sets down the spatula. The tremor starts in her fingers and works its way up her arm, subtle but visible to anyone watching. She turns back to the stove, her movements careful and deliberate, pretending to check something that doesn't need checking.

"Sweet, Emily," Clare says, holding back tears. Her voice catches on her daughter's name. She clears her throat, tries again. "You must be tired. Maybe you didn't sleep well."

Vincent sees how Clare grips the edge of the counter, holding herself steady. The knuckles go white, then red, then white again as she adjusts her grip. She reaches for a plate, and it rattles against the counter before she steadies it. Every movement requires visible effort, like she's puppeting her own body through the motions of normalcy.

"Enough!" Ryan's fork hits his plate with a clatter that makes Vincent jump. His usual slouch straightens, shoulders squaring as he turns to face his sister. "What the hell is wrong with you?"

Emily blinks rapidly, confusion flooding her features. The hardness drains away, leaving her looking young and lost. "I..." She looks around the table, taking in everyone's frozen positions, their careful not-looking. "Mom, I'm sorry. I didn't mean..."

The apology trails off into nothing. Emily stares at her hands like they belong to someone else, turning them over, examining the fingers that just moments ago gripped the syrup bottle with such unnecessary force.

"It's fine, dear," Clare says, still not turning around. "Just eat your breakfast."

Ryan chooses to deflect from his sister and leans back in his chair, that studied casualness that means he's about to say something cutting. His eyes find Vincent, measuring him with the kind of assessment that always precedes cruelty.

"Nice shirt, Dusboy," Ryan says, his smirk audible in his voice. "Is that what passes for fashion in your swamp? Or did you borrow it from someone who actually has shoulders?"

Vincent feels heat rise in his chest but keeps his expression neutral. Ryan continues, warming to his theme.

"Seriously, you're like a scarecrow someone forgot to stuff. All poles and angles. Bet you have to run around in the shower just to get wet." Ryan laughs at his own joke, the sound harsh in the tense kitchen. "No wonder you spend all your time with Mira. She's the only one who makes you look normal by comparison."

"Ryan," Clare says, finally turning from the stove. Her face has composed itself into something like calm, but Vincent can see the effort it takes. "What is with you two? Apologize. Now."

"Just making conversation," Ryan says, but something flickers in his expression. A moment of uncertainty, like he's not entirely sure why he felt compelled to attack Vincent just then.

Through all of this, Mira hasn't moved. She sits across from Emily, her dark eyes fixed on the other girl with an intensity of one studying a yet-undiscovered creature. She doesn't eat, doesn't drink, just watches. Her stillness is different from her usual quiet observation. This is focused, clinical, like she's documenting symptoms of a disease.

Emily reaches for her fork, and Mira's eyes track the movement. Emily cuts her pancake, and Mira watches the knife slide through. Every gesture, every breath, every blink is catalogued in Mira's unwavering gaze. It should be uncomfortable, being watched like that, but Emily doesn't seem to notice. Or maybe she notices but can't bring herself to care, that hollow confusion still clouding her features.

Forks scrape against plates with too much force. Coffee cups clink against saucers like punctuation marks in an argument no one's having. Clare moves between table and stove, her hands still trembling slightly, dropping more food on plates that already have too much.

Angela hasn't moved from her doorway position. Her lips

continue their counting, and Vincent catches fragments. "Stay present," she whispers. "One day at a time. One sixty-four." The mantras of recovery mixing with her daily count, a shield against the tension that fills the kitchen like smoke.

Vincent forces himself to eat, though the eggs taste like nothing and the pancakes sit heavy in his stomach. He thinks about the fungus at the mill, those pale blooms Emily touched yesterday. The spores that swirled around her hand, settling on her skin, finding their way inside. Is this what they do? Eat away at the connections between thought and feeling, leaving people to say cruel things without understanding why?

The kitchen feels smaller with each passing minute, the walls pressing in, the air thickening despite the open window. Even the morning light seems perverse, filtered through clouds and fog until it carries no warmth, only the bare minimum of illumination needed to see the damage being done.

———

The path to St. Dymphna's cuts through the older part of Marrowick, where houses lean against each other like drunks trying to stay upright. Vincent follows Clare's determined stride, watching how she navigates the cracked sidewalks with unconscious precision, her feet finding the stable spots between buckled concrete and invasive moss. The afternoon has brought no improvement to the weather, just a lighter shade of gray that passes for daylight here.

"Saint... Dimf..." Angela pauses, her tongue struggling with the unfamiliar name. "How do you say it again?"

"Dimf. Nuh," Clare corrects gently, her voice carrying the patience of someone who's explained this before. "Saint Dymphna. She's the patron saint of mental illness, nervous disorders, and family happiness." She touches the small cross at her throat as she speaks, a gesture so automatic she probably doesn't realize she's doing it.

Angela nods, mouthing the name silently, adding it to her collection of things to remember. Vincent sees her lips move through the syllables, practicing, the same careful attention she brings to counting days. "Saint Dymphna," she finally says aloud, getting it right.

Ryan kicks a stone ahead of them, sending it skittering into a puddle. "Patron saint of crazy people. Perfect for this town."

"Ryan," Clare's voice carries a warning, but it's mild, tired.

The church appears around a bend, and Vincent's first thought is that it looks like something that's been fighting a losing battle for decades. The stone walls wear their age badly, streaked with dark stains where water has run down for so many years it's carved channels in the rock. Moss grows thick on the northern side, so dense it looks like fur, green and dripping. The steps leading to the entrance are cracked, grass pushing through, puddles collecting in the depressions.

The wooden doors hang slightly askew, the hinges rusted and complaining when Clare pushes them open. Water drips from the eaves in a steady rhythm, has been dripping so long there are grooves worn in the stone beneath. The whole structure seems to be slowly dissolving back into the earth, returning to component parts of stone and wood and memory.

"Watch the threshold," Clare says, stepping over a portion where the stone has crumbled.

Vincent expects the inside to match the outside, expects that familiar Marrowick smell of damp and decay, the fungal undertone that colors everything here. His foot crosses the threshold, and the change is so immediate, so complete, that he actually stops walking.

The air inside St. Dymphna's is clear. Not just clear, but

actively clean, carrying the scent of beeswax and old wood and something else, something that reminds him of morning frost, sharp and pure. No moisture clings to these walls. No mildew darkens the corners. The very atmosphere feels different, lighter, as if the weight that presses down on all of Marrowick stops at the door.

Vincent breathes deeply, and it's the first full breath he's taken since arriving in this town. His lungs expand without that feeling of breathing through wet cloth. The air moves freely here, circulating in patterns that have nothing to do with decay.

The interior contradicts everything the exterior promised. Wooden pews gleam with polish, their surfaces reflecting the light from windows that should be grimy but aren't. The floor, old stone worn smooth by generations of footsteps, shows no sign of the moisture that plagues every other building in town. Even the corners, those spaces where dampness usually collects and breeds, are dry and clean.

Candles burn at the corners of the room, their flames steady and straight, not flickering in drafts. The smoke rises in perfect columns, disappearing into the heights of the ceiling without spreading that fungal smell that smoke usually carries in Marrowick. Instead, it smells like frankincense and myrrh, ancient and somehow protective.

"How?" Vincent says, not meaning to speak aloud.

Elias, who's been silent since they left the house, actually responds. "The church is maintained by the diocese. They send someone to clean weekly." But even his clinical explanation sounds uncertain, like he knows this level of preservation goes beyond normal maintenance.

Mira moves away from the group, drawn toward the center of the nave. She stands there with her eyes closed, head tilted slightly, that gesture she makes when she's listening for something others can't hear. Her hands hang loose at her sides, fingers spread slightly, as if feeling the air itself.

"It's quiet here," she says, and Vincent understands she doesn't mean the absence of sound. She means the absence of that thing, that presence that seems to inhabit every other space in Marrowick. Whatever feeds on the town, whatever grows in the mill and spreads through the streets, it stops at these doors.

Emily, who's been brittle and sharp all day, seems to soften in the church's atmosphere. The tension drains from her shoulders, the hard set of her jaw relaxes. She moves closer to Clare, and then, in a gesture that seems to surprise them both, leans her head against her mother's shoulder.

Clare's hand comes up automatically, smoothing Emily's hair with the kind of unconscious affection that speaks of years of such gestures. Emily doesn't pull away, doesn't stiffen, just rests there like she used to when she was younger, before whatever began growing inside her started eating away at their connection.

"I'm tired, Mom," Emily whispers, and she sounds like herself, truly herself, for the first time since yesterday at the mill.

"I know, sweetheart," Clare murmurs back, her arm coming around Emily's shoulders.

For this moment, in this space, they look like what they're supposed to be: a mother and daughter who love each other, not two people being slowly hollowed out. The sight makes Vincent's chest tight with something that might be hope or might be grief for what's being lost.

Angela stands beside Elias near a bank of votive candles, their small flames creating a constellation of light against the stone. She reaches into her purse, finds some coins, drops them into the offering box with a soft clink. Then she lights a candle, her lips moving in what might be prayer or might be her eternal counting. Elias watches her with an expression Vincent can't read, something between confusion and recognition.

Ryan lounges in a pew, trying to maintain his air of indifference, but even he seems affected by the atmosphere. His usual sneer has softened to something merely skeptical, and he's stopped making commentary about everything being stupid or boring.

The church holds them in its clean air and steady light, a pocket of resistance against whatever is consuming Marrowick. Vincent finds himself reluctant to leave, to step back through those doors into the gray world where things grow wrong and people lose pieces of themselves without knowing why.

But they can't stay here forever. This is temporary sanctuary, not solution. Outside, the rain continues its patient work of dissolution. The fungus spreads through wood and stone and flesh. And Emily, leaning against her mother in this moment of peace, still carries spores inside her that will resume their work the moment they leave this protected space.

Clare begins to move toward the door, Emily still close beside her. "We should go. I need to start dinner."

They file out slowly, each of them taking one last breath of that clean air before stepping back into Marrowick's persistent dampness. Vincent is the last to leave, pausing at the threshold to look back at the gleaming pews, the steady candles, the impossible preservation of this space.

Then he steps outside, and the weight of the town settles back onto his shoulders like a familiar, unwelcome coat.

The peace of St. Dymphna's lasts exactly as long as it takes them to reach the first bend in the path home. Vincent feels it leave like warmth draining from his skin, replaced by that familiar dampness that characterizes everything in Marrowick. The group spreads out along the narrow path, Clare and Angela ahead discussing dinner plans, Elias following with his measured stride, Ryan kicking stones into puddles with renewed aggression.

Emily falls into step beside Vincent. At first it seems natural enough, the random redistribution of walking positions that happens in any group. But she matches his pace too precisely, maintains a distance that's slightly too close, her shoulder occasionally brushing his arm in a way that feels deliberate.

"Your shirt's soft," she says, and before Vincent can process the strange comment, her hand is on his arm, fingers running along the fabric of his sleeve.

The touch starts at his elbow and travels up toward his shoulder, slow and exploring. Her fingers press through the thin material, finding the shape of his arm underneath. It's not a casual touch, not the brief contact of teenagers who barely know each other. There's something searching in it, intimate in a way that makes Vincent glance towards Mira.

He pulls away, stepping sideways to put distance between them, but Emily follows. Her face wears an expression he can't read, part smile, part confusion, like she's not entirely sure what she's doing but can't stop doing it.

"Did you know," she says, her voice taking on a quality that doesn't sound like her, "that skin is the largest organ? All those nerve endings, all that sensitivity. We feel so much with our fingertips, but it could be more."

Her fingers find his wrist where his sleeve ends, skin against skin now, and her touch is cold despite the afternoon's warmth. She traces the veins visible through his pale skin, following their blue lines with a focus that feels clinical and deceiving.

Vincent jerks his arm away completely this time, stepping off the path to put a puddle between them. His chest feels tight, his breathing shallow. Not from attraction, but from the absurdness of it, the sense that Emily is touching him but it's not really Emily doing the touching.

"What are you doing?" The words come out harsher than

intended, loud enough that Angela glances back with concern.

Emily blinks, her hand still extended toward where Vincent's arm was, fingers grasping at empty air. She looks at her own hand with the same confusion she had at breakfast after snapping at her mother. That disconnection between action and intent, like someone else is moving her body while she watches from inside.

"I don't..." She trails off, pulling her hand back to her chest, cradling it like something injured.

Her voice sounds young suddenly, scared. The strange quality that colored her words moments ago has vanished, leaving just a teenage girl who doesn't understand her own behavior. She looks between Vincent and her still-extended hand, then takes a step back, then another, putting distance between them as if proximity itself is dangerous.

Vincent glances at Mira, who's been walking behind them, observing everything with that stillness she's perfected. Her dark eyes move from Emily to Vincent, taking in his discomfort, Emily's confusion, the space that now exists between them. She doesn't speak, doesn't offer comfort or explanation, just watches with an intensity that suggests she's adding this to her growing catalog of things she notices about Emily.

Ryan recognizes the tension and laughs, but it's not his usual mocking sound. There's uncertainty in it, like he's laughing because he doesn't know what else to do. "Em's getting weird. Weirder than usual, anyway."

"Shut up," Emily says, but without force. She wraps her arms around herself, fingers digging into her upper arms through her sweater, holding herself together or holding something in.

The walk home continues in strained silence. Emily stays far from Vincent now, walking alone between groups, her head down. Every few steps she looks at her hands, turning them over, examining them like evidence of a crime she doesn't remember committing. Clare calls back to ask if she's alright, and Emily responds with automatic assurance that means nothing.

Vincent keeps his distance too, his arm still feeling the ghost of her touch, too intimate, too searching. He thinks about the spores from the mill, how they settled on her skin yesterday. Is this what they do? Not just eat away at emotional connections but create new ones, wrong ones, connections that shouldn't exist?

The house appears through the trees, and everyone seems to exhale with relief. They scatter immediately upon entering, fleeing to separate rooms as if distance might help, might stop whatever is happening to Emily from spreading to the rest of them. Vincent climbs the stairs to his room, still feeling the cold track of Emily's fingers on his skin.

Night comes early to Marrowick, or maybe it never fully leaves, just varies in intensity of darkness. Vincent lies in bed, listening to the rain that started again after dinner, trying not to think about Emily's touch, the way her fingers pressed through fabric like she was trying to reach something deeper than skin.

Sleep comes in fragments, broken by the radiator's clanking and the house's settling and dreams of pale fingers reaching through the dark. He wakes to find the room colder than it should be, his breath visible in small puffs that dissipate into the darkness.

Mira sits at the window.

She's so still Vincent thinks at first she might be sleeping upright, but then he sees her eyes are open, reflecting what little light filters through the fog outside. She's wearing the same clothes from dinner, hasn't changed for bed, like she's been sitting there for hours watching something in the gray nothing beyond the glass.

"Can't sleep?" Vincent asks, his voice rough with interrupted dreams.

"I got enough," Mira says without turning. "I'm working through it. The fungus is just the medium. He's using it just as he used Muldrath."

The words don't make immediate sense, but with Mira, they rarely do. Vincent sits up, blanket pulled around his shoulders against the cold. The window glass is beaded with moisture, condensation running down in streams that distort the world outside into abstract suggestions of trees and sky.

"What do you mean?"

Mira's hand rises to the glass, her palm flat against the cold surface. Where her skin touches, the condensation clears in a perfect handprint, revealing the fog beyond with startling clarity.

"It's not there," she says, and Vincent thinks she means the fungus, the presence that seems to inhabit everything in Marrowick. But then she continues, her voice dropping to barely above a whisper. "What he wants is here."

She moves her hand from the window to her chest, laying it flat over her heart. The gesture is precise, deliberate, like she's indicating a specific location on a map.

"Yes, it's true. I can be in two places," she says, turning finally to look at him. Her eyes in the darkness are deep and certain. "Here, talking to you. And somewhere else, seeing things I need to see. It's always been this way, but it's stronger here. The boundaries are thinner."

Vincent thinks about seeing her in the hallway that first night, translucent, facing the wall while also sleeping in her bed. Two Miras, dual purpose. He wants to ask more, but something in her expression stops him. This is all the explanation she can give, maybe all the explanation that exists.

"What do you see when you're somewhere else?" he asks instead.

Mira turns back to the window, her hand still over her heart. "The spaces between things. Where the fungus grows. Where it came from. Where it's going." She pauses, her head tilting in that bird-like way. "He's patient. He's been waiting so long, people have forgotten that he exists. But he found a crack in Emily. Her touch, her reaching. He's using her to get what he wants."

The room feels colder still, and Vincent pulls the blanket tighter. Outside, the fog presses against the window like something trying to get in, and Mira sits watching, observing the world as he struggles with her knowledge that he understands more like riddles.

CHAPTER
SEVEN

The drizzle has thinned to something that's more suggestion than actual rain, leaving the Holt backyard heavy with moisture that clings to everything like a second skin. Vincent stands on the porch, watching Clare gesture toward the depleted stack beside the back door, her movements carrying the efficiency of someone who's managed wood supplies through decades of damp winters.

"Ryan, we need more wood for tonight," she says, not looking at her son but at the gray sky, gauging whether the weather will hold. "Take Vincent with you. Show him where we keep the good pieces."

Ryan pushes off from the wall where he's been slouching, his perpetual air of barely contained irritation sharpening into something more focused. "Sure, Mom. Love playing tour guide."

The sarcasm rolls off Clare like water. She's already turning back to the house, her mind on dinner preparations or laundry or any of the dozen tasks that keep her moving through each day. Vincent catches the slight tremor in her hands, still there from this morning's breakfast confrontation with Emily, but she grips the door handle and steadies herself before disappearing inside.

"Come on, Dusboy," Ryan says, already heading toward the far corner of the yard. "Try not to hurt yourself."

Vincent follows, his shoes squelching in the saturated grass. The backyard stretches longer than it looked from the house, sloping down toward a grove of cedars that mark the property line. Everything here wears a coat of green, moss creeping up fence posts, algae staining the concrete blocks that mark the garden beds, lichen spreading across every surface that stays still long enough.

The woodpile sits under a makeshift shelter, three walls of corrugated metal that do little to keep out the persistent damp. The logs glisten with moisture despite the covering, their cut ends dark with rot that's working its way inward. An ax leans against a weathered stump, its blade spotted with rust, handle worn smooth from years of use.

Ryan grabs the ax with the kind of casual familiarity that comes from growing up in a place where splitting wood is as routine as brushing teeth. He sets a log on the stump, raises the ax in one smooth motion, and brings it down with perfect economy of movement. The blade bites deep. CRACK! The log splits clean, two halves falling away from each other like something surrendering.

"See?" Ryan says, though Vincent hasn't asked for demonstration. "Easy."

He holds out the ax handle toward Vincent, that smirk playing at his lips that means he's about to enjoy himself at someone else's expense. Vincent takes the ax, surprised by its weight, the way it wants to pull his arms down. The handle is slick with moisture and who knows what else, requiring a tighter grip than seems necessary.

Vincent positions a log on the stump, trying to mirror Ryan's stance. He lifts the ax, feeling immediately that his form is wrong, his balance off. The swing comes down crooked, the blade glancing off the side of the log instead of biting into it. The deflection sends the ax head toward his leg, and he has to jump back to avoid catching the blade in his shin.

Ryan barks out a laugh, sharp and delighted. "Nice foot-work. Very graceful."

Heat rises in Vincent's face, but he repositions himself, adjusts his grip. The second attempt is no better, the ax bouncing off the log entirely, sending a shock up through his arms that makes his shoulders ache. The log rolls off the stump, unmarked except for a small dent where the blade failed to penetrate.

"So," Ryan says, leaning against the shelter's post with studied casualness, "you're really into my emo cousin? That's your thing?"

Vincent sets another log on the stump, not responding, concentrating on the placement. But Ryan continues, warming to his theme.

"What do you two even do? Sit in the dark and write poetry about death? Stare at walls together? Compare who has the most tragic backstory?"

The ax comes down wrong again, barely grazing the log. Vincent's hands are starting to blister from the wet handle, the skin burning where it rubs deep. He can feel Ryan watching, enjoying every failed attempt, storing up material for future mockery.

"I mean, I get it," Ryan continues, his voice taking on a false sympathy that's worse than straight cruelty. "She's pretty in that whole broken doll way. But man, the family baggage."

Vincent adjusts his stance, trying to find the right angle, the right force. The ax feels heavier with each swing, his arms already tired from the unfamiliar motion. Sweat mixes with the mist on his face, dripping into his eyes, making it harder to aim.

"Her mom just walked out, didn't she?" Ryan's voice has

shifted, carrying an edge that cuts deeper than mockery. "Couldn't handle living with her and her dad being so weird. Just up and left one day. What kind of mother does that?"

The words hit Vincent like cold water, washing away the embarrassment of his incompetence with the ax, replacing it with something harder and sharper. His knuckles go white around the ax handle, and for a moment he imagines swinging it in a different direction, seeing how Ryan's smirk would look split down the middle.

But Vincent knows the truth that Ryan never will. Mira's mother didn't abandon them. She sacrificed herself to save Duswood, to protect her daughter from something that would have consumed them all. That truth sits heavy in Vincent's chest, a secret that's not his to tell, a burden he carries alongside Mira's strange grief.

"Guess it runs in the family," Ryan continues, oblivious to the way Vincent's entire body has gone rigid. "The weird, I mean. Apple doesn't fall far from the tree. Or in this case, doesn't fall at all, just hangs there being strange and making everyone uncomfortable."

Vincent sets the ax down with careful, controlled movements. His hands shake slightly, but not from exertion. He turns to face Ryan fully, meeting his eyes with a steadiness that seems to surprise them both.

"You have no idea what happened," Vincent says, his voice flat and empty of emotion. "But…whatever helps you sleep at night, man."

Ryan's smirk falters for just a moment, something flickering behind his eyes. Uncertainty maybe, or recognition that he's pushed into territory he doesn't understand. But the moment passes, and the smirk returns, satisfied with having gotten under Vincent's skin even if he doesn't quite understand how or why.

"Touched a nerve, huh?" Ryan says, but there's less confidence in it now.

Vincent doesn't respond, just turns and starts gathering the few pieces of split wood, carrying them back toward the house. His shoulders burn from the failed attempts with the ax, his hands throb where blisters are forming, but these physical discomforts are nothing compared to the weight of carrying truths that can never be spoken.

Neither of them notices the figure on the porch, half-hidden in the shadow of the doorway. Mira stands perfectly still, having witnessed the entire exchange. Her expression remains unreadable, that particular blankness she wears when she's processing information that exists in multiple layers of meaning. She watches Vincent approach with the wood, watches Ryan kick at the remaining logs with renewed aggression, watches the space between them fill with unspoken tensions that smell like rust and rot and things better left buried.

———

Emily announces her plan with the determination of someone who needs movement to escape their own skin, her voice carrying that brittle brightness that's become her default since yesterday morning's strange cruelties. "We're going back to the cove," she says, already pulling on her yellow rain jacket. "There's more to see. Caves on the north end we didn't get to last time."

No one argues. The house feels too small with too much tension, the walls pressing in with accumulated grievances and unspoken fears. Even Ryan seems eager to escape, shoving his hands into his pockets and heading for the door without his usual complaints about Emily's enthusiasm.

The path to Ashen Cove seems shorter this time, or maybe Vincent's feet are learning the rhythm of root and stone, the places where the ground gives way to mud and where it holds firm. The drizzle has stopped entirely, leaving just the fog, thick and low, moving through the trees like something searching. It clings to their clothes, beads on their hair, makes everything more than a few feet away look like a watercolor painting left in the rain.

They emerge from the tree line onto the beach, and Vincent feels again that sense of entering an alien landscape. Ashen Cove stretches before them in shades of gray that have no names, each one bleeding into the next until it's impossible to tell where the stones end and the water begins. The tide is lower than before, exposing more of the beach's architecture, the way the shale layers itself in sheets that crack and shift underfoot.

Driftwood piles along the high tide line like the bones of ancient creatures, bleached white by salt and sun that rarely shows itself here. Some logs are massive, wider than Vincent is tall, worn smooth in places, splintered and raw in others. Kelp tangles around the rocks in ropes thick as his arm, dark and slick, still moving slightly as if animated by more than just the wind.

The tidepools spread before them like mirrors to a gray sky, their surfaces disturbed only by the occasional bubble rising from hidden depths. Vincent peers into one and sees anemones closed tight against the air, barnacles sealed in their tiny fortresses, crabs scuttling sideways into crevices too small to follow. Everything here knows how to hide, how to protect itself from exposure.

Seagulls wheel overhead, their cries distorted by the fog into something that sounds almost like language, words stretched and twisted until they lose all meaning. They dive and rise, dive and rise, but never land, as if the beach itself repels them. Vincent notices how they avoid certain areas entirely, whole sections of shore that look no different from the rest but must carry some invisible warning.

Emily leads them north along the waterline, jumping from rock to rock with practiced ease. Her yellow jacket makes her easy to track in the gray monotony, a spot of color that seems almost violent against the muted landscape. She calls back directions, warnings about loose stones and slippery patches, but her voice sounds thin, swallowed by the fog almost as soon as it leaves her mouth.

The rocks grow larger as they move north, requiring actual climbing rather than just careful stepping. Vincent's hands find purchase on barnacle-crusted surfaces that tear at his palms, leave them stinging with tiny cuts. The smell here is stronger, that mixture of salt and decay that coats the inside of his nose, makes everything taste like the ocean.

Ryan climbs with aggressive efficiency, taking the hardest routes as if to prove something. He pulls himself up onto a particularly tall boulder, stands at its peak like he's conquered something meaningful. Mira moves more carefully, testing each handhold before committing her weight, her dark clothes making her almost invisible against the wet stone.

"And there's the weirdo," Emily says, pointing across the curve of shore.

Vincent follows her gesture and sees it, though at first his brain refuses to process it as a structure built by human hands. The shack leans against the tree line like something that grew there rather than was constructed, its walls a patchwork of driftwood and rusted tin that speaks of decades of repair with whatever the beach provided. The roof sags in the middle, and Vincent can see gaps where the weather has torn away sections, covered over with blue tarp that flaps in the wind like diseased skin.

A thin wisp of smoke rises from a pipe that might be a chimney, might be something else, the smoke dispersing into the fog almost immediately. The windows, what few Vincent can see, are covered with what looks like newspaper or cardboard, blocking any view inside. A collection of objects surrounds the shack, things pulled from the water or the woods, arranged in patterns that might have meaning or might just be the accumulation of years of scavenging.

"That's where Jonah Kells lives," Ryan says, and there's something different in his voice now, the mockery replaced with what might be respect or might be fear.

"Who?" Vincent asks, though something about the name feels familiar, like something overheard but not quite remembered.

Ryan jumps down from his boulder, landing with a splash in a tidepool. "Local crazy person. Used to be smart, Dad says. Knew Mira's dad back in school or something. But he went sour, started talking about things that don't make sense. Lives out here like some kind of hermit, collecting garbage and talking to himself."

"He's not crazy," Emily says, but quietly, like she's not sure she believes it. "He just sees things different. And people see him as different. Or…I don't know. Just…ya know. Weird."

"Yeah, that's what crazy means," Ryan responds, but he's looking at the shack with an expression Vincent can't read. "Dad says he used to be normal. Had a real job, real life. Then something happened, no one really knows what, and he just… opted out. Started living rough, started saying things about the town that made people uncomfortable."

"What kind of things?" Vincent asks.

Ryan shrugs, but it's forced casual. "Weird stuff. About things growing where they shouldn't. About the town being sick. About how we're all feeding something without knowing it." He kicks at a piece of kelp. "Crazy talk."

Vincent feels a chill that has nothing to do with the ocean wind. The words sound too familiar, too close to what he's been observing since they arrived. He looks at Mira, expecting her to say something, to make one of her cryptic observations that explains nothing but suggests everything.

But Mira just stares at the shack with that perfect stillness she has, her head tilted slightly as if listening to something the rest of them can't hear. Her lips move slightly, might be counting, might be prayer, might be something else entirely. She takes a step toward the shack, then another, drawn by something invisible.

"We should go," Emily says suddenly, her voice sharp with urgency. "The tide's turning."

Vincent looks and sees she's right. The water that seemed distant minutes ago now laps at rocks that were dry when they arrived. The fog has thickened too, closing in from the ocean, swallowing the furthest rocks, creeping toward them with intent that feels deliberate.

They scramble back the way they came, but the rocks are different now, slicker, the barnacles sharper, the gaps between stones wider. The fog pursues them, or maybe they're just moving through it, but either way, visibility drops to mere feet. Emily's yellow jacket once again their beacon, the only point of reference in a world suddenly made of gray nothing.

Behind them, already invisible in the fog, the shack remains. Vincent imagines he can still see that thin line of smoke, can feel eyes watching from behind those covered windows. Jonah Kells, whoever he is, whatever he knows, waiting in his driftwood shelter while the tide comes in and the fog swallows everything.

They reach the tree line just as the fog becomes impenetrable, following the path more by memory than sight. Vincent glances back once, but Ashen Cove has disappeared entirely, might never have existed at all except for the salt smell on his clothes and the small cuts on his palms from the barnacles.

———

The ceiling above Vincent's bed has become too familiar, every crack and water stain mapped in his mind through hours of sleepless study. He follows one particular line that branches like a river system, splitting and rejoining in patterns that might mean something or might just be the random artwork of moisture and time. The radiator has gone quiet for once, leaving only the house's settling sounds, those creaks and sighs that could be wood adjusting to temperature or could be something else moving through the walls.

Again, sleep refuses to come. Every time Vincent closes his eyes, he hears Ryan's voice, casual and cruel, tossing out those words about Mira's mother like they're nothing more than local gossip. "Her mom just walked out, didn't she? Couldn't handle living with her and her dad being so weird." The words replay with perfect clarity, each syllable carrying that particular tone Ryan uses when he thinks he's being clever, when he thinks he understands something he couldn't possibly comprehend.

Vincent turns onto his side, the sheets twisting around his legs in a way that feels like being held down. Through the gap between curtain and window frame, he can see the fog pressed against the glass, so thick it might be solid. No moon visible, no stars, just that gray presence that's become Marrowick's constant companion. It moves slightly, swirling in patterns that seem deliberate, like something breathing against the window, trying to find a way in.

The truth about Mira's mother sits in Vincent's chest like a stone, heavy and sharp-edged. She made her choice. She walked into the swamp knowing she wouldn't walk out, knowing that her sacrifice was the only thing that could stop what was growing in Duswood's dark heart. She didn't abandon anyone. She saved everyone, saved Mira most of all, though the cost was leaving her daughter to grow up with only half the story, the half that hurts without the half that explains.

Mira, young as she was, seemed to understand something the adults didn't, seemed to know her mother was gone in a way that meant more than just missing. The town created its own story, as towns do, filling the absence with assumptions and whispers. Unstable. Troubled. Couldn't handle the pressure. The kind of mother who just leaves.

But Vincent knows better. He carries the truth like a second skeleton inside his own, a framework of facts that can never be spoken aloud. Not because they're secret, exactly, but because they're impossible. How do you explain that someone walked into another dimension to fight something that feeds on human grief? How do you tell people that their comfortable lie is safer than the truth?

He shifts again, kicking at the sheets that seem determined to strangle his legs. His feet find cool spots on the mattress, then those spots warm and he has to move again, searching for comfort that doesn't exist. The pillow feels flat no matter how he arranges it, his neck aching from the wrong angle that every angle seems to be tonight.

Ryan's words weren't just cruel, they were precisely wrong, the exact opposite of truth. Mira's mother left because she loved too much, not too little. Loved enough to walk into something that would consume her, knowing her daughter would grow up wondering, possibly hating, certainly hurting. That kind of love doesn't fit into Ryan's understanding of the world, where everything is surfaces and sarcasm, where depth is just another word for weird.

Vincent thinks about the confrontation by the woodpile, how his hands wanted to use that ax for something other than splitting logs. The violence of the impulse surprised him, the way rage rose so quick and hot at Ryan's casual cruelty. But violence wouldn't change anything, wouldn't make Ryan understand, wouldn't bring Mira's mother back or ease the weight Mira carries.

The weight. Vincent can see it sometimes, the way Mira moves through the world like she's carrying something invisible but substantial. Not just the grief of loss, but the burden of knowing things others don't, seeing things others can't. Her ability to be in two places at once is a gift, but it's another kind of weight, another way of being separated from the normal world and normal people.

He turns onto his back again, staring at that familiar ceiling. The water stain that looks like a bird in flight, or maybe a hand reaching for something it can't quite grasp. His own mother counts days sober, one hundred sixty-four now, each number a small victory against a past that tried to drown her. But Mira counts something else, something Vincent can't quite identify. Maybe the days since her mother left. Maybe the moments between being here and being there. Maybe something that has no numbers at all.

Across the room, Mira sleeps. Vincent listens to her breathing, steady and deep, finding comfort in its gentle rhythm. The moonlight filtering through the fog catches on her eyelashes, casting delicate shadows across her cheeks. Even in sleep, her face holds that quiet intensity he's come to treasure, the slight furrow between her brows, the way her lips sometimes part as if about to reveal a secret. He watches her and feels that familiar ache in his chest, a tenderness so complete it almost hurts.

The fog shifts against the window, and for a moment Vincent thinks he sees a shape in it, a suggestion of something almost human. But when he looks directly, it's just fog, just moisture suspended in air, just another piece of Marrowick's perpetual gray. Still, the feeling remains that something watches, something waits, something feeds on the secrets people carry and the truths they can't tell.

Afternoon comes to Holt House like an illness, gray light filtering through windows fogged with condensation that never quite clears. Vincent sits at the kitchen table, watching Clare move through her domain with movements that want to be efficient but keep stuttering, her hands pausing mid-reach as if she's forgotten what she was reaching for. She arranges dishes that don't need arranging, stacks plates that are already stacked, her fingers trembling in ways that have nothing to do with the damp cold that seeps through every wall.

Something simmers on the stove, might be soup, might be stew, the smell thick and meaty but wrong somehow, like ingredients that shouldn't go together have been forced into the same pot. Steam rises and mingles with the moisture already hanging in the air, making everything feel underwater, submerged in something heavier than atmosphere. Clare stirs in the infinity shape, the wooden spoon moving in circles that seem to count something, mark time to a rhythm only she hears.

Ryan slouches at the far end of the table, his body radiating the particular hostility of teenage boys who feel trapped. His phone lies face-down beside him, ignored or deliberately avoided. His fingers drum against the wood in patterns that speak of barely contained agitation, each tap harder than the last, building toward something that hasn't arrived yet but will.

Emily sits across from him, flipping through what looks like an old cookbook, its pages warped with age and moisture. She laughs at something, might be a recipe title, might be an illustration, the sound bright in the heavy kitchen. Too bright. It cuts through the thickness like glass breaking.

"Can you shut up?" Ryan's voice comes out sharp enough to draw blood. "Nobody cares about a stupid cookbook."

The words hit harder than they should, carry more venom than sibling irritation typically holds. Emily's laughter dies instantly, her face going still in that way Vincent has started to recognize, that moment before something shifts, before whatever's growing inside her takes another piece.

"I was just..." Emily starts, but Ryan cuts her off.

"You're always just. Just talking, just laughing, just existing too loud. It's exhausting." He shoves back from the table, the chair legs scraping against the floor with a sound like fingernails on stone. "This whole house is exhausting."

Clare pauses in her stirring, just for a moment, her shoulders tightening. But she doesn't turn, doesn't acknowledge the cruelty, just continues her circles with the spoon, round and round, as if the motion itself might smooth over the sharp edges filling the room.

Emily's face undergoes that transformation Vincent has witnessed too many times now. Her eyes go flat, the warmth draining out like water from a punctured balloon. When she speaks, her voice carries that hollow quality, words without the person behind them.

"Your cooking tastes like disappointment, Mom," Emily says, the words falling into the kitchen like stones into still water. "Every meal, the same bland nothing. Like you're trying to make food as empty as your prayers. Do you think if you make everything tasteless enough, God might finally notice you? Might finally care that you're drowning in this pathetic house, pretending Dad's death meant something when really he just wasn't careful enough with a saw?"

The spoon stops moving. Clare's hand grips the handle so tight her knuckles go white, then red, then white again. She doesn't turn around, but Vincent can see her other hand find the edge of the counter, holding on like it's the only thing keeping her upright.

"That's enough, Emily," Clare says, her voice steady but stretched thin, the note of warning sharper than before. She hesitates, watching her daughter as if seeing someone she almost recognizes and almost doesn't. "You look… worn out, sweetheart. Why don't you go lie down for a while? I think you need it."

It's the same excuse she always makes, the same deflection, the same refusal to acknowledge that something is wrong, genuinely wrong, not just teenage moodiness or family tension but something invasive, something feeding. Vincent watches her shoulders rise and fall with breaths that want to be steady but catch in places, little hitches that betray the effort it takes to maintain this facade of normalcy.

Emily blinks, that confused look replacing the cruelty, her hand coming up to her mouth as if she could catch the words and stuff them back in. "I didn't... Mom…"

"It's fine, dear. Just the weather. Makes us all say things." Clare turns finally, and her smile is terrible in its determination, pulled across her face like a wound that won't heal. "Why don't you go lie down?"

Angela hovers in the doorway, neither in nor out, finding that liminal space she occupies everywhere now. Her lips move in their endless count. "One sixty-four," she whispers, then "sixty-five," though it hasn't been a full day yet. The numbers have started to blur, to mean something other than days sober. They're just sounds now, a mantra against whatever it is that fills every room.

She watches Clare with eyes that carry their own weight of concern, recognition maybe, one woman who's fought to hold herself together watching another start to fracture. Her fingers tap against her thigh, three times, pause, three times, pause. The rhythm doesn't match Clare's stirring, doesn't match Ryan's drumming, doesn't match anything except its own internal logic.

Vincent feels the walls pressing in, the air thickening with each breath. The floorboards creak beneath his chair though he hasn't moved, the wood swollen with moisture, expanding and contracting with sounds that might be settling or might be something moving between the boards. Above the doorway, the crucifix catches what little light filters through the fogged windows, Christ's face carved in permanent agony, shadows stretching his suffering across the wall in shapes that look diferent, too long, too twisted.

The condensation on the windows runs in streams that blur the outside world into abstract suggestions. Trees become dark smears, the yard dissolves into gray nothing. Everything beyond this kitchen might have ceased to exist, leaving just this room, these people, this slow dissolution of family bonds that the fungus feeds on, growing stronger with each cruel word, each confusion, each trembling hand that grips a counter to stay upright.

Vincent stands, the movement sudden enough that everyone looks at him. He can't stay here, can't watch another moment of this careful pretense that everything is normal when nothing is, when something is eating them all from the inside out. His chair scrapes back, adding to the symphony of pitiful sounds that fills the kitchen.

"I need some air," he says, though no one asked for explanation.

He moves toward the door, toward escape, and through

the fogged glass of the porch door he sees her. Mira sits alone on the porch, still as always, a dark shape against the gray afternoon. The sight of her feels like breathing after being underwater, like finding solid ground after falling. He reaches for the door handle, cold and damp under his palm, and behind him the kitchen continues its broken rhythm. Clare stirring, Angela counting, Emily confused and sorry, Ryan radiating anger that might be his or might be something else's.

The porch door closes behind Vincent with a soft click that feels like crossing into another world, one where the air moves differently, where the pressure that filled the kitchen can't quite reach. The fog has rolled in thick from the sea, sliding across the yard in streams that move with purpose, wrapping around fence posts and tree trunks like something searching. The dampness here is different from inside, cleaner somehow, without that fungal undertone that clings to the walls of Holt House.

Mira sits on the old bench that runs along the porch railing, her back straight, her hands resting on the weathered wood. She traces the grain with her fingertips, following lines worn smooth by decades of other hands, other moments of escape. She doesn't look up when Vincent approaches, doesn't acknowledge him with words, but something in her posture shifts, a subtle opening that means he's welcome.

He stands there for a moment, uncertain, the way he often is around her, never quite sure if his presence is wanted or merely tolerated. The fog swirls between them, thin tendrils that dissipate when he moves through them. From inside comes the muffled sound of Clare's voice, the words lost through glass and wood and the weight of everything unsaid.

Vincent sits beside her, careful to leave space between them, that careful distance teenagers maintain when they're not sure what they are to each other. The bench creaks under his weight, a sound that blends with all the other sounds of this place, wood adjusting to moisture, to pressure, to time. He pulls the blanket from his shoulders, the one he grabbed without thinking when he left his room this morning, and drapes it around them both.

The gesture feels too intimate, too presumptuous, and he almost pulls back. But Mira shifts closer, letting the blanket settle around her shoulders, and after a moment that stretches like held breath, she leans against him. The weight of her is slight but warm, real in a way that nothing in the kitchen felt real. Her hair smells like rain and something else, something that reminds him of Duswood, of home.

They sit in silence for a while, watching the fog thicken, watching the yard disappear into gray nothing. Somewhere out there is the woodpile where Ryan mocked him, the path to Ashen Cove where they saw the hermit's shack, the town where people drain of feeling while their hands join in empty gestures. But here, now, there's just this bench, this blanket, this quiet that isn't empty but full of things that don't need saying.

"Ryan said something," Vincent finally says, his voice low enough that the fog seems to swallow it. "About your mother."

Mira's hand stills on the railing. She doesn't tense, doesn't pull away, but something changes in her stillness, becomes more deliberate, more controlled.

"He doesn't know anything," she says, her voice soft but steady, carrying that certainty she has about things others can only guess at. "People need stories for the spaces they don't understand. His story is easier than the truth."

Vincent wants to tell her that the truth about her mother's sacrifice sits in his chest like a second heart. He wants to explain the burden of carrying that truth, that he sees her mother's courage in her strange gifts, to see things others miss. But the words tangle in his throat, too big for speaking, too heavy for this moment.

Instead, he turns toward her, his hand finding her face, fingers gentle against her cheek. She looks up at him, and in her dark eyes he sees that she knows he knows, that she's always known, that this is just another thing that exists between them without needing words. He leans down, hesitates for just a moment in case she wants to pull away, but she doesn't. Their lips meet, brief but certain, a touch that says more than any explanation could.

When they part, Mira rests her forehead against his, her eyes closed, her breathing steady. The fog swirls around them, creating a pocket of privacy, a space where the rest of the world can't intrude. Vincent feels her hand find his, their fingers interlacing with the ease of things that are meant to fit together.

"Look," Mira says, not moving, not opening her eyes, but Vincent follows her meaning anyway, looks down at the porch floor where her other hand points.

Between the boards, pushing up through a gap, a pale bloom grows. It's perfect in its depravity, waxy white petals arranged in a symmetry that nature doesn't usually achieve. It pulses slightly, that breathing rhythm Vincent has come to recognize, opening and closing like something tasting the air. This close, he can see the fine dust of spores that cling to its surface, ready to release at the slightest disturbance.

Mira pulls away from him, stands with deliberate purpose. She looks down at the bloom with an expression Vincent can't read, might be anger, might be recognition, might be something else entirely. Then she brings her boot down on it, hard, crushing it with a thoroughness that goes beyond necessary. The bloom splits under her heel, releasing a small cloud of spores that the fog immediately catches and disperses. She grinds her foot, making sure nothing remains but a pale smear on the wood.

She turns back to Vincent, takes both his hands in hers,

pulls him to his feet. Her grip is stronger than he expected, urgent in a way that makes his heart beat faster.

"It wants us," she says simply, her voice carrying that certainty again. "Both of us. Apart."

Vincent doesn't ask what she means, doesn't need to. He can feel it too, the way the fungus responds to their proximity, the way it grows toward them like plants toward light. It feeds on broken connections, on love turned empty, on families fracturing. But their connection is different, newer, not yet worn down by years of proximity and disappointment. They're something it wants but hasn't learned how to consume yet.

From inside the house comes Emily's voice, sharp and cold, saying something that makes Clare's quieter response sound like crying. A door slams upstairs, Ryan's probably, the sound reverberating through the walls. The house continues its slow dissolution, the fungus feeding on every harsh word, every confusion, every trembling hand that tries to maintain normalcy.

But out here on the porch, Vincent squeezes Mira's hands tighter, and she squeezes back. The fog thickens around them, muffling the sounds from inside, creating a barrier between them and the slow catastrophe of Holt House. They stand together in their pocket of quiet, two people who know truths that can't be spoken, who carry weights that can't be shared, who found each other in the midst of something that wants to consume everything real and leave only empty gestures behind.

The mist envelops the house completely now, and in this gray nothing, they exist, together, real, resistant to whatever wants to hollow them out. For now, that's enough. For now, they hold on.

Elias finds Vincent in the mudroom, examining his shoes for traces of the pale smear Mira left on the porch boards. His approach carries that processed determination Vincent has come to expect, each footstep measured, but something else moves beneath the surface today. A nervousness that makes his fingers tap against his thigh in patterns that echo Angela's counting.

"I need to go into town," Elias says, the words coming out too fast, then a pause, then more slowly: "For supplies. Would you help me carry things?"

Vincent knows this is a lie before Elias finishes speaking. Not the going to town part, but the needing help and the supplies part. Elias has never needed help with anything, handles everything with that same clinical efficiency. But something in his eyes, the way they don't quite meet Vincent's, says this invitation is about something else entirely.

"Sure," Vincent says, setting down his shoe.

The car smells of leather and disinfectant, too clean for Marrowick, like Elias wages constant war against the encroaching damp. Vincent settles into the passenger seat, watching condensation already begin to fog the edges of the windshield. The engine turns over with a reluctant cough before settling into a steady rhythm.

They pull away from Holt House, gravel crunching under tires, and the fog swallows them immediately. Elias drives with both hands on the wheel, knuckles prominent through pale skin. The windshield wipers beat their steady rhythm, pushing aside drizzle that reforms instantly, an endless cycle of clearing and obscuring.

The road winds through trees that press too close, their branches scraping the car's roof with sounds like fingernails. Vincent watches Elias from the corner of his eye, notes how his jaw tightens when they pass certain landmarks. A rusted mailbox. A driveway overgrown with blackberry vines. The sign for Bridgeport Mill Road.

At that last one, Elias's knuckles go white. Not gradually, but all at once, like something inside him seizes. The car drifts slightly toward the center line before he corrects, overcorrects, then finds the lane again. His breathing has changed, shorter, controlled, the way people breathe when they're trying not to panic.

"The mill closed fifteen years ago," Elias says suddenly, though Vincent hasn't asked. "Clare's husband worked there. Most of the town did. And then they didn't"

The words hang in the fog between them, explanation and deflection both. Vincent doesn't respond, just watches the trees thin as they near town, replaced by buildings that lean against each other for support. Everything here looks tired, worn down by constant moisture and something else, something that makes the paint peel in patterns too regular to be natural.

The Net & Keel squats between a bait shop and what might have been a pharmacy once, its windows now covered with newspaper. The pub's sign swings on rusted chains, the painted fish so faded it could be any creature, could be nothing at all. Elias parks with unnecessary precision, adjusting twice before turning off the engine.

Inside, the pub reeks of fry oil gone rancid and rope left too long in salt water. The ceiling hangs low, forcing taller patrons to duck between beams draped with fishing nets that haven't seen ocean in decades. Tables bear scars of initials and burns, the wood so saturated with spilled beer and grease that it feels soft under Vincent's palms.

The lunchtime crowd goes quiet when they enter. Not silent, which would be obvious, but that particular reduction in volume that means people are listening while pretending not to. Conversations continue, but the words become meaningless, just sounds to fill space while attention focuses elsewhere.

Elias chooses a table in the corner, back to the wall, view of the door. Old habit or new paranoia, Vincent can't tell. They sit on chairs that creak with every small movement, the sound too loud in the hushed pub. A waitress approaches, won't meet their eyes, takes their order for chowder with the efficiency of someone who wants this interaction over.

By the window, a fern sits in a cracked pot, its fronds brown at the edges. But at the soil line, where the stems meet earth, white fuzz spreads in delicate patterns. Not mold exactly, but something with that same pale substance Vincent recognizes from the mill, from the beach, from the space between Holt House's porch boards. It pulses slightly in the dim light, or maybe that's just his eyes trying too hard.

The door opens with a grinding of hinges that need oil, letting in fog and the smell of low tide, and with them comes Jonah Kells. His presence changes the temperature of the room, not warmer or colder but different, charged with something that makes the already quiet pub go quieter still. Conversations don't stop but hollow out, become scripts people recite while their attention fixes on the man in the doorway.

He wears a jacket stiff with salt, the kind of garment that's been soaked and dried so many times it holds its shape without a body inside. Mud cakes his boots, not regular mud but the gray-black slurry from the tide line, studded with broken shells and dried strings of kelp. He stands there for a moment, scanning the room with eyes that see too much, catalog too precisely.

The locals don't shun him, nothing so obvious. They just become very interested in their drinks, their phones, the patterns in the wood grain of their tables. A man at the bar shifts his stool slightly away. A woman pulls her purse closer. Small movements that add up to a circle of avoidance.

Elias stands when Jonah's gaze finds them, the motion too formal, like he's greeting a dignitary instead of a man who lives in a shack made of driftwood and salvage. His hand extends, hangs there for a moment before Jonah takes it, their handshake brief and awkward, like two people who've forgotten how the gesture works.

But Jonah's eyes land on Vincent first, really looking, the kind of assessment that feels like being turned inside out. His mouth quirks into something that's not quite a smile, more like recognition of a joke only they understand.

"Elias Thorn. Never thought I'd see you back in a place like this. Guess I should have known better." There's the ghost of a smile, a little wry, a little tired, but real. "You still drive like you're being chased by the devil?"

Elias exhales, tension leaking out just a little. "Old habits."

Jonah nods, tapping a cigarette from his pocket but not lighting it. "Some things stick. Good to see you, anyway. Even if it's not for the best reasons."

The waitress returns with their chowder, sets the bowls down too quickly, one of them sloshing slightly onto the scarred table. She takes Jonah's order without looking at him, without asking what he wants, like she already knows or doesn't care. He gets the same chowder, the same water glass, the same studied indifference.

They stir their soups, the sound of spoons against ceramic too loud. Vincent watches cream swirl into broth, chunks of potato and something that might be salmon but could be anything gray and fleshy. None of them eat, just move their spoons in circles that accomplish nothing while Jonah and Elias catch-up.

"You've been out to the mill," Elias says finally, not a question but a statement that wants confirmation.

Jonah's spoon pauses mid-stir. "Everyone's been to the mill. Even when they haven't."

"You know what I mean."

"Do I?" Jonah leans back, his chair creaking with the movement. "You want to talk about unusual things. Unusual's just usual that hasn't been normalized yet."

Elias's jaw tightens, that muscle jumping beneath skin. He's trying to maintain control of this conversation, but Jonah operates by different rules, speaks in sideways truths that can't be pinned down. Vincent watches them circle each other with words, predator and prey but unclear who's which.

"Have you seen anything?" Elias tries again, his voice carrying that clinical precision he uses like armor. "Growth patterns, spore production, anything that might indicate..."

"You know, Clare's husband went out at that place." Jonah says it flat, without emotion, like stating the weather. "Saw ripped his side clean off. They said equipment failure, but milling equipment doesn't fail like that. Unless the safety trigger failed too. Unfortunate coincidence."

Elias flinches, actually physically pulls back, his shoulder hitting the wall behind him. It's the first genuine emotion Vincent has seen from him, this visceral reaction to words that land like blows. The careful control cracks, just for a moment, showing something raw underneath.

Vincent realizes this is the first time he's heard it said so plainly. Not Clare's careful euphemisms about accidents and God's plan. Not Emily and Ryan's vague references to their father's death. Just the brutal fact of it, a man torn apart by something that was meant to rip material far stronger than human flesh.

At the bar, a couple sits on stools sized for closer proximity, but they maintain maximum distance, their bodies angled away from each other. Their drinks sit untouched, condensation pooling around the bases. Their hands rest on the bar, inches apart but might as well be miles. The woman says something, her mouth moves, but the man doesn't respond, just stares at the mirror behind the bottles, looking at nothing or looking at something only he can see.

The absurdity of it pulls at Vincent's attention, this couple that should be together but exists in separate spaces while occupying the same location. Like the town itself, going through motions that have lost their meaning, maintaining distances that protect nothing because the threat is already inside.

Elias tries to rebuild his clinical walls, straightening in his chair, hands flat on the table like he's about to give a presentation. His voice takes on that measured quality, each word precisely chosen, discussing mold and rot and health risks like these are problems that can be solved with proper ventilation and fungicide. He lists symptoms and treatments, vectors of transmission, statistical probabilities. The language of science, of control, of things that can be understood and therefore defeated.

But Jonah won't allow it. He pushes his untouched chowder aside, the bowl scraping across wood with a sound like bone on stone. His fingers drum once, twice, then still.

"You ever notice how silence carries different in this town?" Jonah asks, cutting through Elias's recitation of spore reproduction rates. "Not quiet. Silence. Like something's wearing it."

The words don't make immediate sense, but Vincent feels their truth anyway. The way conversations stop not because people run out of things to say but because something swallows the words. The way the fog muffles sound but also seems to create its own absence, spaces where noise should be but isn't.

Elias's hands clench slightly, his control slipping again. "We're not here to discuss philosophy."

"Aren't we?" Jonah leans forward, elbows on the table, close enough that Vincent can smell the salt-rot of his jacket. "You want to talk about what's growing without talking about what feeds it. Like discussing a fire without mentioning oxygen."

The pub continues its muted existence around them. The couple at the bar still maintains their careful distance. Someone in the corner stares at their phone too long without scrolling, like they're performing the act of reading rather than actually reading. Everything feels rehearsed, repeated, empty of genuine intention.

"The thing from Duswood," Elias says finally, the words coming out strained, uncomfortable. He doesn't look at Vincent when he says it, this admission that perhaps Jonah knows about what happened there, what they faced there, because he knows what Elias did there and the truth about Mira's mother. "Not Muldrath. Not the creature of stone and soil, but…the static. The way the air breaks."

Vincent's chest tightens. Hearing Elias reference The Adversary, even obliquely, makes him real in a way that Vincent has been trying to avoid. Makes the connection between what happened in Duswood and what's happening here impossible to deny.

Jonah tips his head, considering. "Names are a way to feel brave. Give something a name, you think you understand it. Think you can fight it." He shifts his attention to Vincent, those eyes that see too much focusing with uncomfortable intensity. "You saw him. Maybe not with eyes. But you know when you're being looked at, even in a dark room. That feeling between your shoulder blades, like something's measuring the distance."

Vincent doesn't answer, can't answer, because Jonah is right. He knows that sensation, has felt it in Duswood's swamps, in the spaces between trees, in the moments before everything fell apart. The feeling of being observed by someone or something that doesn't need eyes to see, doesn't need form to be present.

"What should we do?" Elias asks, the question small, almost lost in the pub's ambient noise.

Jonah sits back, his chair creaking with the movement. "Don't feed it."

"That's not helpful."

"Isn't it?" Jonah's fingers trace patterns on the table, following scars in the wood that might be random or might be deliberate. "It eats what's between people. The connections. The feelings. That's the only thing worth eating, if there's nothing else. Love, hate, fear, trust. All the invisible threads that make us more than just bodies moving through space."

Vincent thinks of Emily's cruel words at breakfast, the confusion after. The couple in town, their rage transforming to emptiness. Clare's trembling hands as she pretends everything is normal. All the small disconnections adding up to something larger, something hungry.

"The mill is the heart of it," Elias says, trying again for certainty, for something concrete to focus on.

Jonah's gaze flicks to the door, quick, nervous, like checking for eavesdroppers. When he speaks again, his voice drops low enough that Vincent has to lean in to hear.

"Everything breathes out there. Has been breathing longer than this town's been here. The mill just taught it how to breathe with purpose. How to inhale what it wants and exhale what serves it." He pauses, his eyes moving between

Elias and Vincent. "Now we have to ask, and I think we already know, who taught the mill?"

The question hangs in the air like spores, ready to take root in thoughts that don't want to think it. Because Vincent does know, can feel the shape of the answer even if he can't name it. Someone made choices. Someone opened doors that should have stayed closed. Someone fed the first feeding, setting in motion this slow consumption of Marrowick.

And Elias knows too, his face gone pale, his hands gripping the table's edge like he might fall without its support.

They leave money on the table, too much for soup they didn't eat, and move toward the door through air that feels thicker than when they entered. The other patrons don't watch them go, but Vincent feels their attention anyway, that careful not-looking that takes more effort than staring would. The couple at the bar still sits in their separate togetherness, neither having touched their drinks, neither having moved except to breathe.

Near the door, a fisherman in rubber waders sits alone, nursing something amber in a smudged glass. As Jonah passes, the man nods, just barely, a movement so small it might be involuntary. But Jonah catches it, returns it with equal subtlety. Not greeting exactly, more like acknowledgment of shared knowledge, shared burden, shared understanding that some things can't be said aloud in places where the walls might be listening.

Vincent holds the door, the metal handle cold and slightly sticky with salt air and whatever else accumulates in places like this. Jonah pauses beside him, close enough that Vincent can see the lines around his eyes, deep grooves carved by years of squinting at things others refuse to see.

"You keep close to his daughter, the quiet girl," Jonah says, his voice low, meant only for Vincent. The words come out careful, weighted, like he's thought about them for a long time before speaking. "Things that split usually mean to hold."

Vincent doesn't understand, the words sliding through his mind without finding purchase. But something in Jonah's tone, the way his eyes hold Vincent's for a moment longer than comfortable, says this is important. This is warning or advice or prophecy, maybe all three.

"I don't..."

But Jonah is already moving, heading not back toward his driftwood shack but into the fog that swallows the street, disappearing between one step and the next like he was never there at all. Vincent stands in the doorway, cold air mixing with the warm stale breath of the pub, until Elias's hand on his shoulder pulls him back to movement.

The short drive back to Holt House passes in silence except for the rain on the roof, the wipers beating their endless rhythm. Elias grips the steering wheel with the same white-knuckled intensity as before, but now Vincent understands it better. It isn't just fear of the road or the fog; it's the knowledge of something watching, something neither of them can name aloud. The Adversary is here, and Elias knows the danger isn't in the trees or the dark but in whatever breathes between them, waiting for their guard to slip.

Holt House appears through the fog like something conjured, its windows glowing weakly against the growing dark. Elias parks, turns off the engine, sits for a moment staring at the house like he's gathering strength to go inside. Then he gets out without a word, heading straight for the door, leaving Vincent to follow or not.

But Vincent's attention is already elsewhere, drawn to the figure on the porch. Mira sits on the bench, wrapped in a dark red cardigan that must be Clare's, it looks older than she is, the sleeves hanging past her hands. She doesn't look up when Vincent approaches, but something in her posture shifts, that subtle opening that means he's welcome.

He sits beside her, their shoulders almost touching but not quite, that careful distance that's become their language. The fog curls around the porch railings, thick enough now that the yard has disappeared, might not exist at all. They sit in their bubble of porch light, surrounded by gray nothing.

"Was it what he wanted?" Mira asks, not needing to specify who she means.

"I don't know what he wanted," Vincent says, which is true. Elias's motivations remain opaque, hidden behind that clinical precision he uses like armor.

From inside the house comes Emily's laughter, too sharp, too sudden, like glass breaking. It rises and rises, past humor into something else, something that makes Vincent question her reality. Then silence, abrupt as a slammed door, which follows immediately, the sound reverberating through the walls.

Mira's hand finds his in the growing dark, her fingers cold but real, solid in a way that everything else feels increasingly less so. She doesn't squeeze, doesn't cling, just holds, that simple connection that the fungus wants to eat but hasn't learned how to digest yet.

The fog thickens, and the day dims early, or maybe night comes faster here, eager to swallow what little light remains. Vincent watches the mist curl and shift, sometimes seeming to form shapes, suggestions of figures or faces that dissolve when looked at directly. Beside him, Mira watches too, her expression unreadable as always, seeing things he can't see, understanding things he can't understand.

But her hand in his remains constant, warm now from contact, a single point of connection in a town that's forgetting how connection works. They sit together as darkness falls, as fog erases the world, as somewhere in the distance the mill breathes its patient, purposeful breath, waiting for whatever comes next.

The market square of Marrowick is sorrowful in its ambition, its cobblestones slick with more than rain, reflecting the gray nothing of the sky in broken fragments that shift with each step. Vincent follows Clare's determined stride through the crowd, watching her navigate between fishmongers and vegetable stalls with the precision of someone who's made this journey many days of the week for years. Angela keeps close to her side, counting something under her breath, fingers tapping against her thigh in that rhythm Vincent knows means she's fighting to stay present.

The air tastes of salt and fish guts, rot and brine mixing with the ever-present dampness that clings to everything here. Gulls wheel overhead, their cries sharp and accusatory, diving toward the harbor where fishing boats rock in their moorings like sleepers having bad dreams. Vendors call out their wares with voices gone hoarse from competing with the wind, their words blurring together into a kind of market song that has no melody, just rhythm and repetition.

Ryan kicks at a puddle, sending water splashing toward Emily's boots. She doesn't react, doesn't even seem to notice, her attention fixed on something Vincent can't identify.

Maybe the patterns in the crowd, the way people move around each other without quite touching, maintaining distances that feel practiced rather than natural. Mira walks beside him, not touching but close enough that he can feel the warmth of her through the damp air.

Then Vincent sees it. Or hears it first, a man's voice rising above the market murmur, sharp and wrong.

"You always do this." The man stands near the fishmonger's stall, his face twisted into an expression that doesn't belong in public. His wife shrinks back, her basket dropping, turnips rolling across wet stones. "Twenty years of your stupidity. Twenty years of pretending you matter."

The words carry that same quality Vincent heard at breakfast when Emily turned cruel, that surgical precision of language designed to wound. But this is different too, rawer, like something has stripped away the thin veneer of civility that keeps people from saying what they really think. Or what something else thinks through them.

A woman three stalls over suddenly wheels on her daughter, a girl no more than seven, wearing a yellow raincoat that matches Emily's. "I don't care anymore," the woman says, her voice flat and terrible. "Do you understand? I. Don't. Care. About you, about your needs, about anything." The child's face crumples, but silently, like she's learned not to make noise when the world turns against her.

Two teenage boys who had been examining comic books at a vendor's table suddenly shove each other, not playfully but with real violence. One goes down hard on the wet stones, his elbow cracking against cobblestone with a sound that might require medical assistance. The other boy stands over him, fists clenched, breathing hard, his face confused like he doesn't understand how he got here, how this happened.

Vincent watches the pattern emerge, sees it spreading through the crowd like wind through grass, like waves across water. One couple arguing becomes two, becomes three. A man shouts at a vendor about prices. A woman accuses another of cutting in line. Children start crying, not the normal tears of tired kids but the desperate sobs of abandonment. And it moves, this discord, radiating outward from no single source but everywhere at once, as if the very air carries it.

His chest tightens, breath coming shorter. The sensation reminds him of Duswood, of moments when reality thinned and desperate things pushed through. But this is different, more insidious. Not a single monster but a corruption of the ordinary, turning daily interaction into something toxic.

Mira's hand finds his, grips tight enough to hurt. She doesn't speak, doesn't need to. Her face remains composed, that careful blankness she wears when she's seeing more than what's visible. But her grip tells him she feels it too, it's spreading through the market like spores on the wind.

Emily stands perfectly still in the middle of the chaos, watching with an intensity that makes Vincent think that perhaps that isn't Emily anymore. Not frightened, not confused, but fascinated. Like she's observing something she recognizes, something familiar. Her lips move slightly, like she's remembering a dream.

A couple near them erupts into screaming. The woman's voice cracks as she lists grievances going back decades. The man responds with accusations that cut deeper than any knife. Their faces are purple with rage, veins standing out on necks, spit flying as they tear into each other with words meant to destroy.

Clare's face drains of color. Her hand finds Angela's arm, grips hard enough to leave marks. "We need to go," she says, her voice carrying an urgency that brooks no argument. "Now."

But she doesn't lead them toward home. Instead, she turns toward the narrow street that leads to St. Dymphna's, her feet finding the path with desperate purpose. They follow, leaving the market square and its spreading poison behind, though Vincent can still hear the shouting, the crying, the sound of love turning to hate turning to nothing at all.

The heavy wooden doors of St. Dymphna's close behind them with a sound like sealing, and the change is immediate, complete, like stepping from water into air. Vincent's lungs expand fully for the first time since entering the market, drawing in air that tastes of beeswax and old wood, frankincense and that particular stillness that lives in sacred spaces. No moisture clings here, no fungal undertone colors the atmosphere. The very air moves differently, circulating in patterns that have nothing to do with decay.

The interior contradicts everything about Marrowick. Where the town drowns in dampness, here surfaces gleam dry and polished. The pews reflect candlelight from their worn but cared-for wood, each bench bearing the patina of generations of hands but no trace of rot. The stone floor shows the shallow depressions of centuries of footsteps, but no moss grows in the grooves, no moisture darkens the corners. Even the shadows here feel clean, empty of the weight that presses down everywhere else in town.

Emily moves first, sliding into a pew beside her mother with movements that have lost their recent sharpness. Something in her face shifts, softens, becomes younger. The hardness that's been building behind her eyes for days drains away, leaving her looking like what she is: a sixteen-year-old girl, confused and tired and seeking comfort. She leans against Clare's shoulder, a gesture so natural, so reminiscent of earlier years, that Clare's breath catches.

Clare's entire body releases tension Vincent didn't realize she'd been carrying. Her shoulders drop, her hands unclench, her face loses that careful control she's been maintaining since breakfast. She wraps an arm around Emily, pulls her closer, and for this moment they're just mother and daughter again, not two people being slowly hollowed out.

Ryan slumps in the pew across the aisle, his perpetual hostility muted to mere sullenness. Even he seems affected by the atmosphere, his usual need to mock and challenge reduced to silence. Angela sits behind them, her lips still moving in their count, but slower now, less desperate. The numbers might actually mean days again instead of shields against dissolution.

Vincent leans close to Mira, his lips near her ear. "It feels lighter here." The words come out as barely more than breath, not wanting to disturb the sanctuary's peace.

Mira doesn't answer, doesn't acknowledge he's spoken. Her attention fixes entirely on Emily, watching with an intensity that makes Vincent uneasy. Those dark eyes track every movement, every breath, every flutter of Emily's eyelashes as she rests against her mother. Not protective watching, not concerned watching, but clinical, like observing symptoms of a disease she's tracking.

The votive rack stands against the north wall, rows of small candles, some lit, most dark. Emily pulls away from Clare eventually, drawn toward them with slow, deliberate steps. She stops before the rack, her hand rising toward the matches, then falling. Rising again, almost touching an unlit candle, then withdrawing. She stands there, frozen in indecision or something else, staring at the unlit wicks with such focus that the rest of the church might not exist.

Minutes pass. The candlelight flickers, creating shifting patterns on Emily's face, but she doesn't move, doesn't blink. Her breathing slows until Vincent wonders if she's breathing at all. The concentration on her face isn't peaceful but strained, like she's trying to remember something important, something vital, but the memory keeps slipping away.

Clare watches her daughter with growing concern, the peace of moments ago replaced by a mother's worry. She rises, moves to Emily's side, touches her shoulder with infinite gentleness. "Sweetheart?"

Emily blinks, seems to return from wherever she's been. She looks at the candles, at her mother, at her own hands like she's not sure how she got here. "I wanted to light one," she says, her voice small and confused. "But I couldn't remember why. Or for who."

Clare guides her back to the pew, and they sit in the church's clean silence for a few more minutes. No one speaks. No one wants to leave. This pocket of clarity, of protection, feels too precious to abandon. But they can't stay forever. The afternoon is aging toward evening, and Holt House waits.

They move toward the door with obvious reluctance, each step heavier than the last. Vincent's hand finds the handle, cold metal that seems to carry the outside chill even here. He pulls it open, and the fog rushes in like something that's been waiting, pressing against the threshold with eager persistence.

The moment they step outside, the weight returns. The air thickens with moisture and that fungal smell, coating the inside of Vincent's nose, his throat, his lungs. The fog wraps around them, dense and searching, and the sanctuary of St. Dymphna's might never have existed at all. Emily's face begins to harden again, that confusion creeping back into her eyes. Clare's shoulders rise, tension returning to claim its territory.

They walk back toward Holt House through the fog, leaving the church's protection behind, returning to the slow dissolution that Marrowick promises, that feeds on them with patient, purposeful hunger.

———

The kitchen at Holt House wraps them in false warmth, steam rising from pots on the stove, the air thick with rosemary and thyme that can't quite mask the underlying smell of damp wood and something else, something that shouldn't be there.

Vincent watches his mother work alongside Clare, their movements falling into a rhythm that speaks of shared understanding, the language of women who've learned to communicate through action rather than words.

Angela stirs something in a heavy pot, her wrist rotating in steady circles that match her counting. "One sixty-five," she whispers, so quiet only Vincent catches it. Her other hand rests on the counter, fingers spread wide like she needs to feel something solid, something real. The steam rises around her face, making her look younger for a moment, or maybe just less worn.

Clare chops vegetables with such precision that implies it could be done by memory. The knife hitting the board in a rhythm that doesn't vary. Carrots, onions, celery, each piece exactly the same size, like uniformity might restore order to a house where order has started to slip. She pauses mid-chop, the knife suspended above a half-sectioned potato, and her voice comes out careful, measured.

"My husband was taken by the mill." The words fall between them like stones into water, creating ripples that Vincent feels from across the room. Clare doesn't look up, doesn't elaborate, just continues chopping as if she hasn't spoken at all. "The saw grabbed him. They said the safety failed." Another pause, another careful slice.

Angela's stirring doesn't falter, but something in her posture shifts, recognition maybe, or understanding. She doesn't offer platitudes, doesn't say she's sorry, just continues stirring while Clare continues chopping, both women working through their separate griefs in the steam and herb-scented air.

"We had a decent life," Angela says suddenly, her voice catching on something between confession and defense. The stirring stops for just a moment, her hand gripping the wooden spoon like it might float away. "Vincent's father and I. Not perfect, but I thought..." She resumes stirring, harder. "I thought we knew what we were doing. Then...he just left. His only involvement in Vincent's life now is the monthly deposit in my checking account."

The confession hangs between them, and Vincent sees his mother's shoulders rise and fall with a breath that shakes slightly at the edges. He knows she's thinking about those lost years, the ones before she started counting days, when bottles meant more than air or food, when the counting wasn't days but drinks, then bottles, then blackouts. The weight of it presses against Vincent's chest, this watching his mother navigate around the edges of her past without falling in.

The subject changes without transition, Clare asking about the seasoning, Angela suggesting more salt, both of them pulling back from the edge of something too deep to explore over dinner preparation. They work in this careful harmony until the meal is ready, everything properly cooked, properly seasoned, properly arranged on plates that Clare sets with unnecessary precision.

Dinner passes in the kind of silence that weighs more than words. Forks scrape ceramic with sounds too sharp in the quiet room. Vincent sits between Mira and Ryan, trying to eat while his throat feels too tight to swallow. Emily picks at her food, moving it around her plate in patterns that might mean something or might just be nervous energy looking for outlet. Even Ryan stays quiet, his usual commentary suppressed by the atmosphere that fills every corner of the room.

After dishes are cleared and washed, after Clare retreats to her bedroom and Angela to hers, counting steps up the stairs, Vincent lingers in the living room. The old furniture sits in shadows that seem deeper than the lamplight should allow, and the walls creak with sounds that might be the house settling or might be something else entirely.

He's reading, or pretending to read, when Emily drifts into the room. She moves behind his chair with that too-quiet step she's developed, and suddenly her hand rests on the back, fingers splayed across the worn fabric. The touch lingers too long, carries too much weight for casual contact. She leans down, close enough that her breath disturbs the hair at his neck, warm and cold at the same time.

"You two look so close," she murmurs, and though she means him and Mira, the words carry a different weight, a different intention. Her fingers brush the fabric near his shoulder, not quite touching him but almost, the suggestion of contact more intimate than actual touch would be. "Like you share something. Like you know each other's secrets."

Her smile, when Vincent turns to look, isn't the confused expression from earlier, isn't the childlike softness from the church. It's something sharper, more deliberate, like she knows exactly what she's doing even if she doesn't know why. She walks away humming, the melody tuneless and off, notes that don't belong together forced into proximity. The sound hangs in the air after she's gone, like smoke from a fire that shouldn't be burning.

Vincent finds Mira on the porch, wrapped in the same blanket from before, watching the fog roll across the yard in patterns that might be random or might be purposeful. He sits beside her, and she immediately shifts closer, eliminating the careful distance they usually maintain. Her hand finds his face, turns him toward her, and she kisses him. Not the brief touch from before but something deeper, more grounding, pulling him back from the edge of whatever Emily's proximity threatened to push him toward.

When they part, Mira rests her forehead against his, her breath warm in the cold air. "She's changing," she whispers, not needing to specify who. "It wants her to want things. He's using it to get her to come between us. You must not let him."

From inside the house comes a long, low creak, wood shifting with a sound like breathing, like the whole structure drawing air into lungs it shouldn't have. Vincent pulls back from Mira, something in that sound triggering a need to know, to understand.

He goes inside, kneels by the baseboard in the hallway where the sound seemed strongest. Presses his ear against the wood, and there it is: a low, continuous whisper, like wind through leaves except there's no wind, no leaves. It's the sound of growth, of something spreading through the spaces between walls, mycelial threads reaching and connecting and consuming whatever they touch. The sound of the house being eaten from the inside, slowly, patiently, with the kind of hunger that has all the time in the world.

Vincent pulls back, his heart beating too fast, his skin cold despite the warmth of the house. The fungus isn't just in the mill, isn't just in the town. It's here, in the walls, in the spaces between what they can see, growing stronger with each cruel word, each empty gesture, each connection that breaks and leaves nothing behind.

The pie sits heavy on Vincent's tongue, too sweet, the filling coating his mouth with a cloying film that refuses to wash down even with water. Around the table, forks scrape against Clare's good china with sounds that feel deliberate, aggressive, each clink and scratch carrying more weight than cutlery should bear. The cherry filling looks almost black in the kitchen's yellow light, and Vincent thinks of the dark stains spreading through the walls, the fungus he heard breathing just minutes ago.

Clare's fingers drum against the table, a rhythm that doesn't match her usual patterns. She watches Ryan shovel pie into his mouth with mechanical efficiency, each bite larger than the last, barely swallowing before loading his fork again. The sight triggers something in her face, a tightening around her eyes that Vincent recognizes as the precursor to words better left unspoken.

"Ryan, slow down." Her voice carries that maternal edge that wants to be gentle but comes out sharp. "You're going to choke eating like that."

Ryan's fork pauses halfway to his mouth, loaded with another massive bite. He sets it down with exaggerated care, the tines ringing against the plate. "Sorry my eating offends you." The words slide out cold, calculated. "Should I ask permission before each bite? Would that make you feel more in control?"

The air in the kitchen shifts, it thickens. Vincent sees his mother's hand still on her coffee cup, sees Elias's magazine lower slightly, everyone suddenly focused on this eruption that feels both unexpected and inevitable.

"I'm just concerned…" Clare starts, but Ryan cuts her off.

"No, you're just controlling. Always have been. Dad knew it too, probably why he spent so much time at the mill. Better to risk the saws than another dinner listening to you catalog everyone's failures." Ryan pushes back from the table, his chair scraping across the floor with a sound like tearing. "At least the saw was honest about what it wanted."

The words hang in the air, poisonous and drifting. Clare's face drains of color, her mouth opening and closing without sound. Ryan doesn't wait for a response, just turns and pounds up the stairs, each footstep deliberate, punishing the wood for existing.

In the silence that follows, Angela rises with movements that want to be helpful but just add to the chaos. She gathers coffee cups that still have coffee in them, stacks plates that don't need stacking, her hands moving in patterns that accomplish nothing except motion itself. "More coffee?" she asks no one in particular, already pouring before anyone answers. The pot shakes slightly in her grip, coffee sloshing dangerously close to the rim of cups already too full.

Elias clears his throat, the sound careful and measured, like he's about to deliver some clinical observation that might restore order. His mouth opens, words forming behind his teeth, but then his jaw closes with an almost audible click. Whatever he was going to say retreats back down his throat, swallowed like medicine that tastes too bitter to take. He returns to his magazine, though his eyes don't move across the words, just stare at the same spot while his fingers worry the paper's edge into soft frays.

Vincent catches Mira's eye across the table. She hasn't touched her dessert, the slice of pie sitting pristine on her plate like evidence at a crime scene. Her face maintains that careful blankness she wears when she's processing too much at once, but her hand moves slightly on the table, fingers extending just enough to be invitation. Vincent understands immediately.

They rise together, not suddenly but with the fluid coordination of people who've learned each other's rhythms. No one stops them, no one even seems to notice their departure. Clare stares at the spot where Ryan sat, Angela continues her purposeless movement with dishes, and Elias maintains his pantomime of reading. The kitchen has become a stage where everyone performs their roles without audience, without meaning.

The living room feels different, quieter, though the same sounds of the house settling reach them here. Vincent sinks into the sofa, the cushions compressed from years of other bodies, other moments. Mira follows, tucking herself against his side with an ease that still surprises him sometimes, this girl who usually maintains such careful distances choosing closeness with him.

Her head finds his shoulder, settles there with a weight that feels like anchor, like answer to questions he hasn't asked. The fog outside presses against the windows, thick enough that the world beyond might not exist, but here in this pocket of worn furniture and muted lamplight, something real persists. Vincent's arm comes around her, natural as breathing, and she shifts closer, eliminating whatever space remained between them.

The house creaks around them, those sounds he now knows are more than wood adjusting to temperature. Somewhere in the walls, the fungus continues its patient growth, spreading through spaces that should be empty, feeding on the anger and hurt that fills these rooms. But with Mira against him, solid and warm and choosing to be here, the sounds feel distant, manageable.

Vincent turns his head, finds her looking up at him with eyes that see everything and still choose to stay. He kisses her, not the desperate collision of people trying to feel something, but the certain kiss of two people who've already chosen, already decided, already begun building something the fungus can't quite reach. Her hand finds his, fingers interlacing with practiced ease, and for this moment they exist outside the slow dissolution of Holt House.

"Mira?" Clare's voice cuts through from the kitchen, not sharp but tired, weighted with dishes and duty. "Could you help me with these plates, dear?"

Mira's fingers squeeze Vincent's once before she pulls away, rising with the grace she brings to every movement. She doesn't speak, doesn't need to. The look she gives him says enough: I'll return. This isn't over. We're not over.

Vincent watches her go, her dark hair catching the lamplight as she moves toward the kitchen, toward Clare's exhausted request, toward the mechanical maintenance of a household that's falling apart from the inside. The living room feels colder without her weight against him, the sofa cushions already forgetting the shape of their closeness.

Emily enters the living room without sound, her bare feet finding the spaces between floorboards that don't creak, moving with the deliberate silence of someone who's learned the house's language. Vincent doesn't hear her approach, doesn't sense her presence until she's already behind the sofa, close enough that he feels the air displacement, the subtle change in temperature that means another body has entered his space.

Her hand appears first in his peripheral vision, pale fingers trailing along the sofa's wooden frame, tracing the carved ridges with unnecessary attention. The touch is slow, exploratory, like she's learning the furniture's texture for the first time. Or like she's practicing for something else. Vincent's shoulders tighten, an involuntary response to proximity he didn't invite, doesn't want.

He stays still, hoping stillness might make him invisible, might make Emily lose interest and drift away to wherever her fractured attention takes her next. But she continues her circuit around the sofa, her fingers never leaving the wood, maintaining contact like she needs the furniture to guide her movement. She's behind him now, directly behind, and Vincent can hear her breathing, slow and deep, too controlled to be natural.

"You looked comfortable," she says, her voice carrying that strange quality it's had since the mill, words that sound like Emily but aren't quite Emily, like someone else is borrowing her voice. "With Mira. Like you fit together."

Vincent doesn't respond, doesn't turn to look at her. His hands grip his knees, knuckles going white with the effort of not moving, not reacting, not giving whatever is driving Emily the response it wants. The lamplight throws his shadow across the coffee table, and he watches it, focuses on it, tries to make it the only real thing in the room.

Emily leans down, and Vincent feels her presence like pressure, like the weight of water when you dive too deep. Her hair brushes his shoulder, carrying the smell of Clare's shampoo mixed with something else, something that reminds him of the mill, of those pale mushrooms releasing their spores. She's close enough now that he can feel her breath on his neck, warm at first, then changing, becoming thick and damp, carrying a sour undertone that makes his stomach turn.

The smell intensifies as she gets closer, not quite rot but the promise of rot, the scent of things beginning to break down at the cellular level. It coats the back of his throat, makes him want to gag, but he holds still, holds his breath, holds onto the desperate hope that she'll pull away, that whatever puppet strings are moving her will jerk her in a different direction.

"Your skin looks soft," Emily whispers, and the words slide across his neck like something wet and perverse. "I wonder if it feels the way it looks."

Vincent jerks forward, his body responding before his mind can form the command. His heart hammers against his ribs, each beat painful in its intensity. He turns to find Emily watching him, her head tilted at an angle that makes her look broken, like a doll with a twisted neck. Her smile forms slowly, deliberately, starting at one corner of her mouth and spreading across her face like an infection.

But her eyes aren't on him. They're fixed on something behind him, over his shoulder, locked onto the doorway with an intensity that makes Vincent's blood turn to ice water. He knows before he turns, knows from the way Emily's smile widens, from the way the air in the room suddenly feels sharp and brittle.

Mira stands in the doorway, a tea towel still in her hands, her body frozen mid-step like she's walked into an invisible wall. Her face shows nothing, that careful blankness she wears like armor, but Vincent sees the way her fingers tighten on the towel, sees the fabric bunch and twist in her grip.

Emily moves with dreamlike slowness, leaning down again, her eyes still locked on Mira's. Vincent tries to pull away, but his body won't respond fast enough, muscles turned to stone by the horror of what's happening. Emily's lips press against his neck, cold despite the warmth of her breath, leaving a sensation like a bruise, like a mark that goes deeper than skin.

The kiss lasts forever and no time at all, a violation that Vincent feels in his bones, in the place where his spine meets his skull, in every nerve that screams for escape. Emily pulls away with that same infected smile, her eyes never leaving Mira's face, watching, measuring, feeding on whatever she sees there.

The silence that follows is complete, absolute, the kind of quiet that exists in the space between lightning and thunder. Mira doesn't speak, doesn't scream, doesn't throw the towel or slam the door or do any of the things that might make sense. She simply sets the towel down on the nearest chair with movements so controlled they look choreographed. Her face remains blank, but something behind her eyes shifts, closes, locks itself away where Vincent can't reach.

She turns with the same deliberate control, walks down the hallway with steps that make no sound. Their bedroom door closes with a soft click, barely audible but somehow the loudest sound Vincent has ever heard. It's the sound of something ending, something breaking, something the fungus has been working toward since Emily first touched those pale blooms at the mill.

Vincent sits frozen on the sofa, his neck still burning where Emily's lips touched, the sensation spreading like poison through his veins. He wants to follow Mira, wants to explain, wants to make her understand that he didn't want this, didn't invite it, couldn't stop it. But his legs won't work, his voice won't come, his body betrays him with its stillness.

Emily drifts toward the stairs, her movements liquid and strange, like she's moving through water or dreams. She's humming now, a tune that exists outside of any logical composition. The melody follows her up the stairs, hanging in the air like smoke, like spores, like the promise of worse things to come.

Vincent remains on the sofa, alone in the lamplight, the fog pressing against the windows, the house creaking around him with sounds he now knows are growth, are spreading, are the slow consumption of everything real and good. His neck throbs where Emily kissed him, and he knows without looking that there will be a mark, not visible but there all the same, evidence of the fungus's victory, of its ability to corrupt even the simplest truth of his feelings for Mira.

The hallway stretches before Vincent like a throat, dark and narrow, swallowing the small sounds of his movement as he approaches their bedroom door. His knees hit the floor harder than intended, the impact sending a dull pain up through his thighs, but he doesn't adjust his position, doesn't seek comfort. Comfort feels wrong when Mira is behind that door, unreachable, her silence louder than any accusation could be.

His knuckles rap against the wood, soft, tentative, the kind of knock that apologizes for its own existence. "Mira?" His voice comes out rough, scraped raw by the words he couldn't say earlier, couldn't force past the paralysis that held him to that sofa while Emily marked him with her invasive touch. "Please. Let me explain."

Nothing. Not even the sound of movement from inside, no creak of bedsprings or shuffle of feet. The silence is complete, deliberate, a wall more solid than the door itself. Vincent knocks again, slightly harder, though still careful not to wake the rest of the house. His forehead comes to rest against the wood, and he can smell the old varnish, the years of hands touching this surface, opening and closing, marking the passages between public and private spaces.

"I didn't want it," he whispers to the door, to the silence, to wherever Mira is behind this barrier. "I couldn't move. I couldn't stop her." The words sound pathetic even to him, excuses that carry no weight against what Mira saw, against that moment when Emily's lips touched his neck while her eyes stayed locked on Mira's face.

And then, in the tiniest of voices, Mira responds. "It's eating away at us. I can't make you resist. *You* must do that."

Vincent sinks back, his spine finding the opposite wall, legs stretched across the narrow hallway. The floor is cold through his jeans, that particular cold of old houses where heat never quite reaches every corner. He pulls his knees up, wraps his arms around them, making himself smaller in the darkness. Time passes, marked only by the house's sounds, those creaks and sighs that he's learning to interpret like a new language.

The first creak comes from above, where Emily's room sits directly over this spot in the hallway. It's followed by another, then another, a rhythm that's too regular to be random foot-steps, too deliberate to be the natural settling of wood. The pattern continues, expanding outward from that initial point, moving through the ceiling like something spreading, like roots seeking water, like veins carrying blood or something else through the house's hidden spaces.

Vincent tilts his head back against the wall, listening to this symphony of uncomfortable sounds. Each creak lasts too long, carries too much weight, suggests movement where movement shouldn't be. The walls themselves seem to pulse slightly, a barely perceptible expansion and contraction that he might be imagining except he's not imagining it, can't be, because he felt the same thing at the mill, that sense of a building breathing.

His hand moves almost without thought, finding the base-board where wall meets floor. The wood feels different here, softer, like it's been saturated with something that's broken down its cellular structure. Vincent shifts, lowering himself until he's lying on his side, his ear pressed against the base-board. The position is uncomfortable, undignified, but dignity stopped mattering the moment Mira closed that door.

The sound comes immediately, clearer than ever before. A whisper that isn't wind, isn't water in pipes, isn't any of the things it could be if the world still made sense. It's the sound of growth, of expansion, of something spreading through the spaces between what's visible. The fungus speaks in this hushed voice, not words but intent, not language but purpose. It breathes with the house, or the house breathes with it, the two organisms so intertwined now that Vincent can't tell where structure ends and invasion begins.

He presses closer, trying to understand the pattern, the rhythm. It's not random, this growth. It follows lines of connection, paths between rooms where people move, where they touch walls for balance, where they lean in doorways having conversations. The fungus maps the human traffic of the house, growing stronger in places where emotion runs high, where anger and fear and love leave their invisible residue.

The whisper intensifies near the door to his and Mira's room, becomes almost a hum, a vibration he feels in his bones. Of course it's stronger here. This is where their connection lives, where they've kissed and held each other, where they've built something real and precious that the fungus recognizes as food. It grows toward them like plants toward light, hungry for what they have, patient in its consumption.

Vincent pulls away from the baseboard, his ear ringing with the absence of that horrible whisper. He sits up, back against the wall again, staring at the door that remains closed, that shows no sign of opening. Behind it, Mira exists in her own silence, processing what she saw, maybe feeling the same fungal presence in the walls, maybe understanding better than Vincent what it means, what it wants, what it's already taking from them.

The hallway feels smaller now, compressed between these two impossibilities: Mira's silence and the fungus's whisper. Vincent exists in the space between them, unable to reach either, unable to stop either. His neck still throbs where Emily kissed him, a sensation that goes deeper than skin, marking him as something the fungus has touched, has used, has made part of its slow consumption of everything good in this house.

Above, another creak, longer this time, drawn out like a

sigh or a laugh or something breathing out after holding its breath too long. The sound travels through the walls, down through the structure, until Vincent feels it in the floor beneath him, in the wall at his back, in the air he breathes. The fungus is everywhere now, has maybe always been everywhere, waiting for the right conditions, the right food, the right moment to reveal itself.

Vincent remains on the floor, his body folded into the corner where wall meets wall, making himself small in the darkness. He doesn't knock again, doesn't call out. Just sits and listens to the two silences that define his world now: Mira's deliberate quiet and the fungus's patient whisper. Neither offers comfort, neither offers answers, both promise that tomorrow will be worse than today, that connections will continue to break, that the house will continue its transformation into something that was never meant to be.

The night stretches ahead, hours of darkness before dawn brings its gray light and whatever new horrors the fungus has prepared. Vincent finds himself on the sofa and closes his eyes, though it makes no difference in the darkness, and waits for something to change, for Mira to open the door, for the fungus to stop growing, for Emily to be Emily again instead of this puppet thing that speaks cruelty and touches with wrong intention. But nothing changes. The door stays closed. The fungus keeps whispering. And Vincent remains caught between them, alone in the dark, listening to the sound of everything he cares about being slowly consumed.

CHAPTER
TWELVE

T he fog has pressed so close to the kitchen windows that morning feels like dusk, gray light filtering through moisture that beads and runs in constant streams down the glass. Vincent enters to find the kitchen already occupied, everyone arranged around the table in positions that suggest careful choreography, maintaining distances that protect nothing. The smell of coffee mingles with damp wool and something else, that fungal undertone that clings to every surface now, sweet and mildew like fruit left too long in dark places.

Clare moves through her domain with brittle efficiency, her hands never still, adjusting salt shakers that don't need adjusting, wiping counters already clean. She turns on Ryan with the sudden focus of someone who needs a target for shapeless anxiety.

"Your boots," she says, voice sharp enough to cut. "Look at the mud you've tracked across my rug."

Ryan glances down at the brown smears spreading from the door, shrugs with the particular indifference of teenage boys who've learned that caring about anything makes you vulnerable. "It's just dirt."

"It's not just dirt, it's inconsideration." Clare's voice rises slightly, catches, drops back to controlled irritation. "Every day, the same thing. Every day I have to clean up after you like you're still five years old."

Ryan mutters something that might be an apology or might be profanity, the words too low to parse. He doesn't push back though, doesn't escalate, just slumps further in his chair like he's trying to disappear into the wood. His compliance feels wrong somehow, too easy, like even his rebellion has been eaten away, leaving only the gesture without the fire behind it.

Angela sits at the far end of the table, her presence both there and not there, existing in that careful space she's perfected since their arrival. Her fingers work at buttering toast without a purpose, spreading it edge to edge, corner to corner, though she makes no move to eat it. Vincent watches her other hand where it rests on the tablecloth, fingertips tapping out her count. One sixty-six, or maybe sixty-seven now. The days blur together in this gray place where morning looks like evening and nothing feels entirely real.

Elias clears his throat, that particular sound he makes before attempting normal conversation. "The weather service says the fog should lift by afternoon." The words fall into the kitchen like stones into deep water, creating no ripples, generating no response. He waits a beat, then adds, "Though they've been saying that for three days now."

Still nothing. The silence stretches, fills with the sound of butter knife against toast, coffee percolating, the soft patter of condensation running down windows. Elias retreats behind his magazine, though the way he holds it suggests he's not reading, just using it as a shield against the kitchen's uncomfortable atmosphere.

Mira enters from the hallway, moving with that particular grace she has, making no unnecessary sound. She goes directly to Clare, picks up the coffee pot without being asked, begins refilling cups with the same efficient movements Clare uses, like they're synchronized, like they've rehearsed this dance. But she doesn't look at Vincent. Not once. Not even a glance in his direction, though he knows she knows exactly where he sits, can feel his presence the way he feels hers.

The absence of her attention creates a vacuum in Vincent's chest, a hollow space that aches with each breath. He watches her pour coffee into his mother's cup, watches her fingers steady on the handle, watches the way she tilts her head to avoid meeting his eyes when she has to pass near his chair. The careful navigation around his existence hurts worse than anger would, worse than accusations. This deliberate unseeing makes him feel like he's already disappearing, already becoming one of the empty spaces the fungus leaves behind.

Ryan's fork scrapes against his plate, the sound too loud, too deliberate. Vincent realizes he's doing it on purpose, creating noise to fill the suffocating quiet. Ryan looks between Vincent and Mira with the calculating expression of someone who's found weakness to exploit.

"What, did you two have a fight or something?" Ryan's voice carries that particular tone of false casual interest that precedes cruelty. His fork scrapes again, metal on ceramic like fingernails on stone. "She can't even look at you. Guess the big romance isn't holding up. Told you she was weird."

The words land exactly where Ryan intended them to, right in that hollow space in Vincent's chest. He doesn't respond, doesn't give Ryan the satisfaction of a reaction, but the truth of the observation makes it worse. Everyone can see it, this careful distance Mira maintains, this deliberate apartness that says more than any argument could.

The kitchen door bursts open with enough force to rattle the dishes, and Emily enters like weather, bringing with her an energy that doesn't belong to this gray morning. Her voice fills the space immediately, too bright, too loud, each word cutting through the fog of tension with manic cheerfulness.

"The fog makes such beautiful patterns against the windows! Like lace, like breathing, like the whole world is wrapped in cotton." She spins slightly as she moves toward the table, her movements too fluid, too rehearsed. "And the gulls were screaming this morning, did you hear them? Screaming and screaming like they'd seen something wonderful and terrible and couldn't tell which."

Clare flinches at the volume, at the wrongness of Emily's energy in this muted space. Her hands still on the counter, knuckles white against the edge. Even Angela looks up from her mechanical toast-buttering, a frown creasing her face at this explosion of inappropriate enthusiasm.

Emily continues, oblivious or uncaring, her words tumbling over each other in their rush to fill the air. "I think the fog is trying to tell us something, don't you? The way it moves, the way it breathes. Like it knows things, like it sees things we can't see, like it's been waiting so long to show us what it knows."

"Shut up, Em." Ryan's voice cuts through her rambling with unexpected force. Not his usual mockery but something harder, more desperate. "Just shut up."

The words hang in the air like a slap, and Emily stops mid-gesture, her hand frozen in the air where she'd been illustrating the fog's movement. Her smile doesn't fade but fixes in place, becomes something painted on, empty of whatever force was animating it moments before. She stands there, silent finally, while the rain continues its soft percussion against the windows, the only sound in a kitchen gone still as held breath.

———

Evening settles over Holt House like a wet blanket, the walls seeming to thicken with moisture that dampens every sound. Vincent sits on the sofa, his body creating a depression in cushions that feel damp despite no visible water, everything in this house carrying that persistent transgression of things that never quite dry. The living room lamp casts yellow light that should be warm but isn't, just illumination without comfort, showing the fog pressed against windows like it wants inside.

Clare occupies the corner armchair, her body rigid with a tension that radiates outward, making the air around her feel charged. Her knitting needles click like mechanical beetles, never varying their rhythm, creating row after row of something that might be a scarf or might be nothing, just the motion of making for the sake of having something to do with hands that won't stop shaking when idle. Her jaw clenches between counts, the muscle jumping beneath skin that looks too pale in the lamplight.

Angela hovers near Clare's chair, not quite standing, not quite sitting, caught in that perpetual state of wanting to help but having nothing helpful to do. She reaches for Clare's empty tea cup, but Clare waves her away without looking up from her needles. Angela retreats, advances again, offers to adjust the lamp, to bring a different color yarn, to open a window for fresh air. Each offer meets the same dismissive gesture, Clare's focus locked on the rhythmic motion of needles sliding through wool, building something that will never be worn.

From the hallway comes Elias's measured footsteps, that particular rhythm of someone pacing without admitting they're pacing. He stops at each window, checks the latch, moves to the next, checks that latch, continues his circuit. The sound creates its own pattern, footsteps and pauses, the subtle rattle of locks being tested. Vincent counts seven windows before Elias starts over, beginning his route again as if the latches might have loosened in the minutes since his last inspection.

At the far end of the sofa, Mira perches rather than sits, her body maintaining maximum distance while still technically sharing the furniture. Her attention fixes on the fogged window, though there's nothing to see beyond the gray pressure of moisture against glass. She hasn't spoken since dinner, hasn't acknowledged Vincent's presence except to shift slightly away when he first sat down, a movement so small anyone else might miss it but which feels to Vincent like a chasm opening between them.

The space between them on the sofa might be inches or might be miles, charged with the weight of last night's violation, Emily's lips on his neck, Mira's witnessed betrayal that wasn't betrayal but looked like betrayal, felt like betrayal in the way that matters more than truth. Vincent wants to reach across that space, wants to take her hand, wants to make her understand. But his body won't move, paralyzed by the certainty that any gesture toward connection will be rejected, will make things worse, will confirm that the fungus has succeeded in breaking what they'd built.

Emily's humming precedes her entrance, that tuneless melody that sets Vincent's teeth on edge. She drifts into the room with movements that seem choreographed, too smooth, too purposeful despite appearing aimless. She circles the furniture like something hunting, her path taking her behind Angela, behind Clare, behind the sofa where Vincent sits trying not to tense at her approach.

She stops directly behind him, close enough that he feels the air change, feels her presence like pressure between his shoulder blades. Her hand settles on the sofa back, fingers inches from his shoulder, not touching but threatening touch, promising touch, making the possibility of touch worse than actual contact would be.

Emily leans down, her breath warm against his ear, and

her voice comes out soft enough that only Vincent and Mira can hear, a whisper meant for exactly two audiences, calculated to wound them both.

"You don't have to sleep on the couch again tonight."

The words slither into Vincent's ear like something alive, carrying implications that come with their own invitation. It's perfectly crafted to hurt Mira, to suggest betrayals and possibilities that don't exist but don't need to exist to do their damage.

Vincent jerks away with enough force to rock the sofa, his body responding before his mind forms words. "Stop it, Emily." His voice comes out louder than intended, sharp enough to make Clare's needles pause mid-stitch. But he continues, eyes fixed on the empty air just above her shoulder, addressing not Emily, but the thing he knows is listening. "Don't use us to hurt her!"

The room goes still. Clare's head snaps up, her attention finally pulled from her fruitless knitting. Angela freezes midhover. Even Elias's pacing stops, his footsteps halting somewhere near the hallway door. Everyone stares at Vincent, at his unexpected outburst, at the suggestion that something inappropriate is happening though they can't quite see what.

Mira rises from the sofa with the fluid grace of water finding its level, no sudden movement, no dramatic gesture, just a simple standing and walking toward the door. She doesn't look at Vincent, doesn't look at Emily, doesn't acknowledge that anything has happened. She simply removes herself from the space with the quiet dignity of someone who refuses to be part of a performance they didn't audition for.

Emily's smile doesn't falter, but something in it shifts, twitches at the corner like a glitch in her expression. Not shame, Vincent realizes with a chill. Satisfaction. She's gotten exactly the reaction she or it or *he* wanted, has successfully driven another wedge between him and Mira, has fed whatever hunger drives her now to create these careful cruelties.

She drifts away with that same choreographed smoothness, humming again, that tuneless sound that makes the air feel thick. Vincent turns to Clare, words spilling out before he can organize them properly.

"Something's wrong with Emily. Really wrong. She keeps... she's acting strange, saying things, doing things. The house feels wrong. Everything feels wrong. We need to help her, need to do something."

Clare's expression closes off, becomes the careful blank that adults wear when they're about to dismiss something they don't want to examine. She returns to her knitting, needles resuming their insectile click.

"It's just hormones," she says, her voice carrying that forced casualness of someone reciting a script they've memorized. "Girls her age get like this sometimes. Moody, dramatic. It'll pass."

The dismissal lands with finality, a door closing on any possibility of help, of acknowledgment, of addressing the corruption spreading through the house like those pale blooms in the walls. Vincent sits back against the sofa, alone now despite the room full of people, watching Clare knit, Angela hover, Elias resume his circuit of windows. Everyone performing their roles while something patient and hungry continues its work of hollowing them out, one connection at a time.

The stairs protest under Vincent's weight, each step releasing a groan that the damp air swallows before it can properly echo. His hand slides along the banister, the wood slick with moisture that never quite evaporates, leaving a film on his palm that feels both oily and gritty. The wallpaper beside the staircase shows water stains spreading in patterns that remind him of anatomical drawings, veins and arteries mapping some hidden circulation beneath the surface.

Near the top of the stairs, his fingers encounter something that shouldn't be there. At first he thinks it's just a bubble in the wallpaper, a place where moisture has separated paper from wall. But when he presses, it gives way with a soft, yielding resistance that makes his stomach turn. It's warm, warmer than the wall around it, and it pulses slightly against his touch with a rhythm that might be his own pulse reflected back or might be something else entirely.

Vincent pulls his hand back, sees the wallpaper has split where something pushes through from behind. A pale bloom emerges from the tear, about the size of his handprint, its surface waxy. It looks like the things at the mill, the things growing between the porch boards, but this one seems more developed, more purposeful. The petals, if they can be called petals, arrange themselves in a spiral pattern that hurts to look at directly, creating an optical illusion of depth, like staring into a hole that goes through the wall into some other space.

The bloom pulses with that breathing rhythm, expanding and contracting slightly, and with each pulse a fine dust releases from its center. Spores, Vincent realizes, watching them drift in the dim hallway light, settling on his sleeve, his skin, seeking entry into whatever they touch. The smell reaches him a moment later, sweet and rotten, like fruit forgotten in a drawer, like flesh beginning its return to component elements.

He scrapes at the bloom with his sleeve, not wanting to touch it directly again. The fabric tears through the soft flesh of it easily, too easily, like it wants to be destroyed, wants to release more of itself into the air. The remnants smear across the wallpaper, leaving a stain that looks disturbingly organic, and the smell intensifies, clings to his sleeve with a persistence that makes him want to tear the shirt off, throw it away, burn it.

Vincent continues up the stairs, his contaminated sleeve

held away from his body, the sour smell following him like a midnight shadow. He stops at Mira's door, that barrier that might be wood or might be worlds, separating them more effectively than distance could. His hand rises to knock, hesitates, rises again.

He can feel her in there. Not hear her, not see any light under the door, but feel her presence the way he's always been able to feel her, that particular awareness that exists between them. She's standing just beyond the door, he knows this with certainty, facing away from him, her back to the wood, deliberately turned from any possibility of connection.

His knuckles barely brush the door, the softest knock he can manage. "Mira?" Her name comes out as breath more than word, a question and plea and apology all compressed into two syllables.

The silence that answers feels active, intentional, a wall built from her refusal to acknowledge him. But he knows she hears him, knows she's there, standing so close that if the door didn't exist they could touch. The knowledge makes it worse somehow, this proximity without possibility, this nearness that might as well be absence.

Something shifts in the quality of her presence, a subtle change in the air pressure or the sound of fabric moving. For a moment Vincent thinks she might turn, might open the door, might let him explain about Emily, about the fungus, about how everything is being corrupted and they need to stand together against it. But instead, he hears the soft click of a lock engaging. Not the main lock, which was already turned, but the bolt, the secondary lock that makes a statement about permanence, about decisions made and positions hardened.

The sound of that bolt sliding home carries more weight than any words could. It's Mira saying she knows he's there and chooses this distance, chooses this separation, chooses to let the fungus win this small victory of driving them apart.

Vincent's hand drops from the door, his fingers numb, his chest hollow with a grief that feels premature but inevitable.

He turns to descend the stairs when Emily's humming rises from below, that tuneless melody that seems to come from no human throat. It winds up through the stairwell, thin and brittle, notes carried along to somewhere unknown. But as he listens, Vincent realizes it's not just Emily's voice. There's something else beneath it, or within it, a deeper sound that seems to come from the walls.

He freezes midway down the stairs, one hand pressed against the wallpaper where he scraped away the bloom. The wall feels different now, not just damp but alive, carrying a vibration that runs through the whole structure. It's rhythmic, regular, like something breathing. Like the house itself drawing air into spaces that shouldn't exist, exhaling through cracks that weren't there yesterday.

The humming continues, Emily's voice weaving through this deeper sound, harmonizing with it. Emily and the house are synchronized, breathing together, humming together, existing together in some symbiosis that excludes everyone else. The sound builds, not louder but deeper, more present, until Vincent feels it in his bones, in his teeth, in the hollow spaces of his skull.

His fingers spread against the wall, feeling the pulse of it, the inhale and exhale of a structure that was never meant to breathe but breathes anyway. The house has become something else, something more than wood and plaster and paint. It's an organism now, infected and transformed by the fungus that grows in its walls, spreads through its spaces, its byproduct is the disconnection and cruelty that fills its rooms.

The realization makes Vincent pull his hand back like the wall burned him. He stands on the stairs, trapped between Mira's locked door above and Emily's maleficent humming below, while around him the house continues its patient breathing, drawing in the fog and fear and fractured relationships, exhaling spores and sorrow and the slow dissolution of everything human.

The house inhales, and Vincent feels himself pulled slightly forward. It exhales, and he sways back. He's caught in its rhythm now, part of its breathing, another component in this organism that was once a home but has become something hungry, something patient.

The kitchen windows weep with condensation when Vincent enters, streams of moisture running down glass like the house itself is crying. The fog outside presses so close it might be solid, a gray wall that turns morning into something neither day nor night but suspended between. His feet find the worn spots on the floorboards, those depressions carved by years of the same movements, the same routes between door and table, sink and stove. But the wood feels softer this morning, yielding slightly under his weight in a way that feels as if the house might swallow him.

The family sits arranged around the table like pieces on a board, each in their designated position, maintaining distances that protect nothing. Clare presides at the head, her spoon moving through oatmeal in circles that accomplish nothing, just motion for motion's sake. Angela sits to her left, a bowl of cereal untouched before her, the milk beginning to turn the flakes to paste. Her fingers tap against her wrist.

Ryan slumps in his chair, his body a study in aggressive disinterest. He shovels cereal into his mouth with mechanical efficiency, each bite punctuated by the sharp clink of spoon against bowl. The sound carries too much weight in the quiet kitchen, deliberate and hostile, like he's trying to break something with each contact.

"Isn't the fog beautiful this morning?" Emily's voice cuts through the silence with unnatural brightness, each word too carefully formed, too precisely delivered. She sits forward in her chair, her smile stretched across her face like something painted on. "It reminds me of cotton, or clouds that fell down, or breath on cold glass."

"It reminds me of suffocation," Ryan responds without looking up from his bowl. The words drop into the kitchen like cut crystals, heavy and sharp-edged. "Like the whole town is drowning in its own exhale."

Emily's laugh comes too quick, too high, a sound that doesn't match any emotion Vincent recognizes. "You're so dramatic, Ryan. Always seeing the dark side of everything. Maybe if you looked for beauty, you'd find it."

"Maybe if you stopped talking, we'd all find some peace."

The exchange continues, Emily asking questions nobody wants to answer, Ryan responding with barbs designed to wound. Vincent barely hears them, his attention fixed on the empty space beside him where Mira sits. She might be inches away or miles, the distance between them measured in more than physical space. Her hands rest on the table, fingers spread slightly, palms down, empty of anything. No coffee cup to hold, no spoon to occupy them, just flesh against wood, still as carved stone.

Vincent's own hands mirror hers without meaning to, flat against the table's surface, feeling the grain beneath his palms. The wood carries a film of moisture, everything in this house damp despite the absence of visible water. He wants to reach across the small space between them, wants to touch her hand, wants to bridge this gap that shouldn't exist. But he can't move, paralyzed by the certainty that she'll pull away, that the rejection will be witnessed by everyone, that it will confirm the fungus's victory.

Clare watches them from the head of the table, her eyes moving between Vincent and Mira with the careful assessment of someone who sees everything but chooses silence. Her lips press into a line so thin they might disappear entirely, holding back words that would only make things worse. She returns to her oatmeal, stirring and stirring, creating patterns in the paste that mean nothing.

"We should go into town." Elias's voice erupts into the kitchen with too much volume, like someone who's forgotten how to modulate for indoor spaces. The magazine he's been pretending to read drops to the table with a slap. "I think we all need a treat. Get some donuts at the Bavarian bake shop."

The suggestion hangs in the air, obviously false in its necessity but offering escape from this suffocating kitchen. Everyone agrees without enthusiasm, voices overlapping in mumbled assent, already rising from chairs, eager to be anywhere but here.

Vincent stands, his chair scraping against the floor with a sound that makes him wince. As he moves toward the door, he notices the corners of the room where shadows gather, where the walls meet at angles that seem foreign somehow. The dampness has darkened the paint there, creating patterns that might be water stains or might be something else. In one corner, barely visible, something pale pushes through a crack in the plaster. Not quite a bloom yet, just the suggestion of one, the promise of what's growing in the spaces they can't see.

The road to Marrowick glistens black with moisture, each footstep releasing a soft splash that the fog swallows before it can echo. The family moves in a loose formation, Clare and Angela leading with careful steps, Elias beside them with his hands buried in his coat pockets. Ryan kicks at puddles with renewed violence, sending water arcing into the gray nothing. Emily drifts between them all, her yellow raincoat the only bright thing in this colorless world, humming that tuneless sound that Vincent's grown to despise.

Vincent and Mira trail several paces behind, close enough to be part of the group but far enough to exist in their own pocket of fog and silence. The moisture beads on Mira's dark hair, tiny pearls that catch what little light filters through the gray. Her shoulders remain rigid, her gaze fixed straight ahead, tracking the shadows of the others but never turning toward Vincent. The space between them feels electric with things unsaid, charged like the air before lightning.

The silence stretches until Vincent can't bear it anymore. The words come out rougher than intended, scraped raw by the effort of speaking. "What happened the other night wasn't me. You know that."

Mira's pace doesn't change, her eyes still focused on the fog ahead where the others have become vague shapes, suggestions of people rather than people themselves. When she speaks, her voice carries that particular flatness she uses when she's processing something painful, turning it over in her mind like a stone worn smooth by handling.

"I know it's using Emily…through the fungus. He is. The Adversary." The name falls between them like something physical, making the fog seem to thicken. "But it's important how you respond to it."

The words land like broken glass, feel like accusation despite their measured tone. Vincent stops in the middle of the road, his feet planted in twin puddles that immediately soak through his shoes. The sudden halt forces Mira to stop too, to turn and face him for the first time since that night. Her dark eyes reflect the gray sky, giving nothing away, but her jaw tightens in a way that betrays the effort of maintaining composure.

"You're letting it in," she says, and now there's something beneath the flatness, a tremor of fear or anger or both.

Vincent reaches for her arm, his movement too quick at

first, making her flinch. But he gentles his touch immediately, his fingers barely grazing the wet fabric of her coat. "I'm with you. Only you. Don't let it take that from us."

The words hang in the fog between them, and Vincent sees something shift in Mira's expression, the smallest crack in her careful control. She studies his face with that intensity she has, looking for something beneath the surface, reading him the way she reads everything, searching for truth in the spaces between what's said and what's meant.

For a long moment they stand there, two figures in the middle of a wet road, fog curling around them like something alive. Vincent can hear the others continuing ahead, their voices muffled and distorted by distance and moisture. But here, in this gray nowhere between house and town, there's only him and Mira and the question of whether what they've built can survive what's trying to tear it down.

Mira pulls her arm away, but the gesture is gentle, considered rather than rejection. She doesn't speak, doesn't offer forgiveness or acceptance, but when she starts walking again, the distance between them has shrunk. Not gone, not erased, but smaller. She doesn't walk as far from him, allows their shoulders to exist in the same space, their hands to swing at their sides with the possibility of touching though they don't touch. It's not reconciliation exactly, but it's not the careful apartness of before.

The fog thickens as they continue toward town, pressing closer with each step, until Vincent can barely see his own feet hitting the wet pavement. Buildings begin to emerge from the gray like ships from the sea, their shapes distorted by moisture and distance into something that might be architecture or might be hallucination. Windows glow weakly through the fog, yellow squares that provide no warmth, just markers of human habitation in this drowned world.

Ahead, the others have stopped in front of the bake shop, waiting for Vincent and Mira to catch up. Emily turns to watch them approach, her smile visible even through the fog, that painted expression that belongs to something else wearing her face. But Vincent doesn't look at her. His attention stays on the space beside him where Mira walks, not touching but no longer unreachable, their connection damaged but not consumed, still fighting against what wants to destroy it.

———

Evening settles over Holt House with the weight of wet wool, the air so thick with damp that breathing feels like drowning in slow motion. The walls seem closer than they were this morning, pressing inward with a patience that suggests they have all the time in the world to close completely. Vincent sits in the living room, feeling the moisture seep through his clothes, through his skin, settling into his bones with a chill that no amount of warmth can chase away.

Clare occupies the parlor like an automaton programmed for a single task, her needles clicking like beetle wings. The sound carries through the doorway, steady as a metronome, creating row after row of something that might be a scarf or might be nothing, just yarn twisted into shapes that serve no purpose except to keep her hands moving. Her face wears the blank expression of someone who's retreated deep inside themselves, performing the motions of living without actually being present.

Angela sits beside her, a dish towel in her lap that she folds and unfolds and folds again, the fabric growing softer with each repetition. Her movements carry that particular nervousness of someone who needs to be useful but has nothing useful to do. She smooths the towel flat, creates perfect corners, then immediately destroys her work to begin again. Her lips move in their eternal count, numbers that have lost whatever meaning they once held, just sounds to fill the silence in her head.

Through the window comes the sound of Ryan's voice from the porch, low and constant, muttering into the fog like he's having an argument with the weather itself. The words don't carry clearly through the glass, just the rhythm of complaint, of anger with no target except the gray nothing that surrounds everything. Sometimes his voice rises to almost-shouting before dropping back to that bitter murmur, waves of hostility breaking against the indifferent fog.

Vincent sits on the sofa, the same depression in the cushions from last night, from every night since they arrived. But tonight Mira sits beside him, not at the far end like last night, not maintaining maximum distance. She's left a gap between them, careful space that acknowledges what happened, what was witnessed, what needs healing. But it's a smaller gap than before, one that could be crossed with the smallest gesture, though neither makes that gesture yet.

They don't speak. Words feel too dangerous in this house where the walls might be listening, where Emily drifts from room to room like smoke looking for fire. But their silence isn't empty. It carries the weight of their walk to town, of Vincent's words in the road, of Mira's careful consideration. They exist in the same space without touching, breathing the same thick air, facing the same slow dissolution of everything around them.

Emily's humming precedes her entrance, that tuneless sound that seems to come from no human throat. She drifts through the room with movements that flow like water, too smooth, too purposeful despite seeming aimless. Her path takes her past the window where condensation runs in streams, past Clare's chair where the needles never stop clicking, past Angela's nervous hands working the towel into softer and softer submission.

When she reaches the lamp beside Vincent and Mira, she

pauses. Her head tilts with that bird-like motion that doesn't belong to her, studying them with eyes that reflect the lamplight in ways that seem amiss, too bright, too knowing. Her smile forms slowly, starting at one corner of her mouth and spreading across her face with deliberate construction.

She leans down toward the lamp, her face inches from the glass chimney that protects the flame. Her lips purse, and she releases a slow, deliberate breath across the top. The flame gutters, bends away from her exhale, nearly dying before struggling back to life. The light flickers across her face, creating shadows that make her look older, then younger, then like something that was never human at all.

Emily straightens, that constructed smile still in place, her eyes lingering too long on Vincent and Mira sitting together on the sofa. She doesn't speak, doesn't need to. The gesture with the lamp says everything.

She drifts away, continuing her circuit through the house, disappearing up the stairs with footsteps that make no sound. Her humming lingers after she's gone, hanging in the air like smoke, like spores, like threat.

Mira shivers beside Vincent, the first involuntary movement he's seen from her all day. Without thinking, without planning, they both shift toward each other, eliminating the careful gap. Her shoulder presses against his, solid and warm through the damp clothes. Neither speaks, neither acknowledges the movement, but they stay there, pressed together against whatever wants to separate them.

The house creaks around them, long and low, wood shifting with sounds that suggest breathing, suggest life where life shouldn't be. The walls expand and contract with subtle rhythm, drawing in the fog and fear and exhaling something worse. But Vincent and Mira remain on the sofa, together, their connection damaged but holding, a small warmth in a house going cold.

CHAPTER
FOURTEEN

The porch door closes behind Vincent with a soft click that the fog swallows immediately, turning sound into memory before it can properly exist. Steam rises from the mug in his hands, the heat dissipating so quickly in the clammy air that he wonders if the tea was ever warm at all. The moisture clings to everything, beading on his skin the moment he steps outside, coating him in a film that feels both cold and somehow alive, like being touched by something that shouldn't have the capacity for touch.

Mira sits on the bench against the railing, her dark hair hanging loose around her shoulders, already heavy with the damp. She doesn't turn when he approaches, doesn't acknowledge his presence with words or gesture, but something in her posture shifts, opens, creates space beside her that feels like invitation. The fog wraps around her like it's trying to claim her, tendrils curling through her hair, across her shoulders, dissipating and reforming in patterns that seem too deliberate to be natural air currents.

Vincent settles beside her, the wood of the bench slick beneath him, water pooling in the depressions where countless others have sat before. His jeans immediately begin soaking through, the cold seeping into his skin with patient persistence. The tea in his mug has already cooled to barely lukewarm, the steam gone, leaving just liquid that tastes of nothing but the minerals in Holt House's old pipes. He sets it aside on the bench, the ceramic clicking against wet wood with a sound that feels too loud in the muffled morning.

The railing before them disappears into gray nothing after just a few feet, the yard beyond invisible, might not exist at all except for the occasional sound that filters through. A gull's cry, distorted by distance and moisture into something that barely sounds like a bird. The creak of trees swaying in wind they can't feel. The subtle splash of water dripping from eaves, from branches, from the fog itself as it condenses and falls in an endless cycle of dissolution and reformation.

Mira leans into him with a movement so gradual Vincent almost doesn't notice it happening until her shoulder presses against his, warm through the layers of damp clothing. The contact sends something through him, not quite relief, not quite comfort, but recognition. They're still here, still themselves, still capable of choosing closeness despite everything working to drive them apart. Her hand moves across the small space between them, fingers spreading slightly, palm up in clear invitation.

Vincent takes her hand without hesitation, their fingers interlocking with the ease of practice, of memory, of something deeper than conscious choice. Her skin feels cold at first, chilled by the morning air, but warmth builds where they touch, spreading up through his arm, into his chest, settling somewhere near his heart. He adjusts his grip, pulling her hand into his lap, covering it with his other hand, trying to warm her, protect her, keep this one real thing safe from whatever wants to corrupt it.

They sit in silence for long minutes, maybe longer, time stretching strange in the fog where everything looks the same from moment to moment. Vincent watches the mist move across the porch, swirling in eddies and currents that follow no wind he can detect. Sometimes it seems to reach toward them, pale fingers extending across the boards, only to dissipate just before making contact. Other times it pulls back, creating clear spaces around them like something repelled, like their connection generates a field it can't quite penetrate.

The gulls sound closer now, their cries carrying that mechanical quality Vincent has noticed since arriving in Marrowick, like recordings of birds rather than actual birds. The sound layers over itself, creating harmonics that shouldn't exist in natural calls, building into something that drives a pain into the back of his head. But when Mira's fingers tighten slightly in his, the sound retreats, becomes just birds again, just morning noise from a harbor he can't see.

"Do the others feel it too?" Mira's voice comes so soft Vincent almost thinks he imagined it, words barely louder than breath, meant only for him. She doesn't look at him when she speaks, her gaze fixed on the fog, on the nothing that surrounds them. "It's taking everything."

The words carry weight beyond their simplicity, encompass the slow dissolution of Holt House, the empty faces in the market, Ryan's increasing cruelty, Emily's transformation into something that wears her face but isn't her. The fungus spreading through walls, through air, through the connections between people, feeding on love and leaving nothing behind. The Adversary's patient work, using the corruption to hollow out everything human, everything real.

Vincent doesn't answer with words. There's nothing to say that wouldn't diminish the truth of what she's observed. Instead, he tightens his grip on her hand, pulls her closer against his side, uses touch to say what language can't adequately convey. Yes, the others feel it. Yes, it's taking everything. Yes, they're losing. But also: We're still here. We're still us. We're still choosing each other despite the cost.

The fog responds to their increased closeness, swirling

more aggressively around the porch, tendrils reaching toward their joined hands with something that looks like hunger. But it can't quite touch them, can't quite reach the place where their fingers interlock, where their shoulders press together, where their breathing synchronizes without conscious thought. The moisture beads on their skin, runs down their faces like tears, but the connection holds.

———

Clare moves through the market square like someone who knows exactly where they're going but can't remember why, her steps quick and purposeful even as her eyes dart between the stalls with barely concealed alarm. Vincent follows in the wake she creates, watching her navigate between vendors and shoppers with the precision of long practice, though something in her movements suggests panic held barely in check. The fog hasn't lifted despite the hour, hanging over the square like a lid, trapping them all in this gray-washed world where colors exist only as suggestions.

The corruption hits Vincent gradually, building with each step deeper into the market. At first he thinks it's just quiet, the normal morning lull before commerce truly begins. But as they pass the fishmonger's stall, where the vendor guts mackerel with honed precision, Vincent realizes what's missing. No hawking of wares, no haggling over prices, no gossip exchanged between neighbors. The vendor's knife moves through flesh and bone without commentary, his mouth a sealed line, eyes focused on nothing while his hands perform their practiced motions.

A woman approaches the vegetable stand, points at potatoes, holds up three fingers. The vendor bags them, accepts payment, returns change. The entire transaction occurs in absolute silence, not even a nod of acknowledgment between them. Their faces remain blank, not hostile or unfriendly, just absent, like the part of them that engages with the world has been carved out, leaving only the mechanics of existence.

Vincent watches a child tug at his mother's coat, mouth moving in what should be words, should be requests or complaints or observations. But no sound emerges, or if it does, it's swallowed immediately by the thick air. The mother looks down, her face cycling through expressions that might be responses, might be conversation, but all of it silent, all of it absent of care. Even their footsteps seem muted, the cobblestones that should ring with movement producing only soft, wet sounds like stepping on moss.

Angela stays within arm's reach of Clare, her fingers working against her palm in that counting rhythm that's become her anchor. Vincent catches fragments of numbers when they pass close enough. "One sixty-eight, sixty-nine, seventy." But the count seems arbitrary now, disconnected from days or hours or any measurement that matters. Just numbers to fill the space where thoughts might go, where fear might take root if she stops moving her lips, stops creating this barrier of mathematics between herself and whatever's happening to Marrowick.

Behind them, Elias walks with the particular gait of someone trying to appear casual while fighting the urge to run. His hand emerges from his coat pocket, checks his watch, returns to hiding. Thirty seconds later, the same motion, the same glance at time that means nothing in this fog where morning might be evening, where minutes stretch like years. His other hand grips something in his pocket, might be keys, might be coins, might be nothing at all, just the need to hold something solid while everything else dissolves.

Ryan kicks at a puddle, the water splashing against a vendor's table, but even this small violence produces no reaction. The vendor doesn't look up, doesn't complain, just continues arranging fish on ice that's already melting, creating streams that run between the cobblestones like tiny rivers. Emily drifts between the stalls, her yellow raincoat the only brightness, humming that tuneless melody that seems to be the only sound that can penetrate the silence. But even her humming sounds different here, absorbed by the fog, twisted into something that harmonizes with nothing.

A gull circles overhead, its cry cutting through the silence before dying mid-call, as if the bird forgot what sound it was making. Vincent watches it wheel away into the fog, and suddenly he can't remember if this is the same morning as yesterday, or the day before, or if these distinctions matter anymore. The market square looks identical to how it looked yesterday…was it yesterday? The same vendors in the same positions, the same silent transactions, the same absence where human connection should exist. The fog. The indifference. The days are blurring together.

Clare's hand shoots out, grabs Vincent's wrist with surprising strength. "We're leaving," she says, her voice carrying an edge that cuts through even this muffled air. "Now. All of you. We're going to St. Dymphna's."

She changes direction without warning, turning down the narrow street that leads to the church. Her feet find the path with desperate purpose, like someone drowning who's spotted shore. Angela follows immediately, matching Clare's quickened pace. The others trail behind, pulled along by the sudden urgency, by the promise of escape from this market where humanity has been reduced to empty gestures.

The stone bulk of St. Dymphna's emerges from the fog gradually, its spire disappearing into the gray above. The heavy wooden doors stand like a promise, like a border between this new world and something that might still be held over. Clare reaches for the handle, pulls it open with both hands, the hinges groaning with a sound that feels too loud after the market's silence.

At the threshold, Elias stops. His foot hovers over the boundary between outside and in, his body rigid with hesitation. He turns to look at Vincent, and in that glance Vincent sees recognition, understanding, maybe even fear. Elias knows what the church means, knows what crossing this threshold represents. His eyes hold Vincent's for a moment that stretches too long, asking permission or seeking reassurance or acknowledging something that can't be spoken.

Then he steps inside, and they all follow, leaving the silent market behind.

The change washes over Vincent like stepping from water into air, his lungs expanding fully for the first time since entering the market. The heavy doors close behind them with a sound like sealing, shutting out the fog and silence of Marrowick. Here, the air moves differently, carries the scent of beeswax and old wood. The vaulted ceiling rises into shadows, but they're clean shadows, empty of the weight that presses down everywhere else.

Clare doesn't pause to adjust to the change, doesn't acknowledge the relief that passes across everyone's faces. She takes Emily's hand with gentle firmness, leading her daughter down the center aisle toward the front pews. Their footsteps echo properly here, leather on stone, the sound traveling up into the rafters and returning transformed but not twisted. Emily follows without resistance, without that strange fluidity that's marked her movements lately. She walks like a sixteen-year-old girl again, slightly uncertain, allowing herself to be led.

They reach a pew near the altar where candles burn in straight lines, flames steady and vertical, undisturbed by drafts. Clare guides Emily down, and they kneel together on the worn cushions that bear the impressions of countless knees over countless years. Clare's hands find her rosary, the beads clicking softly as she begins to murmur prayers Vincent can't quite hear, words worn smooth by repetition, by generations of the faithful seeking comfort in their rhythm. Ryan slumps in the back pew with his arms crossed.

Emily bows her head, and her hair falls forward like a curtain, hiding her face from view. Her shoulders drop, losing that unnatural tension that's held them high and rigid for days. She looks smaller suddenly, younger, her yellow raincoat too big for her frame, more like a child playing dress-up than the sharp-edged creature she's become. Her hands fold in something approaching prayer, fingers interlaced, thumbs crossed. For this moment, she could be any daughter beside any mother.

Vincent watches from halfway down the aisle, unable to move closer, unable to look away. Beside him, Mira's hand finds his again, her fingers sliding between his with that easy familiarity they've developed, that natural fit that feels like coming home. Her grip remains steady, firm, anchoring him while they witness this transformation that might be real or might be performance or might be something else entirely. The warmth of her palm against his creates its own small sanctuary within the larger one, a pocket of connection that remains untouched by doubt.

Behind them, Angela drifts toward the back pews, her movement dreamlike, drawn by something only she perceives. She sits, then slides to her knees, her counting finally ceased. Her eyes close, her face tilting upward slightly, and for the first time since they arrived in Marrowick, her features relax completely. The lines around her mouth soften, the furrow between her brows smooths. She breathes deep, holds it, releases it slow, and with that exhale seems to release something else, some burden she's been carrying since before Vincent can remember. Her lips move, but not in counting now, might be prayer, might be gratitude, might be simple acknowledgment that peace still exists somewhere.

Clare rises from her knees with the careful movements of someone whose joints protest the action. She touches Emily's shoulder gently, a reminder to stay, to continue praying, to hold onto whatever grace has found her in this moment. Then she moves to the bank of votive candles against the north wall, their small flames creating a constellation of light against the shadows. She takes a long match from the holder, lights it from one already burning, holds it to a fresh wick until it catches.

The new flame rises straight and true, adding its light to the others, and Clare leans close to whisper something. Vincent can't hear the words, but he sees Emily's head turn slightly, listening. Whatever Clare says takes time, not a quick prayer but something longer, more complex, maybe instruction, maybe confession, maybe just a mother's desperate attempt to reach a daughter who's been drifting away. Clare returns to the pew and whispers something to Emily. She nods once, barely perceptible, and Clare's hand rests briefly on her hair, smoothing it with infinite tenderness before pulling away.

Clare turns toward the door, and the others begin to follow, their movements reluctant, nobody eager to leave this pocket of normalcy for whatever waits outside. Angela rises last, her face carrying a peace that makes her look years younger, decades of worry temporarily erased. They gather near the door, waiting, but Emily doesn't move. She remains kneeling at the pew, staring at the bank of votive candles with an intensity that makes Vincent hesitate.

"Emily?" Clare's voice carries gentle concern. "We should go, dear."

Emily rises with that same mechanical smoothness that's become her signature, turns toward them with a smile that doesn't reach her eyes. She walks toward the door, passing the votive candles, and Vincent thinks she'll continue past. But she stops, turns back, stands before the flames with her head tilted in that bird-like way that doesn't belong to her.

Her lips press together, then part. She leans forward slightly, and releases one slow, deliberate breath across the nearest flame. The candle gutters, flickers, dies. Smoke rises in a thin spiral, dissipating into the church air, carrying with it some quality of sanctity that can't be recovered. The absence of that one small flame seems to darken the entire space, not dramatically but noticeably, like the first star disappearing at dawn, herald of coming change.

Vincent sees it happen, watches the deliberate nature of it, the calculated violation of this sacred space. Clare's hand stills on her rosary, her shoulders tensing with recognition she immediately suppresses. But Emily is already walking toward them, face calm and innocent, that tuneless humming beginning again, soft and perverse in the church's acoustic perfection.

The fog rushes back the moment they cross the threshold, pressing against them with renewed hunger, as if it's been waiting, gathering strength while they sheltered in the church. Vincent feels it immediately, the weight settling on his shoulders, the moisture coating his throat with each breath, the fungal undertone that makes everything taste of decay. The market square has emptied completely now, not even the silent vendors remaining, just wet cobblestones reflecting nothing, leading nowhere.

Vincent's hand finds Mira's before the church door fully closes behind them, their fingers interlocking with desperate purpose. Not the gentle connection from the porch this morning, but something fiercer, more necessary, like if they let go they might lose each other in the gray nothing that surrounds them. Her grip matches his intensity, her fingers pressing between his until their palms meet completely, no space remaining where the fog might intrude. The contact generates its own small warmth in the cold damp, a single point of certainty in a world that's losing definition.

Clare leads them with absolute certainty, her feet finding the familiar path without conscious thought. Her back remains rigid, shoulders squared against something more than cold. The rosary beads click in her pocket, an irregular rhythm that speaks of fingers working without awareness, seeking comfort in repetition that brings no comfort. She doesn't look back, doesn't check that others follow, just moves forward with the grim determination of someone who knows retreat is impossible but advances anyway.

Ryan walks with his hands shoved deep in his pockets, his head down, watching his feet strike wet pavement with unnecessary force. Each step sends small splashes of water up his legs, darkening his jeans, but he doesn't adjust his gait, doesn't seek drier paths. The anger that usually radiates from him has turned inward, compressed into something denser, more dangerous. His jaw works like he's chewing words he won't speak, grinding them between his teeth until they're powder.

Angela stays close to Elias, but not touching, maintaining that careful distance of people who want comfort but don't know how to ask for it. Her lips move in what might be prayer now instead of counting, though Vincent can't hear the words. Maybe she's trying to carry some piece of the church's peace with her, hold it like a shield against what waits at Holt House. But with each step away from St. Dymphna's, her shoulders rise higher, tension creeping back into her frame like water soaking through cloth.

Elias checks his watch again, then again, the gesture now completely divorced from any interest in time. His other hand emerges from his pocket, adjusts his collar, returns to hiding. He walks with the measured pace of someone thinking too hard about walking, each step calculated, considered, consciously performed. Sometimes he glances at Vincent, quick looks that might be checking his presence or seeking something else, some confirmation that what they witnessed in the church matters, means something, changes something.

Behind them all, Emily drifts like smoke, her path weaving slightly though the road runs straight. Her humming follows them through the fog, sometimes seeming to come from ahead, sometimes from beside, sometimes from the fog itself, as if the moisture carries it, spreads it, makes it part of the atmosphere they're forced to breathe.

Vincent can't stop replaying the moment in his mind, that deliberate breath across the candle flame, the way the light died, the smoke rising like a soul departing. The image burns behind his eyes with each blink. Emily's face afterward, calm and satisfied, like she'd accomplished something necessary. Not childish mischief but something calculated, something that understood exactly what it was doing, what it was violating, what it was claiming.

The fungus has grown strong enough now that even the church can't completely repel it. That single extinguished flame feels like a foothold, a breach in defenses that have held for longer than the town itself. If St. Dymphna's can be touched, corrupted, even in that small way, then nowhere is safe. No sanctuary remains except what Vincent and Mira create between their joined hands, and even that feels fragile, temporary, something the fog tests with each step.

The buildings thin as they leave the town center, replaced by trees that loom through the gray like tombstones. The road beneath their feet changes from cobblestone to cracked asphalt to gravel, each surface announcing their progress toward Holt House though Vincent wishes they could walk forever, never arrive, never face what waits in those walls that breathe with corrupted life. His free hand finds the place on his neck where Emily kissed him, expects to feel something, some mark or wound, but there's only skin, unmarked but somehow still violated.

Mira's thumb moves against his hand, a small stroke that might be comfort or might be her own need for reassurance that they're still themselves, still choosing each other despite the corruption spreading through everyone around them. Vincent squeezes back, tries to put everything he can't say into that pressure. That he sees what's happening, feels it too, won't let it take them without fighting. Though what fighting means against something that feeds on human connection, that grows stronger with each cruel word, each empty gesture, he doesn't know.

The fog parts gradually, reluctantly, and Holt House materializes from the gray like something that's been waiting for them, patient and hungry. The windows glow weakly through the moisture, yellow eyes that watch their approach with what feels like anticipation. The structure seems larger than when they left, or maybe Vincent's perception has changed, can see now how the walls have swollen with what grows inside them, how the roof sags with weight that isn't water, how the entire building has become something other than shelter.

Emily's humming stops as they approach the door, the silence somehow worse than the sound. She pushes past them all, reaches for the handle with eager fingers, pulls it open wide like welcoming them to her domain. The darkness inside seems to reach out, to pull at them, to promise more of the slow dissolution that the church briefly interrupted but couldn't prevent.

They enter one by one, Vincent last, still holding Mira's hand as they cross the threshold back into the patient hunger of Holt House.

CHAPTER
FIFTEEN

Morning seeps through Holt House's windows like something sick, the light gray and thick with moisture that never burns off, never clears, just hangs there making everything damp to the touch. Vincent enters the kitchen to find Clare at the stove, her movements sharp and brittle, stirring something that smells of oatmeal but looks too thick, like paste that's been left to congeal. The wooden floor beneath his feet gives slightly with each step, soft in places where the moisture has worked its way deep into the grain, creating depressions that hold the shape of footprints longer than they should.

Angela sits at the table, her fingers working against her wrist in that endless count. Her lips move silently, numbers that have lost all meaning, just sounds to fill the space where thoughts might gather if she let them. A plate of toast sits before her, untouched, the bread already going soft in the humid air, edges curling like something dying. Elias reads the same magazine, his eyes fixed on the same spot while his jaw works, muscles jumping beneath skin that looks gray in this light.

The kitchen door swings open with too much force,

banging against the wall hard enough to rattle dishes in the cupboard. Emily stands in the doorway, and Vincent's breath catches at the sight of her. Dark strands of seaweed tangle through her hair, wet and glistening, dripping saltwater onto the floor in a steady patter. Sand cakes her boots, not the fine sand from the town's small beach but coarse, gray-black grit that looks dredged from deeper places. Her nightdress clings to her legs, soaked through, transparent in places that make Clare gasp and rush forward.

"Emily, what have you done?" Clare's voice cracks, fear making it high and thin. Her hands hover near her daughter, wanting to touch but afraid of what she might feel. "Where have you been? You're soaking, you're filthy, you're..."

Emily shrugs, the motion too fluid, like her shoulders aren't properly connected to the rest of her. Water runs from her hair down her neck, pooling in the hollow of her collarbone before spilling over, creating dark stains on fabric that spreads like infection. "I was walking."

The simplicity of the answer makes it worse somehow. Clare's face tightens, lines deepening around her mouth as she fights for control. "Walking where? The beach? In your nightdress? In the middle of the night?"

Vincent watches Emily's face, searching for some sign of the girl she was before the mill, before the fungus, before whatever inhabits her now took residence behind her eyes. "Where did you go, Emily?"

She turns to him with a unnatural smoothness. Her head tilts at an angle that necks shouldn't achieve, too far to one side, like something inside has come unmoored. The seaweed shifts with the movement, revealing shells tangled in the strands, tiny things with edges sharp enough to cut. Her lips curve into something that isn't quite a smile, more like someone practicing the expression without understanding its purpose.

"I don't remember." The words fall from her mouth with

careful precision, each one placed deliberately. But that not-smile widens slightly, a tell that says she remembers every-thing, every step through the fog, every moment of wherever she's been, whatever she's touched or what's touched her.

Ryan's fist connects with the cupboard door, the crack of impact making everyone jump. The wood splinters slightly under his knuckles, a small fissure that immediately begins to darken with moisture seeping from inside. "She's lying." His voice carries the particular rage of someone who sees the truth but can't make others acknowledge it. "Look at her. She knows exactly where she's been."

The cupboard door swings on its hinge, creaking with a sound that goes on too long, like the house itself protesting the violence. Or maybe savoring it, Vincent thinks, remem-bering the whispers in the walls, the breathing between the boards.

Angela rises with jerky movements, her counting inter-rupted by the need to be useful, to do something normal in this morning that's anything but. She sets a plate before Emily with unnecessary care, toast and eggs arranged with precision that speaks of desperate attempts at order. The eggs bleed yellow across the white porcelain, yolk running in patterns that remind Vincent of the fungus's pale blooms.

Emily sits without acknowledging the food, her wet night-dress creating a spreading puddle on the chair, dripping steadily onto the floor. She doesn't shiver despite the cold that must be seeping into her bones. Instead, she begins to hum, that tuneless melody. The sound fills the kitchen, not loud but pervasive, worming into every corner.

Vincent recognizes something in the pattern now, the way the notes rise and fall. It's like breath moving through hollow wood, through spaces that should be solid but aren't anymore. Like the house's whispers given voice, made audible through Emily's throat. The sound makes his bones feel soft, makes him want to cover his ears but he can't, can't show that weakness, can't let the thing wearing Emily's face know how much it affects him.

The family eats in silence broken only by the scrape of forks against plates, the careful clink of cups set down too gently, everyone afraid that normal sounds might shatter something already cracked. Emily's humming continues, weaving through the quiet, claiming all the space where conversation might exist. Her eggs remain untouched, the yolk now cold and congealed, while seaweed continues to drip from her hair, each drop marking time like a clock counting down to something none of them want to name.

The fog waits for them beyond Holt House's door, patient and thick, wrapping around their bodies the moment they step outside. Vincent feels it immediately, the way it clings to his skin, infiltrates his clothes, makes every breath taste of salt and something else, something that coats the back of his throat like oil. Clare leads them with grim determination, her shoulders squared against the gray nothing, though Vincent notices how her steps pull slightly to the left, toward the distant suggestion of the mill's direction.

The streets of Marrowick have changed. Not the buildings, not the cobblestones slick with perpetual moisture, but the people. They stand in tight clusters at street corners, three or four pressed close enough to touch but maintaining careful inches between their bodies. Their faces carry the same expression, or lack of expression, eyes unfocused, mouths slightly open like they're waiting for words that won't come. Vincent watches a group of fishermen who should be heading to the docks, should be checking nets, preparing boats. Instead they stand in a circle, facing inward but looking at nothing, their hands hanging loose at their sides, fingers occasionally twitching with movements that might be memory of work or might be something else.

No one speaks. The silence feels deliberate, orchestrated, like the whole town has agreed to stop using words without anyone saying so. A woman passes them pushing a carriage, but Vincent can't hear the wheels on the stones, can't hear the baby if there is one, can only see her mouth moving in what might be a lullaby sung without sound. Her lips shape sounds with perfect precision, but nothing emerges, or if it does, the fog swallows it before it can travel.

Angela walks close to Elias, her counting finally stopped, replaced by a vigilance that makes her head swivel constantly, taking in the corruption but unable to process it. Ryan kicks at puddles, but even his small rebellions seem muted, the water barely splashing, the sound absorbed immediately. Emily drifts between them all, her cleaned hair still damp, still smelling faintly of salt and deep water despite Clare's desperate morning efforts with soap and hot water.

Near the pharmacy, a young couple walks side by side. Their hands hang at the same level, fingers almost touching, that millimeter of space between them feeling vast as oceans. They move in perfect synchronization, left foot, right foot, their pace identical, but they never look at each other, never acknowledge the other's presence. The woman's wedding ring catches what little light filters through the fog, but it might as well be jewelry on a mannequin for all the meaning it carries. The man's hand twitches toward hers, an involuntary movement immediately suppressed, pulled back like something burned him.

Vincent recognizes them from earlier visits to town, remembers them laughing over coffee at the cafe, her hand on his arm, his fingers playing with her hair. Now they exist in parallel isolation, together but fundamentally apart, the connection between them severed so cleanly that not even habit remains.

The harbor emerges from the fog gradually, the sound of water lapping at hulls the only noise that penetrates the silence. Boats rock in their moorings, nets draped over sides, everything prepared for work that isn't happening. A fisherman stands at the edge of the dock, his net hanging slack in his hands, the weights at its edges clicking softly against each other with the subtle movement of his breathing. But he doesn't seem to notice it, doesn't check it for tears, doesn't do anything but stare into the fog where the sea should be.

Vincent approaches carefully, his footsteps loud on the wet wood. The fisherman doesn't turn, doesn't acknowledge the presence of another human. His eyes remain fixed on the gray nothing, but Vincent sees they're tracking something, following movement in the fog that isn't there, or isn't visible, or exists in some other way of seeing. The man's body lists slightly to the right, a subtle lean that would eventually topple him into the water if continued. The same direction as the mill, Vincent realizes. Everyone tilting toward it like plants toward diseased light.

The fog itself moves autonomously. Vincent's noticed it before but now it's obvious, undeniable. Instead of drifting randomly with wind currents, it flows with purpose, streams of it moving between buildings, around corners, all in the same direction. Toward Bridgeport Mill. The moisture doesn't eddy or swirl but maintains its course, patient and steady, carrying something Vincent can almost see, almost taste, spores or intent or both.

On the walk back to Holt House, the family maintains their own silence, infected by the town's muteness or afraid to break it. Vincent watches his feet strike the wet pavement, notices how each step wants to veer left, how he has to consciously correct his path to walk straight. The pull is subtle but insistent, like magnetic north shifted, like the world tilted without telling anyone.

Mira moves closer to him, her shoulder brushing his with each step. The contact feels deliberate, necessary, an anchor against the pull. She leans in, her breath warm against his ear in the cold fog, and whispers with a voice that barely disturbs the air: "They're all leaning toward something."

The words settle into Vincent's chest like stones, heavy with truth he's been avoiding. He doesn't respond, can't respond without acknowledging what they both know. The town isn't just sick, isn't just infected. It's being called, drawn toward the mill with the same inexorable patience that pulls tides toward the moon. And everyone feels it, fights it or surrenders to it, but no one escapes it.

Vincent reaches for Mira's hand, finds it already reaching for his. Their fingers lock together with desperate strength, creating their own small resistance against the pull. But even as they grip each other, Vincent feels the subtle pressure against his left side, the suggestion of direction, the patient insistence that eventually, everyone goes to the mill.

———

Night presses against the windows of Holt House with weight that feels personal, like something trying to get in. Vincent sits in the living room's deepest chair, unable to sleep, watching the fog shift and curl beyond the glass in patterns that might be random or might be deliberate. The house creaks around him with sounds he's learned to interpret: the whisper of growth in the walls, the settling that isn't settling but expansion, the soft exhale of a structure that breathes when it shouldn't.

Movement in the yard catches his eye, a pale shape drifting through the darkness. At first Vincent thinks it's fog condensing into something almost solid, a trick of tired eyes and paranoid imagination. But the shape moves with purpose, with direction, and he recognizes the white flutter of Emily's nightdress, the fall of her hair against the pale fabric. She walks barefoot across the grass, her feet leaving dark prints in the dew that seem to linger too long, like the ground remembers her passage.

Her steps carry that bizarre rhythm Vincent's come to

dread, each foot placed with exact deliberation, maintaining a straight line toward the fence that borders the property. The nightdress trails behind her, the hem already dark with moisture, dragging through grass that seems to reach for it, to cling. Her arms hang at her sides, fingers loose, palms facing backward in a position that looks uncomfortable, unnatural, like her joints have been rearranged.

Vincent pushes up from the chair, his body stiff from sitting too long in one position. "Ryan!" His voice cracks through the house's silence, urgent enough to carry but not loud enough to wake everyone. He needs Ryan's stubborn strength, his refusal to accept the impossible even when it's right in front of him. "Ryan, get up. Emily's outside."

Footsteps pound overhead, then on the stairs, Ryan taking them three at a time. He appears in the doorway wearing boxers and nothing else, his face twisted with irritation that shifts immediately to alarm when he sees Vincent's expression. "What do you mean outside?"

Vincent points through the window where Emily has covered half the distance to the fence. Ryan curses, something vicious and protective, shoving his feet into unlaced boots. He yanks the door open hard enough to bounce it off the wall, cold air rushing in carrying the smell of fog and something else, something that reminds Vincent of the mill, of those pale blooms releasing their spores.

They run across the wet grass, Vincent's socks immediately soaked through, the cold shooting up through his legs. Ryan gets there first, his longer stride eating up the distance. But he stops short of touching Emily, something in her posture warning against contact. She stands perfectly still now, inches from the fence, her face turned toward the road that leads to Bridgeport Mill though the fog obscures everything beyond a few feet.

"Emily." Ryan's voice carries a desperation Vincent's never heard before, the older brother who acts like he doesn't care revealing how much he does. "Em, come on. Wake up. You're scaring everyone."

She doesn't respond, doesn't even twitch at the sound of her name. Her lips move in silent conversation, shaping words that Vincent can't read, having a discussion with something that isn't there or isn't visible or exists in some other space. Her head nods occasionally, small movements like she's agreeing with whatever she's hearing. The fog swirls around her ankles, rising higher, reaching up her nightdress with tendrils that look too deliberate, too hungry.

Ryan reaches for her shoulder, but Vincent catches his arm. There's something about Emily's stillness that feels dangerous, like interrupting whatever's happening might cause something worse. Her bare feet press into the grass, and Vincent notices the ground beneath them has changed color, darker, like something's seeping up from below or down from above, meeting where her skin makes contact with the earth.

"Emily!" Ryan yells now, panic overriding caution. His voice echoes off the fog, returns distorted, multiplied, like several voices calling at once. "Stop this. Whatever you're doing, stop it!"

The fog thickens, condensing around Emily until she's barely visible, just a white shape in gray nothing. Vincent feels the pull now, stronger than during the day, the insistent tug toward the mill that makes his feet want to follow Emily's path. Ryan feels it too, Vincent can see it in the way he plants his feet wider, fighting against the subtle suggestion of movement.

A figure emerges from the fog with no warning, no footsteps announcing approach. Jonah Kells stands there like he's been waiting all along, his coat soaked through, water running from the edges in steady streams. His eyes carry that knowing look, that recognition of things others refuse to see. He doesn't speak, doesn't explain his presence. Instead, he moves with surprising speed for someone his age, his hand clamping down on Emily's shoulder with enough force to break whatever holds her.

"You're not going there." His voice comes out low, fierce, carrying an authority that has nothing to do with volume and everything to do with certainty. His fingers dig into Emily's shoulder, not gentle, not careful, the grip of someone who understands that sometimes pain is the only thing that can call someone back from where they're going.

Emily's body jerks like she's been electrocuted. Her eyes blink rapidly, awareness flooding back in stages: confusion, fear, recognition. She looks at Jonah's face, at his hand on her shoulder, at the fence she's standing against. Her mouth opens, closes, opens again, but no sound emerges except a small whimper that might be fear or might be disappointment at being pulled back.

"Emily!" Clare's voice cuts through the night from the porch, raw with terror that mothers reserve for moments when their children stand at the edge of something irreversible. She runs across the grass in her nightgown and slippers, her face a mask of barely controlled panic.

Emily turns toward her mother's voice and collapses, not dramatically but completely, like whatever was holding her upright has been severed. She folds into Clare's arms with a pliancy that seems boneless, like a puppet with cut strings. Clare pulls her close, rocks her, murmurs prayers or comfort or both while Emily's body remains limp, too accepting of the embrace, too willing to be shaped into whatever position Clare arranges her in.

Jonah steps back, water still dripping from his coat, his eyes moving between the family and the fog that continues to flow toward the mill. His presence feels both necessary and intrusive, like he belongs here and doesn't, exists in the space between guardian and threat.

Inside Holt House, water pools beneath Jonah's feet as he wrings his coat sleeves with methodical precision. Each twist releases streams that patter onto the wooden floor, the sound too loud in the tense silence that fills the living room. The droplets spread immediately, finding grooves between boards, disappearing into the house's hungry spaces. Vincent watches the water vanish too quickly, absorbed by wood that should be saturated already but somehow always has room for more moisture, more corruption, more of whatever feeds the growth in the walls.

The fire Clare built crackles in the hearth, flames that should warm but don't, just create moving shadows that make everyone's faces look hollow, consumed. Jonah positions himself close to it, though the heat doesn't seem to reach him, his clothes still dripping, still carrying the cold of the fog inside. His eyes move around the room with that careful assessment Vincent's noticed before, cataloging exits, checking corners, reading the space like text written in a language most people don't know exists.

"It's breathing heavier now." Jonah's words come out barely above a whisper, meant for the room but directed at no one, or maybe at the walls themselves. His fingers work at his coat buttons, movements automatic, practiced, the gestures of someone who's been wet and cold too many times to count. "The mill's calling."

Elias steps forward from his position by the fireplace, his face drawn with concern that he's trying to shape into clinical interest. The magazine he's been holding drops onto the side table with a soft slap, pages splayed open to an article about mold remediation that seems laughably inadequate now. "Why?" His voice carries that forced calm he uses when he's trying to maintain control of situations that can't be controlled. "What's changed? Why now?"

Jonah doesn't answer directly, never does when questions get too close to truths that hurt to speak. Instead, his gaze shifts to Emily, who sits curled in Clare's lap despite being too old for such comfort, her body folded into impossible angles to fit in the space of her mother's arms. She's shivering now, or appears to be, though her skin doesn't show goosebumps, doesn't show the normal signs of cold. The tremors run through her in waves that don't match any natural rhythm, starting at her feet and rolling upward, making her whole body undulate slightly.

The humming begins again, soft at first, barely audible over the fire's crackling. That tuneless melody that comes from somewhere deeper than Emily's throat, using her voice but not originating from her. The sound fills the room and makes the walls seem to pulse in response, as if the house recognizes the tune, harmonizes with it. Vincent feels it in his teeth, in the hollow spaces of his bones, vibration that shouldn't exist from such a quiet sound.

Clare rocks Emily gently, her face a mask of desperate maternal normalcy, pretending this is just comfort for a frightened child rather than an attempt to hold onto something that's slipping away. Her lips move in words too quiet to hear but visible in the shape of her mouth, the same phrases repeated like a shield against what she knows but won't acknowledge.

Ryan paces by the window, his fists clenched so tight his knuckles show white through the skin. Each circuit takes him past the same spots: window, bookshelf, doorway, back to window. His bare feet slap against the floor with unnecessary force, like he's trying to punish the house for existing, for failing to be the sanctuary it pretends to be. Water darkens the wood where he steps, his feet still wet from the grass, leaving prints that linger too long before the house drinks them in.

Angela hovers near the kitchen doorway, a tray in her hands bearing coffee no one asked for, cups that steam but won't be drunk. Her fingers shake slightly, making the cups rattle against saucers with a sound like chattering teeth. She sets the tray down, picks it up, sets it down again, unable to complete the gesture of hospitality because hospitality has no place here, not now, not with Emily humming and Jonah dripping and everyone pretending they don't feel the pull toward the mill.

Jonah moves closer to Vincent with that sideways approach of someone who doesn't want to be obvious about their intention. He stops just within speaking distance, close enough that Vincent can smell the salt-rot of his coat, the deep water scent that clings to him like he's been swimming in places where light doesn't reach. When he speaks, his voice drops low enough that only Vincent can hear, words meant for him alone.

"Next time she won't come back."

The statement hangs between them, not threat but prophecy, not warning but certainty. Jonah's eyes hold Vincent's, and in them Vincent sees the weight of knowledge, of patterns observed, of endings witnessed. There's no doubt in that gaze, no hope that things might turn out differently. Emily will go to the mill again, will answer its call, and when she does, whatever returns won't be Emily anymore, might not even pretend to be. That is, if she returns.

Vincent wants to ask how Jonah knows, wants to demand explanations, solutions, something more than cryptic warnings. But Jonah is already moving away, his message delivered, his part in this scene complete. He heads toward the door with movements that suggest he was never really here, just a momentary intersection of their crisis with his perpetual vigilance.

The humming continues, Emily's voice weaving through the room's thick air, and Vincent notices how everyone unconsciously sways slightly with its rhythm. Even Ryan's pacing has adjusted to match the melody's tempo, his circuits timed to its rises and falls. They're all being tuned to its frequency, shaped by its pattern, prepared for something Vincent doesn't want to imagine.

The fire gutters suddenly, flames bending away from some

unfelt draft, and in that moment of dimness Vincent sees Emily's eyes are open, staring at nothing or everything, pupils dilated so wide they look black. She's here but not here, present but absent, Emily but not Emily. The humming continues, but her lips don't move, the sound emerging from her without her participation, using her as conduit rather than source.

Clare pulls her closer, tighter, as if physical proximity might anchor what's drifting away. But Vincent sees the truth in Jonah's warning, feels it in the way the house breathes around them, knows it in the pull that grows stronger with each passing hour. Next time Emily goes to the mill, she won't come back.

CHAPTER
SIXTEEN

The walls of Holt House press closer with each passing hour, or maybe it's just Vincent's perception shifting, his awareness of their imprisonment sharpening as evening deepens into night. The fog outside has thickened to the consistency of wet cotton, pressed against every window like something trying to suffocate them slowly. Vincent sits on the sofa, watching Clare hover near Emily with the desperate attention of someone guarding a flame in wind. Her hands flutter constantly, adjusting Emily's collar, smoothing her hair, touching her shoulder, each gesture a small attempt to confirm her daughter still exists in some reachable way.

Emily sits at the dining table, folding linens with movements so precise they look rehearsed. Each towel receives exactly eight folds, corners aligned with mathematical perfection before being set in a growing stack. Her fingers work without pause, without variation, while her eyes remain fixed on the fog beyond the window. Sometimes her lips move slightly, shaping words that produce no sound, having conversations with something only she perceives in that gray nothing.

"Don't even think about it," Ryan snaps when Emily rises from her chair, drifting toward the kitchen door with that liquid grace that doesn't belong to her anymore. His voice cracks with exhaustion and fear worn down to sharp edges. He plants himself between her and the exit, arms crossed, jaw clenched so tight the muscles jump beneath his skin. Emily stops, tilts her head, studying him with eyes that reflect the lamplight wrong, too bright, too knowing. Then she turns back to the table, resumes folding, and Ryan's shoulders don't relax even slightly.

"Maybe we should tie her to a chair," Ryan mutters, the words dropping into the room like mice in a bucket. No one laughs. No one even acknowledges he's spoken, but Vincent sees Clare flinch, sees the way her fingers tighten on the dishcloth she's been wringing for the past hour. The suggestion hangs in the air with the weight of possibility, of desperation approaching that threshold where unthinkable things become necessary.

The house creaks around them with sounds that have grown familiar and terrible. Long, low groans of wood that shouldn't be expanding but is, drawing in moisture and something else, something that feeds the pale blooms Vincent can see pushing through cracks in the baseboards. They've multiplied since morning, waxy petals unfurling in the shadows where walls meet floor, pulsing with that subtle rhythm that matches no heartbeat, no breath, just the patient consumption of everything solid.

Angela moves through the space in stuttering bursts of activity, reorganizing cupboards that don't need organizing, wiping surfaces already clean. Her fingers pause occasionally at her wrist, tapping out a count that Vincent recognizes has changed. Not days anymore, not the proud accumulation of sobriety. Hours now, maybe minutes, marking time until something she won't name but they all feel approaching. She pulls dishes from one cabinet, stacks them in another, then moves them back, the porcelain clicking with sounds too sharp in the thick air.

Elias makes his circuit of the windows for the dozenth time tonight, checking latches that haven't loosened, peering through glass that shows nothing but gray. His fingers test each lock with the thoroughness of someone who understands the futility but needs the ritual, needs to feel like he's doing something even if that something accomplishes nothing. At the large window overlooking the yard, he pauses longer, his breath fogging the glass as he searches for movement in the fog, for shapes that might be Emily walking away, might be something else approaching.

Vincent feels Mira shift beside him on the sofa, her shoulder pressing more firmly against his. Their hands find each other without conscious thought, fingers interlocking with the desperate strength of drowning people gripping the same piece of driftwood. Her thumb moves against his palm in small circles, a gesture that might be comfort or might be her own need for confirmation that something real and warm and human still exists. The contact generates its own small heat in the cold dampness of the room, a pocket of connection that the fungus hasn't reached, hasn't corrupted, though Vincent can feel it trying, testing the boundaries of their closeness.

The grandfather clock in the hallway hasn't worked properly in years according to Clare, its mechanism damaged by decades of coastal moisture. But at the stroke of midnight, it releases three hollow chimes that shouldn't be possible from broken clockwork. The sound reverberates through the house, through the walls, through Vincent's bones. Three chimes for midnight, wrong in every way, the sound lasting too long, echoing in spaces that don't exist.

Every head turns toward the hallway, toward that impossible sound. Emily's humming stops, the first interruption in hours. Her hands pause mid-fold, a towel hanging suspended between her fingers. For a moment, just a moment, her face shows something like confusion, like the Emily who existed before the mill trying to surface through whatever uses her now. Then it's gone, replaced by that empty focus, and the humming resumes at a different pitch, harmonizing with echoes that shouldn't still be audible.

Clare rises with movements that suggest tremendous effort, like the air has thickened to water around her. "We should all get some sleep," she says, though her voice carries no conviction that sleep is possible, that rest exists anymore in this house where walls breathe and clocks chime impossible hours. She touches Emily's shoulder, guides her toward the stairs with gentle insistence that barely masks desperation.

They follow one by one, a funeral procession toward beds that offer no comfort. The final echo of that third chime lingers as they climb the stairs, hanging in the air like smoke, like spores, like promise of worse things waiting in the dark hours before dawn.

———

The stairs creak with a sound Vincent knows too well, that particular weight and rhythm that means someone is descending in the dark. His eyes snap open, body already moving before his mind fully processes what's happening. The room feels too cold, and when he reaches across the space between beds, he finds Mira already sitting up, her silhouette rigid against the darker black of the wall. She doesn't speak, doesn't need to. They both know what that sound means, have been waiting for it since the clock's impossible chiming.

Vincent's feet hit the floor, the wood ice-cold and slightly soft, that give that means the moisture has worked deep into the grain. He doesn't bother with shoes, doesn't bother with anything except getting to the hallway where Mira joins him, her hand finding his in the darkness with the sureness of magnetism. Together they move toward the stairs, toward the sound of the front door that shouldn't be open but is, its hinges crying out in the silence.

The door stands wide, fog pouring through like water breaking a dam. It flows across the threshold in visible currents, pooling on the floor, rising to ankle height before dispersing into the house's eager spaces. The cold hits Vincent's lungs with each breath, coating his throat with moisture that tastes of salt and decay. Through the doorway, through the thick gray nothing, a pale shape moves with terrible purpose.

Emily's nightdress glows faintly in the darkness, the white fabric catching whatever light exists in this drowned world. She's already past the gate, her bare feet silent on the wet road, each step placed with the same exact programmed movements she used folding linens. Her arms hang at her sides, fingers loose, palms facing backward. She doesn't hurry, doesn't run, just maintains that steady pace toward the only destination that matters anymore.

"Emily!" Ryan's voice tears through the night as he shoves past Vincent, nearly knocking him into the wall. He's wearing nothing but boxers and untied boots, his bare chest already slick with fog-moisture as he sprints through the door. His feet slam against the wet ground, sending up sprays of water that the fog swallows immediately. "Emily, stop! Come back!" The desperation in his voice cracks it like adolescence reversing, turning his shouts into something raw and broken.

Ryan closes in on Emily, boots slipping on the water-logged grass. Halfway across the yard, his foot catches in a tangle of wet roots and he goes down hard, knees and palms hitting the ground with a dull smack. For a moment he's sprawled in the cold mud, breath knocked out of him, fog swirling close. Then he scrambles up, soaked and gasping, and keeps running, shouting her name into the gray.

Emily doesn't turn. Doesn't pause. Doesn't acknowledge that anyone has called her name. She continues forward with the inevitability of tide, pulled by something stronger than family, stronger than her will, stronger than the brother who's always pretended not to care but whose voice now breaks with caring too much.

"Emily!" Clare appears on the porch in her nightgown, her cry sharp enough to cut through fog, through night, through the careful composure she's maintained for days. The sound carries a mother's specific terror, the recognition that her child is walking toward something from which there is no return. She starts down the steps, stumbles, catches herself on the railing with hands that shake visibly even in the darkness.

Vincent and Mira run after them, the cold fog soaking through their clothes instantly, turning fabric to wet weight that clings and drags. Vincent's feet slip on the slick road, finding no purchase on the smooth dirt that feels more like ice, like something actively trying to prevent pursuit. Mira grabs his arm and it is the only thing that keeps him upright, her balance somehow sure despite the treacherous surface.

Ahead, Emily's silhouette grows fainter with each step, the fog claiming her incrementally, erasing her from feet up like she's dissolving into the gray. Her nightdress floats behind her, the last visible part, a white flag of surrender or victory depending on whose perspective matters. Ryan's still shouting, his voice growing hoarse, words devolving from her name to "Please" to wordless sounds of grief.

Vincent searches the fog for another presence, for the figure that should emerge from the mist like last time. But there's no Jonah tonight. No weathered face materializing from gray nothing, no firm hand to clamp down on Emily's shoulder, no gruff voice to break whatever spell pulls her forward. The fog remains empty except for their futile chase, their voices that accomplish nothing, their feet that can't close the distance no matter how fast they run.

They reach the curve where the road bends toward Bridgeport Mill, where the fog thickens from mere blindness to something solid, something that pushes back against their bodies like a physical barrier. Emily's form has reduced to suggestion, to the faintest luminescence of white fabric that might be nightdress or might be fog condensing into almost-shape. Then even that vanishes, swallowed completely, leaving them staring at nothing while knowing exactly where she's gone.

Clare collapses to her knees on the wet road, the impact painful-sounding, her nightgown immediately soaking through. Her hands fumble for the rosary that's always in her pocket, beads clicking against each other as her fingers shake too hard to properly grip them. The prayers that emerge from her clenched teeth aren't the smooth Latin she usually murmurs but broken fragments, English and Latin mixed with gasps that might be sobs or might be the struggle to breathe in air that feels too thick for lungs. The beads fall loose in her hands.

Elias appears behind her, his pajamas clinging to his thin frame, his clinical composure crumbling into something raw and human. His hands find Clare's shoulders, grip them with a desperation that has nothing to do with comfort and everything to do with needing something solid to hold while the world dissolves. His fingers dig in hard enough that Clare should protest but doesn't, both of them needing the pain to confirm they're still real, still here, still capable of feeling anything besides the hollow horror of loss.

Ryan stands trembling at the road's edge, his whole body shaking with cold or rage or grief. His fists clench and unclench at his sides, knuckles white, tendons standing out like cables about to snap. "We can't just let her..." His voice breaks on the last word, unable to name what they're letting happen, what they're powerless to prevent.

Vincent feels the words rising in his throat, the truth that everyone knows but no one wants to speak. It emerges without his permission, flat and certain as stone. "She won't stop." The statement hangs in the fog between them, neither accusation nor absolution, just acknowledgment of what Emily has become, what the mill has made her, what she's chosen or what's chosen her.

Mira approaches Clare, who has collapsed in the gravel, her sobs wracking the quiet night. The rosary has slipped from her grasp, lying half-buried in the damp dirt. Without a word, Mira bends to retrieve it, brushing the grit away with careful fingers. She presses the beads gently into Clare's trembling hands, folding Clare's fingers around them and meeting her eyes. Mira's own gaze is steady, resolved, an unspoken promise passing between them in the hush, as if to say: we're not finished yet.

The fog continues to flow toward the mill, carrying Emily with it, into it, making her part of its substance and purpose. They stand at the edge of pursuit, knowing the futility of following, the danger of that path, the certainty that Emily is already gone in every way that matters. The road stretches into gray nothing, and somewhere in that nothing, Emily walks with perfect mechanical steps toward whatever waits at Bridgeport Mill.

———

The kitchen receives them like a mouth, swallowing their fog-drenched bodies into its familiar cavity. Water runs from their clothes in steady streams, pooling on the floor where the wood drinks it eagerly, always thirsty, never satisfied. Vincent feels the moisture seeping through his socks, between his toes, cold that goes deeper than skin, settling into bones like it plans to stay. They arrange themselves around the table without speaking, each taking the same positions they've held for days, as if maintaining these assignments might restore some order to a world that's lost all structure.

The silence weighs more than sound would, thick and suffocating as the fog outside. Clare's prayers continue in whispered fragments, her fingers working the rosary with movements that have lost their smooth rhythm, catching and stuttering like a broken mechanism. The sound of forced habit. The Latin dissolves into English, into wordless sounds that might be God's names or might be Emily's, the two concepts blurring in her desperation. Her nightgown clings to her where she knelt on the wet road, the fabric dark with moisture that won't dry in this house where nothing ever truly dries.

The walls creak around them with that persistent breathing Vincent's grown to recognize, the inhale and exhale of a structure that shouldn't be alive but is. Each sound lasts too long, carries too much weight, suggests movement in spaces that should be solid. The fungus has grown bolder in their absence, or maybe their leaving gave it permission to reveal what was always there. Pale blooms push through the seams where wallpaper meets, unfurling with visible patience, their waxy petals catching the kitchen's yellow light and reflecting it back distorted.

Angela stands at the counter with rigid purpose, filling the coffee pot with water that runs brown from the tap for a moment before clearing. Her hands shake as she measures grounds, spilling dark grains across the counter that she doesn't bother to clean. The coffee begins to percolate with sounds too loud in the quiet, aggressive bubbling that seems to mock the idea that normal routines matter anymore. She pours cups no one asked for, sets them before people who won't drink them, the gesture empty of meaning but necessary for her hands that need tasks, need motion, need anything besides stillness that might let reality settle in.

Her counting has changed again, Vincent notices. Not days now, not even hours. She whispers numbers that might be minutes, might be heartbeats, might be the seconds until dawn that won't bring relief, won't bring clarity, will only reveal how much worse things have become in darkness. "Four hundred thirty-two, thirty-three, thirty-four." The numbers pour from her lips without pause, a shield of mathematics against the chaos that can't be quantified.

Ryan paces the kitchen's perimeter with violent energy seeking outlet. His bare feet slap against the floor, leaving wet prints that the house absorbs immediately, erasing his passage as fast as he makes it. He stops at a corner where a particularly large bloom has pushed through the baseboard, its surface pulsing with that rhythm that matches nothing natural. His foot draws back, connects with the growth in a kick that speaks of rage at everything he can't fight, can't fix, can't protect his sister from.

The fungus tears easily, too easily, its flesh soft and yielding. The impact releases a cloud of spores that hang visible in the air, drifting with purpose rather than air currents. Ryan coughs immediately, stumbling backward, his hand covering his mouth too late. The spores settle on his skin, his hair, dissolving into moisture that might be absorbed or might simply wait for better conditions to grow. He backs against the far wall, eyes wide with recognition of his mistake, of how the fungus uses even violence against it as opportunity to spread.

The remaining pieces of the bloom continue pulsing, unconcerned with their damage, already beginning to regenerate from the edges inward. More blooms become visible as Vincent's eyes adjust, seeing them in corners, along ceiling edges, pushing through outlets where electricity should flow but now only corruption emerges. The house has become more fungus than structure, more infection than shelter, and they sit at its center like food being slowly digested.

"The mill." Elias's voice cuts through the silence with clinical flatness, two words that carry the weight of decision already made. His magazine lies forgotten on the table, pages curled with moisture. His hands rest flat on the table, fingers spread, pressing down as if trying to anchor himself to something solid while everything else dissolves.

Clare's head snaps up, her eyes finding his with desperate denial. She shakes her head, quick, sharp movements that send water droplets from her hair spattering across the table. Her mouth opens, closes, opens again, but no words emerge. What argument could she make? What alternative could she offer? Emily has gone to the mill, and the mill doesn't return what it takes. Everyone knows this. Everyone has known this since Emily first touched those pale blooms, since she started humming that tuneless song, since she began her transformation into something that wears her face but isn't her.

Vincent remembers Jonah's warning with sudden, perfect clarity. The words echo in his mind with the weight of prophecy fulfilled: "Next time she won't come back." Not a threat but a promise, not a warning but simple statement of fact. Jonah knew because Jonah has seen this before, watched the mill call and claim, witnessed the slow consumption of everything human in Marrowick. And now Emily has answered that call for the final time, walked into the fog with inhuman steps that will never return to Holt House.

Vincent turns to find Mira watching him, her dark eyes steady in the kitchen's yellow light. She sees his recognition, his understanding, reads the decision forming in his mind before he's fully conscious of it. Her hand moves across the small space between them, fingers spreading in clear invitation. He takes it without hesitation, their hands linking with the desperate strength of people who know they're about to walk into something from which they might not return.

"Then we follow." Mira's voice comes quiet but certain, not a question but a statement of inevitable action. Her words hang in the air, and Vincent feels everyone in the room shift, feels the decision crystallize from possibility into certainty. They can't leave Emily to whatever waits at the mill. They can't abandon her to the fungus and the fog and the mastery of The Adversary. Even if it's too late, even if what they find isn't Emily anymore, they have to try.

No one argues. The acceptance spreads through the room, settling on everyone with equal weight. Clare rises first, movements stiff but determined, water still dripping from her nightgown. She opens drawers with quick efficiency, pulling out flashlights that probably won't penetrate the fog but might provide the comfort of doing something, preparing something, fighting back even in this small way.

Angela stops counting, the numbers finally failing as shield against what must be faced. She moves to the sink, runs water over her hands though they're already clean, the gesture automatic, something to do while her mind processes what comes next. Her reflection in the window above the sink shows a face Vincent barely recognizes, aged by days that have felt like years, the careful composure she's maintained cracking like old paint.

Ryan stops pacing, his body suddenly still in that way that means decision rather than rest. He disappears upstairs, returns moments later wearing jeans and a jacket, boots properly laced this time. His movements carry new purpose, the aimless rage transformed into something directed, something with a target. He doesn't speak, doesn't need to. His presence at the door says everything.

Clare wraps herself in the old wool coat that hangs by the door, the one that smells of years of coastal storms, of salt and age and memories of better times. Her fingers fumble with buttons, the simple task made difficult by hands that won't stop shaking. Vincent watches her mouth move in what might

Emily's name repeated like a mantra, like saying it enough times might summon her daughter back from wherever she's gone.

They gather at the threshold, the house at their backs breathing its last damp sigh. No one looks at each other; there's nothing left to say. With Vincent and Mira leading, they leave behind what's left of safety, walking into the night, bound by love, fear, and the faintest hope that Emily can be saved.

SEVENTEEN

The road to Bridgeport Mill sucks at Vincent's feet with each step, black mud rising through cracks in the crumbled asphalt like the earth itself has gone soft with rot. The fog wraps around them thicker than before, not just obscuring but pressing, weighing down on shoulders and heads with physical force that makes every movement feel like swimming through syrup. Vincent leads because someone has to, though his body fights against the forward motion, some deep instinct screaming that this path leads nowhere good, nowhere human, nowhere survivable.

Behind him, the others struggle through the same resistance. Clare's breathing comes ragged, punctuated by fragments of prayer that dissolve into the fog before they can form complete thoughts. Angela's counting has stopped entirely, replaced by small sounds of effort as her feet sink ankle-deep with each step. The mud releases their shoes with obscene sucking sounds, reluctant to let them go, eager to pull them down into whatever feeds beneath the surface.

The landscape itself has changed, or maybe Vincent's perception has shifted enough to see what was always there. The trees lean toward the mill with unnatural angles, their trunks bent like genuflecting figures, branches reaching in the same direction with desperate yearning. Fence posts that should stand vertical tilt at forty-five degree angles, their wood swollen and splitting, pale fungus erupting from the cracks in phosphorescent clusters. Even the telephone poles bow toward their destination, the wires between them humming with a frequency that is now ubiquitous, carrying not electricity but something else, some communication between the mill and the corrupted world around it.

Salt rides the air, but mixed with sweetness that belongs to no ocean, no natural decay. It coats Vincent's throat with each breath, thick enough to taste, leaving residue that won't be swallowed away. Beneath it runs something worse, the fungal reek that's become familiar but intensified here, concentrated, like breathing in the essence of decomposition itself. His lungs rebel against it, wanting clean air that doesn't exist anymore, might never have existed in this place where corruption has taken root so deep it's become the foundation.

Through the fog, a shape begins to form. Not emerging but revealed, as if it's always been there waiting for them to get close enough to see. Bridgeport Mill rises from the gray nothing like something geological, less building than outcropping, its edges irregular and deceptive. The structure looms larger than Vincent remembered, swollen somehow, expanded beyond its original dimensions by what grows within and without. Broken windows puncture its bulk at intervals that follow no architectural logic, and through them pulses a light that shouldn't exist, gray-green luminescence that brightens and dims with the rhythm of breathing, of heartbeat, of something alive that shouldn't be.

Movement in the fields catches Vincent's eye, shapes that resolve into human figures as they get closer. They stand scattered across the muddy ground like markers, like headstones, completely motionless despite being upright. A farmer in overalls, his clothes so saturated they hang like weights. A woman in a shopkeeper's apron, the fabric plastered to her body by moisture that never stops accumulating. Children in school clothes, their small bodies rigid as posts, faces turned toward the mill with expressions of perfect blankness.

None of them acknowledge the group's passage. Their eyes remain fixed on the mill's entrance, pupils dilated so wide the irises have nearly disappeared, leaving black circles that reflect nothing. Water runs from their hair, their clothes, pooling around their feet in spreading circles, but they don't shiver, don't shift weight, don't show any sign of discomfort or awareness. They've become part of the landscape, human trees rooted in place by whatever calls from within those breathing walls.

Vincent counts at least twenty of them, maybe more lost in the fog, all maintaining that terrible stillness. Their presence makes the air feel thicker, harder to breathe, as if they're using up what little oxygen remains. Or maybe they're not breathing at all, Vincent realizes with a chill that has nothing to do with cold. Maybe they're past the need for air, sustained by something else, something the mill provides in exchange for their presence, their witness, their slow transformation into whatever they're becoming.

At the mill's entrance, a figure in white stands out against the dark wood and darker shadows. Emily's nightdress has become something else through its journey, no longer white but gray-green with moisture and worse things. Seaweed tangles through her hair in deliberate braids, shells clicking against each other with each small movement. Mud cakes her bare feet up to the ankles, but darker stuff stains the fabric, spreading upward in patterns that look too deliberate to be random, too purposeful to be accident.

Clare breaks from the group with a cry that tears from her throat raw and desperate. Her hands reach for Emily, fingers locking around her daughter's wrist with force that speaks of pure maternal desperation. Vincent sees Clare's knuckles go white, sees the crescents her nails leave in Emily's skin, sees the way she pulls with her whole body, trying to drag Emily back from the threshold she's about to cross.

Emily turns her head with unemotional smoothness, looking at her mother's hand on her wrist like it's something foreign, something she doesn't quite recognize. Then she jerks free with surprising strength, the motion so sudden Clare stumbles backward. Emily's bare feet find the wet ground again, toes spreading in the mud like she's rooting herself, drawing strength from the corrupted earth.

Ryan surges forward with a sound that's half rage, half grief, his boots sending up sprays of black water. But Elias's arm bars his path, catching him across the chest with enough force to drive the air from his lungs. "Wait," Elias says, the word emerging brittle and sharp, his suit jacket hanging heavy with moisture that makes him look smaller, defeated. But his arm remains firm, holding Ryan back from whatever waits beyond that dark entrance.

Vincent feels Mira's presence beside him, her hand finding his in the darkness. Her fingers are cold, slick with fog-moisture, but the contact grounds him, reminds him he's not alone in this nightmare. They share a look, and in her dark eyes he sees his own dread reflected, his own certainty that they're walking into something that might not release them, might transform them like it's transformed Emily, like it's transforming the whole town one connection at a time.

The mill's breathing grows louder as they approach, that rhythmic pulse of light behind broken windows matching some vast circulation Vincent doesn't want to understand. The smell intensifies, coating his sinuses, making his stomach turn with its sweetness, its promise of consumption and transformation. His feet want to stop, want to turn back, but Emily continues forward, and they have no choice but to follow her into the waiting darkness of Bridgeport Mill.

The air inside the mill hangs thick as wet wool, pressing

against Vincent's face the moment he crosses the threshold. Each breath feels like drowning in slow motion, moisture coating his throat, his lungs, condensing in places air should flow freely. The floorboards give beneath his weight with a dangerous softness, wood gone spongy with rot and growth, transforming into something between solid and liquid. Water drips from overhead beams in steady streams, not clean rain but something thicker, darker, leaving trails that glisten in the strange light that seems to come from everywhere and nowhere.

Pale networks of mycelium web across every surface, their filaments spreading in patterns too deliberate for chaos, too organized for nature. They pulse with visible life, expanding and contracting in waves that travel from floor to ceiling, through walls, across the spaces between boards where they've eaten away the boundaries between structure and organism. The threads glow faintly, phosphorescent white-green that makes Vincent think of deep sea creatures, of things that live in places where light never reaches.

The sound hits him next, that deep breathing he's heard in Holt House's walls but magnified here, unrestrained, filling the vast space with its rhythm. It comes from below, from above, from the walls themselves, a sound that bypasses the ears and resonates in the chest cavity, in the hollow spaces between ribs. Vincent feels it sync with his own breathing, tries to resist, but his lungs betray him, falling into the same pattern, the same inhale and exhale that makes him part of the mill's circulation.

Spores drift through the air like snow, visible in the shafts of that sick light, swirling in currents that follow no wind. They settle on his jacket, his hair, dissolving into moisture that soaks through fabric with unnatural speed. He tastes them with each breath, sweet and putrid, coating his tongue with flavors he'd rather not know. Angela coughs behind him, sharp and desperate, her hand covering her mouth too late. The spores have already found their way in, already begun whatever work they do in human lungs.

Emily moves through this corrupted space with perfect ease, her bare feet finding stable spots on rotted boards, her body navigating obstacles without looking. Her right hand trails along the wall as she goes deeper, fingers spreading against the wood with each touch. Where her skin makes contact, prints bloom in pale light, handprints that glow with their own luminescence before fading back into darkness. But they don't disappear completely. Vincent can still see them, afterimages burned into his vision, creating a trail of where she's been, where she's going.

Her face carries that empty serenity that's replaced everything Emily used to be, lips parted in what might be a smile or might be preparation for words that never come. Her eyes catch the fungal light and throw it back doubled, pupils so dilated they've consumed the iris entirely, leaving just black circles that see everything and nothing. She doesn't look back at them, doesn't acknowledge their presence. Her attention fixes on something deeper in the mill, something that pulls her forward with invisible strings.

"Emily!" Ryan's voice cracks through the breathing silence, raw with desperation that borders on hysteria. He lunges forward, boots slipping on the wet boards, arms outstretched. His fingers close around Emily's arm just above the elbow, grip tight enough to leave marks. "Emily, stop! Look at me! It's Ryan, it's your brother!"

The wall beside them shudders like muscle, like flesh disturbed by unwanted touch. A section of fungus swells outward, pale and wet, extending toward Ryan with purpose. The growth unfurls into something like a tendril, like an arm, wrapping around Ryan's wrist with a touch that looks gentle but isn't. Ryan gasps, a sound of surprise that transforms immediately into something worse, something that speaks of strength being drained, of will being sapped, of essence being pulled out through skin.

His shoulders slump forward, his grip on Emily loosening as his fingers go slack. The tendril pulses, tightening its hold, and Vincent can see something traveling through it, some exchange between Ryan and the fungus that shouldn't be possible but is happening right in front of him. Ryan's face goes gray, not just pale but gray like ash, like something fundamental has been extracted.

Vincent starts forward to help, but a figure crashes between them with violent purpose. Jonah Kells appears like he's been there all along, just waiting for the right moment to reveal himself. His coat drips with fresh mud, not just damp but soaked through, as if he's been swimming in the earth itself. His hair plasters to his skull, water running down his face in streams that make him look half-drowned, but his eyes burn with fierce urgency.

Without hesitation, Jonah grabs the fungal tendril with both hands and tears. The sound it makes coming apart is wet and foul, like ripping meat, and it releases Ryan with a snap that sends him stumbling backward. Jonah shoves Ryan away from the wall with more force than seems necessary, putting distance between him and the wounded fungus that's already beginning to regenerate, already reaching out again.

"Don't touch her." Jonah's voice comes out raw, scraped. "It feeds on connection. Every touch, every attempt to reach her, it grows stronger. He grows stronger through it."

The words land with the weight of truth Vincent has been avoiding. The fungus doesn't just corrupt; it weaponizes love itself, turns connection into consumption, makes every attempt at rescue into further feeding. Vincent catches Ryan as he staggers, pulls him back toward the entrance, away from Emily who continues deeper into the mill as if nothing has happened, as if her brother didn't just nearly lose himself trying to save her.

Mira presses close to Vincent's side, her presence solid and necessary in this space where everything else feels fluid, uncertain. Her eyes track between Emily and Jonah, reading patterns Vincent can't see, understanding connections he's only beginning to grasp. The mill breathes around them, patient and hungry, and Vincent knows with terrible certainty that they've walked into something that's been waiting for them, something that knew they would come, something that's already begun to feed.

Beyond the scattered debris of old machinery, the mill opens into a vast chamber where the fungus has given up all pretense of subtlety. It swells from floor to ceiling in a massive column of pale flesh, pulsing with that familiar rhythm but stronger here, visible as waves of light that travel through its translucent mass. The growth has consumed the mill's actual heart, whatever machinery once operated here now just skeletal remains poking through fungal tissue like bones through skin. The air tastes of metal and ash, coating Vincent's tongue with flavors that speak of burning without fire, of oxidation without air.

The wet floor quivers with each pulse, connected to the central mass by veins of mycelium that branch and spread like a circulation system. Vincent feels it through his shoes, through his bones, that deep throb that wants to synchronize with his heartbeat, wants to make him part of its rhythm. The walls themselves have become more fungus than wood, breathing in time with the central column, drawing in the fog through broken windows and releasing something else, something that makes the air shimmer with barely visible spores.

At the base of the massive growth, the fungus shifts and reforms, its surface rippling like water disturbed by wind. Shapes emerge from the pale mass, suggestions of form that shouldn't be there. A shoulder, perhaps. The curve of a jaw. Features that almost resolve into familiarity before dissolving back into formlessness. Then, with deliberate slowness, it sculpts itself into something more defined. Not quite a man, but the impression of one, edges blurred by static, by interference, by the impossibility of simple organic matter holding human shape.

Emily stands before it with her head tilted back, studying the formation with eyes that reflect its pulsing light. Her bare feet have left a trail of glowing prints across the floor, each one lingering longer here, as if the fungus recognizes her, welcomes her, has been waiting for her specifically. She raises one hand toward the shape, fingers spreading in a gesture that might be greeting or might be surrender.

"Dad." The word falls from her lips soft as breath, carrying a terrible certainty that makes Vincent's chest constrict. She takes another step forward, her nightdress dragging through puddles of condensation that glow faintly where they touch the fabric. "He's waiting for me."

The sound Ryan makes isn't quite human, somewhere between sob and scream, torn from a place deeper than throat or lungs. He lurches forward, tears streaming down his face, mixing with the moisture that clings to everything here. "Emily! That's not Dad! Dad died, Dad's gone, Dad's not there..." His voice breaks completely, dissolving into gasps that shake his whole body. "Fight against it, Emily! Please, please fight!"

The words pour out of him in a flood of desperation, years of anger and abandonment and love compressed into seconds. He drops to his knees in the wet filth, hands reaching toward his sister even though he can't touch her, Jonah's warning still echoing in the space between them. His shoulders shake with sobs that sound too large for his body, grief that's been held back by rage finally breaking free.

Clare tears away from Elias's grip with strength born of maternal desperation. Her nightgown swirls around her as she stumbles forward, arms outstretched toward Emily. "Emily!" The name rips from her throat raw and bleeding, a mother's last attempt to call her child back from an edge she's already crossed.

Jonah moves faster than his age should allow, his arm catching Clare around the waist with force that lifts her feet from the ground. His face has gone pale beneath the mud and water, jaw clenched with the effort of holding her back. "You can't reach her," he says through gritted teeth. "It'll take you too. He's using her, using what she thinks she wants, what she thinks she lost."

Clare's fingers claw at Jonah's arm, nails breaking against the wet fabric of his coat. Her legs kick, seeking purchase on the slippery floor, her whole body fighting against the restraint. The sounds coming from her throat aren't words anymore, just raw expression of loss, of failure, of love that can't save what it most wants to protect.

With a final wrench that tears something in Vincent's chest to witness, Clare breaks free. But instead of running toward Emily, she spins and flees toward the entrance, her wail echoing through the mill's breathing spaces. She disappears into the fog beyond the doorway, swallowed by gray nothing before anyone can react.

"Clare! Clare!" Angela's voice cracks with panic, her careful composure finally shattered completely. She starts toward the entrance, but Elias catches her arm, holds her back even as his own face shows the desire to follow, to flee this place where love becomes weapon.

Ryan tries to stand, tries to follow his mother, tries to do something, anything, but his legs won't hold him. Vincent catches him as he falls, arms wrapping around Ryan's chest, holding him back from whatever futile gesture he's about to make. Ryan fights against the grip, but it's weak, drained, the struggle of someone who knows they've already lost but can't stop trying.

Mira's hand finds Vincent's shoulder, her fingers pressing hard enough to hurt through his jacket. Her eyes close for a moment, her whole body trembling with effort Vincent doesn't understand until he realizes she's fighting something too, some pull toward the fungal mass that affects her differently, more directly. When her eyes open, they're focused on Emily with an intensity that speaks of recognition, of understanding something about what's happening that the others can't see.

The fungal mass pulses brighter, and Emily takes another step toward it. Her smile is serene, empty, the expression of someone who's found what they were looking for even if what they've found will destroy them. The shape in the fungus becomes clearer for a moment, features that might be familiar, might be remembered, might be completely fabricated from Emily's need to see them.

"He says it doesn't hurt," Emily says to no one, to everyone, to the breathing walls around them. "He says it's like going home."

The spores rise with each pulse now, thick enough to see without trying, drifting up toward the broken ceiling, out through the windows, carrying whatever they carry to the fog, to the town, to the world beyond. Vincent feels them settling on his skin, trying to find entry, trying to make him part of this communion that Emily has already joined.

The mill inhales, long and deep, and Vincent knows with absolute certainty that they're running out of time. Whatever Emily is becoming, whatever the fungus intends, it's almost complete. The transformation that started at Holt House, that continued through their time in Marrowick, is reaching its conclusion here in this breathing chamber.

Vincent tightens his grip on Ryan, feels Mira's presence beside him, and prepares for whatever comes next. Because Emily is still moving toward the fungal mass, still smiling that empty smile, and they're going to have to decide soon whether to follow her all the way in or accept that she's already gone.

The night tears at Clare's nightgown as she runs, fabric catching on branches she can't see, thorns she doesn't feel until they've already drawn blood. Her bare feet slam against wet pavement, then grass, then stone, the ground changing beneath her without warning while her lungs burn with each breath of thick air that tastes of salt and decay. She has no direction except away, no destination except not there, not that breathing chamber where her daughter walks toward something wearing her dead husband's face.

The ground tilts upward suddenly, nearly sending her sprawling. Her hands scrape against rough stone, finding purchase on what feels like steps, worn smooth by generations of feet seeking the same thing she seeks now. Sanctuary. Refuge. A place where the world still makes sense according to rules she understands. Through the gray nothing, a shape materializes above her, solid and angular against the formless fog. St. Dymphna's rises like a promise kept, its spire disappearing into darkness but its doors visible, real, reachable.

Clare's legs give out on the third step. She collapses forward, knees cracking against stone with pain that feels clean, honest, nothing like the creeping nothingness that saturates everything else in Marrowick. Her fingers find the edge of the door, pull at the heavy wood with strength that comes from somewhere deeper than muscle. The hinges groan, a sound that carries weight and age and persistence, and the door swings inward to release a wash of air that makes her gasp.

It smells of refreshed life and crisp citrus, of incense that clings to stone, of centuries of prayer soaked into the very foundations. The fog stops at the threshold like it's been forbidden entry, pooling outside but unable to cross into this space that remains uncorrupted. Clare pulls herself across that border on hands and knees, her nightgown leaving wet streaks on the floor, blood from her feet mixing with water to create patterns she doesn't look back to see.

Inside, the church breathes differently. Not the fungal pulse of the mill, not the wet wheeze of Holt House, but the quiet circulation of air through high spaces, the natural movement of atmosphere undisturbed by spores or corruption. Candles burn in straight lines along the walls, their flames vertical and steady, producing light that actually illuminates instead of just revealing shadows. The pews stand in their ordered rows, wood polished by touch rather than eaten by moisture, maintaining the shapes they were carved into rather than warping into new configurations.

Clare pushes herself upright, her body protesting every movement, and starts down the center aisle. Her feet leave bloody prints on the stone, but even these seem less like violation than offering, evidence of what she's endured to reach this place. The altar draws her forward, that focal point where suffering transforms into something else, where human pain meets divine possibility. She needs that transformation now, needs to believe that what's happening to Emily can be undone, reversed, redeemed.

Movement in the front pew stops her mid-step. A figure kneels there, dark hair falling forward, hands working through beads with practiced precision. Clare's mind refuses to process what she sees at first, insisting on impossibility, on hallucination, on anything except the truth that Mira kneels in the front pew when Clare knows, knows with absolute certainty, that she left Mira at the mill with Vincent and the others.

But there's no denying the evidence of her eyes. Mira's shoulders rise and fall with steady breathing. Her fingers move through the chaplet beads with deliberate care, each bead receiving its due attention before passing to the next. The soft click of wood against wood creates a rhythm that fills the church's silence, not disrupting but enriching it, adding another layer to the centuries of prayer that permeate these walls.

Clare approaches on unsteady legs, her mind trying to construct explanations that make sense. But sense has abandoned Marrowick, abandoned her life since the moment Emily first touched those pale blooms. She stops beside the pew, looking down at Mira's bowed head, at the Holy Face chaplet in her hands. Clare remembers noticing it years ago, lying on Mira's mother's dresser during a rare visit. The sight tugs at her, the memory sharp: a small, delicate thing, carried through dark times by a woman Clare barely knew.

Mira doesn't look up, doesn't acknowledge Clare's presence with words. Instead, she shifts slightly, creating space on the kneeler, an invitation that needs no explanation. Clare sinks down beside her, her knees finding the worn grooves in the wood where countless others have knelt before. The familiarity of the position, the muscle memory of genuflection, brings tears that she's been holding back since Emily walked into the fog.

Her voice emerges cracked and raw when she tries to speak the familiar prayers. The Latin comes in fragments at first, interrupted by gasps that might be sobs or might be the struggle to breathe air that finally feels clean. But Mira's voice continues beneath hers, steady as bedrock, maintaining the rhythm when Clare falters, carrying the prayer forward when grief makes words impossible.

———

The vast fungal bloom pulses with light that makes Vincent's eyes water, not from brightness but from confusion, from colors that shouldn't exist in any spectrum he knows. It rises before them like a living wall, its surface shifting between states, sometimes solid, sometimes permeable, always breathing with that deep rhythm that he feels deep within his chest. Emily stands at its base, her white nightdress now stained with patterns that mirror the mycelium networks spreading across the mill's walls, as if she's already becoming part of this vast organism.

The pull starts subtle, almost gentle. Not the violent wrenching Vincent expected but something worse, a slow leaching of concern that happens so gradually he doesn't notice until his fingers have already begun to loosen in Mira's grip. It's not that he stops caring about her, about Emily, about any of them. The caring simply grows thinner, more distant, like watching events through frosted glass. His hand relaxes without his permission, fingers beginning to slip from hers as the bloom's light washes over him in waves that feel almost warm, almost welcoming.

But Mira's hand tightens with unexpected force, her fingers locking between his with strength that surprises him. There's something else there too, a sensation he can't quite name, like her palm carries two sources of warmth instead of one. As if another hand presses through hers, reinforcing her grip, refusing to let him drift into the bloom's patient hunger. The doubled warmth spreads up his arm, pushing back against the emptying sensation, keeping him anchored to himself, to her, to the horror of what they're witnessing.

Ryan's voice cracks through the mill's breathing silence, thin and desperate, barely recognizable as the angry boy who kicked at puddles and slammed doors. "Emily." Her name emerges broken, split into syllables by sobs he can't control. "Em, please. Please look at me."

He steps forward, and the floor responds immediately, rippling outward from his feet in circles that disturb years of accumulated moisture and decay. Spores rise around his ankles in clouds that catch the bloom's sickly light, swirling up his legs, seeking entry through cloth, through skin, through any boundary they can breach. His boots sink slightly into floorboards gone soft as flesh, but he doesn't stop, doesn't hesitate, just continues toward his sister with arms outstretched.

Emily turns with unsettling fluidity, her head rotating before her body follows. For a moment, her eyes remain black and empty, reflecting the bloom's light without recognition. Then something shifts, flickers, like a candle flame fighting through wind. Her pupils contract suddenly, irises becoming visible again, brown and familiar and filled with terrible understanding.

"Ryan?" His name comes out small, confused, the voice of the sixteen-year-old girl who used to tease him about his music, who stole his fries at dinner, who existed before the fungus claimed her. Recognition floods her face, followed immediately by horror as she sees where he's standing, how close he's come to the bloom's reach.

She moves faster than she has in days, her hands connecting with Ryan's chest in a shove that carries surprising force. "No." The word emerges fierce and final as she pushes him backward, away from the bloom, away from her, away from the fate she's already accepted. Ryan stumbles, his boots slipping on the wet floor, arms windmilling as he falls backward into Vincent.

Vincent catches him, arms wrapping around Ryan's chest

as Jonah appears beside them with that sudden presence he has, moving through space like he belongs to it differently than others. The older man's face sets in lines of grim determination, water still dripping from his coat, creating pools on the floor. Without pause, without word, Jonah lunges forward toward Emily.

His hand clamps around Emily's wrist with the grip of someone who understands this might be the last chance, the final moment before she crosses a threshold from which there's no return. He pulls with his entire body, teeth bared with effort, cords standing out in his neck as he fights against not just Emily's resistance but the bloom's pull, the mill's will, the patient hunger of whatever waits within that pale mass.

The floor heaves in response, boards buckling upward as pale filaments burst through, rising like vines seeking sun. They wrap around Jonah's arms with deliberate purpose, not violent but insistent, tightening with each pulse of the bloom's light. More emerge from the walls, from the ceiling, converging on this point where human will contests something older, hungrier, more patient than any human emotion.

Within the bloom's translucent mass, a shape clarifies, features that suggest a face without quite achieving one. The static-man impression that haunts Vincent's nightmares, that builds itself from absences rather than presence. Jonah's eyes lock onto it with recognition that speaks of old knowledge, of patterns observed across years of watching Marrowick's slow consumption.

"Let her go." The words come out through gritted teeth, directed not at Emily but at the thing wearing the suggestion of her father's face, the thing that promises reunion while offering only dissolution.

———

In St. Dymphna's, the candles burn higher without wind to feed them, their flames stretching toward the vaulted ceiling as if drawn by invisible hands. Clare feels the heat bloom against her cheek, warming skin still cold from fog and fear. The chaplet beads click faster through Mira's fingers, though her voice maintains its steady cadence, each prayer precise and full despite the quickening rhythm. Their words layer over each other, not competing but weaving, Clare's desperate pleas threading through Mira's measured devotion to create something stronger than either alone.

In the mill, Mira's body trembles with an effort Vincent doesn't fully understand until he feels it through their joined hands. A second rhythm pulses beneath her natural heartbeat, steadier, deeper, as if another heart beats within her chest, reinforcing her own. She pulls him closer, her dark eyes finding his with fierce certainty that cuts through the bloom's patient dissolution.

"We stay." Her voice carries unexpected authority, not loud but dense with purpose. "We hold."

The words seem to create their own space, a pocket of resistance where the fungal pull slides past them like water around stone. Vincent feels it testing their boundaries, probing for weakness, for the crack where doubt might enter. But Mira's grip remains absolute, that doubled warmth in her palm spreading through him, creating a circuit of connection the bloom can't break.

Emily meets Jonah's eyes with perfect clarity, the fog of possession lifting for one terrible moment to reveal the girl underneath. "It's easier." The words emerge soft as exhale, carrying not defeat but a kind of exhausted acceptance. Her gaze shifts past him to where Mira stands with Vincent, and something like understanding passes between them. "I'll keep him from you. Please… don't follow."

The simplicity of it breaks something in the mill's atmosphere. Not dramatic declaration, not final goodbye, just quiet acknowledgment of a journey already begun. Jonah's grip loosens involuntarily, his fingers suddenly nerveless as Emily steps backward into the bloom's embrace. The fungal mass doesn't seize her, doesn't pull. She yields to it like entering sleep, her body relaxing into its pale light.

The transformation happens with terrible gentleness. Light folds around Emily like fabric, like water, like something between states. Her white dress seams with pale threads that might be mycelium or might be light itself, the boundaries between her and the bloom growing indistinct. Her form blurs at the edges first, feet and hands becoming suggestions rather than certainties, then working inward until only her face remains clear, eyes closed, expression peaceful.

Jonah makes one final wrenching attempt, throwing his whole body forward, hands grasping at Emily's disappearing form. His fingers pass through where her arm should be, finding only cool light that clings like cobweb. The filaments that wrapped his arms earlier return with purpose now, climbing his shoulders, his throat, no longer restraining but claiming. They pulse with the bloom's rhythm, and with each pulse, Jonah seems to grow lighter, less substantial, as if the fungus feeds on his very density.

His head turns toward Elias with effort that makes tendons stand out in his neck. Their eyes meet across the breathing space of the mill, and in Jonah's gaze Vincent sees not fear but apology. Sorry for not being strong enough. Sorry for failing where success might have been possible. Sorry for leaving Elias to witness another loss in this place that takes everything.

The filaments reach Jonah's jaw, his mouth, gentle as scarves but inexorable. He doesn't fight anymore, doesn't struggle, just maintains that look with Elias until the pale threads cover his eyes. Then the bloom draws him in with the same patient hunger that took Emily, his form dissolving into its mass like salt into water, leaving only the wet marks where he stood.

In the church, Clare's careful prayers fracture into a sob that echoes off stone walls. Her forehead presses against the altar rail hard enough to leave marks, her hands white-knuckled on the wood as grief tears through her in waves. But Mira's voice continues beneath the sound of breaking, maintaining the litany when Clare can't, carrying the prayer forward with determination.

The candles gutter suddenly, all of them at once, flames bending as if pressed by enormous wind. For a moment, the church plunges toward darkness, shadows rushing in from corners to claim the space. Clare gasps, her hands flying to her rosary, but before the darkness can complete its consumption, the flames return. Not just return but blaze, standing taller than before, straighter, burning with light that pushes the shadows back to their proper places.

The mill's light swells in response to something distant, something it recognizes as opposition. The bloom pulses brighter, trying to complete whatever work it began with Emily and Jonah, to spread its influence beyond these breathing walls. But there's resistance now, invisible but absolute, as if the prayers rising from St. Dymphna's create their own boundary, their own refusal to let the corruption spread unchecked.

The bloom's light dims like a lantern running out of oil, its pulse slowing, weakening, until the vast mass shudders once and begins its collapse. Not violent implosion but gradual surrender, the fungal tissues losing cohesion, releasing their hold on the mill's structure with soft tearing sounds that might be organic matter separating or might be resignation given voice. The air that tasted of ash and metal goes suddenly flat, thin, as if whatever charged it has withdrawn, leaving only ordinary atmosphere that burns Vincent's lungs with its mundane purity.

The rafters groan overhead, long beams that the fungus held in unnatural positions now remembering their weight, their age, their tendency toward falling. Dust and spores rain down in sheets, coating everything in pale powder that tastes of endings. Vincent pulls Mira against him, shielding her with his body as chunks of rotted wood begin to fall, striking the floor with wet impacts that send up clouds of dissolution.

The mycelium networks that webbed every surface lose their luminescence first, their pale threads going dark, then gray, then crumbling into ash that the mill's last breathing disperses. Without their support, boards that seemed solid reveal themselves as shells, eaten hollow from within, collapsing at the slightest pressure. The floor beneath them ripples, buckles, entire sections falling away into darkness below where the fungus retreated to die.

Ryan stands frozen where Emily disappeared, staring at the space that held his sister, that now holds only dimming light and drifting ash. His body refuses movement until Elias grabs him with both hands, shaking him once, hard, before dragging him toward the entrance. Ryan's legs move mechanically, without his participation, his eyes still fixed on that absence until the fog of falling debris obscures it completely.

"Move! Everyone move!" Angela's voice cuts through the collapse like a blade, sharp with urgency that brooks no hesitation. She stands in the doorway, one hand braced against the frame, the other beckoning frantically. Her counting has stopped entirely, replaced by this singular focus on escape, on survival, on getting them all out before the mill completes its transformation from structure to memory.

They stumble through the doorway in a tangle of limbs and desperation, Vincent's hand locked with Mira's, neither willing to release despite the difficulty it creates navigating the threshold. The fog outside feels different immediately, thinner, less oppressive, as if whatever gave it substance has begun to dissipate. They collapse on the wet ground, coughing, gasping, their lungs working to expel spores and dust and the taste of corrupted air.

Behind them, the mill continues its slow surrender. Not the dramatic crash of movie destructions but the patient folding of something whose time has passed. Beams lean into each other, walls bow inward, the whole structure sagging like an exhausted animal finally allowed to rest. Through the fog, Vincent watches its silhouette change, become smaller, less defined, until it's just another shadow in Marrowick's gray morning.

In St. Dymphna's, the prayer ebbs like tide pulling back from shore. Clare's sobs have gentled to quiet weeping, her body trembling with exhaustion that goes beyond physical, that touches something fundamental in her soul as a mother. Mira's hand finds Clare's shoulder, grip firm but gentle, offering comfort that transcends words. The chaplet lies warm between them, beads still carrying the heat of desperate handling.

When Clare looks up, her eyes swollen and red, she finds Mira watching her with expression that carries too much understanding for someone so young. They study each other in the candles' steady light, and Clare sees something remarkable in Mira's gaze.

"Ryan needs you." Mira's words come soft but certain, not suggestion but gentle command. "They all need you now."

Clare rises on unsteady legs, her hand finding Mira's one last time, squeezing with gratitude that has no adequate expression. She doesn't question how Mira knows, doesn't ask how she'll follow, just accepts this strange gift of presence that helped hold the darkness back, if only for a moment, if only enough to matter.

The survivors meet on the path back to town, two groups converging as if drawn by invisible threads. Vincent sees Clare first, her nightgown filthy and torn, her feet bleeding, but her face carrying something that wasn't there before. Not peace exactly, but acceptance, the kind that comes after fighting the unfightable and surviving, if not winning.

Mira stands beside Vincent, ash dusting her dark hair, her eyes rimmed with exhaustion but steady. When Clare sees her, something passes between them, recognition of shared experience that defies logical explanation. They don't speak of it, don't need to. Some truths exist better in silence, in the spaces between what can be said.

Above them, the fog lifts higher than they've seen since arriving in Marrowick. Not gone, not defeated, but retreating, revealing sky that carries the suggestion of sun, the promise that somewhere beyond this gray, light still exists. They stand together on the wet path, diminished by loss but not broken, while morning tries to remember what it means to dawn.

CHAPTER
NINETEEN

The blue overhead feels stark after weeks of gray, a violation of the natural order Vincent's body has accepted. He stands on Holt House's porch, blinking at sky that shouldn't exist, not here, not after everything. The fog lifted during Emily's funeral, pulling back like a tide finally remembering its rhythm, leaving Marrowick exposed beneath light that makes everything look smaller, more ordinary, more broken. Vincent's lungs work against air that tastes of nothing, just oxygen and salt, the absence of spores and moisture so notable his throat feels raw from breathing clean.

The morning carries sounds that weren't there before. Gulls crying with actual bird voices, not the hollow recordings they'd become. Wind moving through trees without that wet whisper of fungal growth. His footsteps on the porch boards ring clear, no longer muffled by the thick atmosphere that pressed against everything. The normalcy of it sits heavy in his chest, a weight that shouldn't exist from something as simple as sunshine breaking through clouds.

Vincent descends the steps, his shoes finding ground that's still damp but firming, no longer the soft corruption that threatened to swallow every step. The road stretches before him, visible for the first time since they arrived, leading toward town and to where Bridgeport Mill once stood. He walks without destination, just needing movement, needing to feel his body work against something that isn't dissolution.

The mill reveals itself gradually as he rounds the bend, or what remains of it. The structure has completed its collapse, no longer the breathing monument to corruption but a heap of wet timber and twisted metal. Barbed wire circles the ruins, metal thorns against the dark wood, keeping the curious at safe distance from boards that might still harbor spores, from spaces that might still remember what grew there. Smoke rises from one corner where someone tried to burn the worst of it, the fire struggling against wood too saturated to properly combust.

Vincent stops at the mill's edge, studying the absence of what terrorized them. The mill is just debris now, dangerous only in the ordinary way of collapsed buildings, full of nails and splinters and unstable beams. No pale light pulses from within. No breathing disturbs the morning. Emily walked into that darkness and never walked out, and now even the darkness is gone, leaving just hazard and memory.

The walk back to Holt House takes longer, his feet dragging against gravel that's developing proper rivulets again, no longer sealed by fungal growth. The house waits unchanged on the outside, its windows reflecting sky instead of gray nothing, but Vincent knows the difference lives inside, in the spaces between people who've lost too much to ever properly heal.

The kitchen receives him with its familiar dimensions, though the air moves differently now, no longer thick with moisture that wouldn't dissipate. Clare sits at the table where she's been since dawn, since before dawn, since they came back from the cemetery where they put Emily's absence in the ground. Her nightgown has been replaced by a black dress that hangs loose on her frame, as if she's shrunk in the days since the mill fell. The rosary beads press deep into her palm, leaving marks that might be permanent, might never fade. Her lips don't move in prayer, don't move at all, just remain slightly parted as if she started to speak Emily's name and forgot how to finish.

Angela hovers near the counter, her hands working through the motion of preparing coffee like a distraction. Pour water, add grounds, wait for percolation, pour into white ceramic cups. Three cups sit cooling on the table, films forming on their surfaces, while Angela prepares a fourth with the same careful attention. Elias picks one up and sips from it. His eyes meet hers with a comforting soft smile. Her counting has stopped, replaced by this desperate desire to serve and please, as if keeping her hands busy might prevent her from thinking about the girl who won't drink coffee again, about the empty chair that used to hold Emily's restless energy.

Through the window, Vincent sees Ryan on the porch steps, his body a rigid line against the morning light. He faces the road toward the mill, toward where his sister disappeared into fungal embrace, and his stillness carries the weight of waiting. Not hope exactly, but inability to accept finality, to stop watching for a figure in white to emerge from distance and explain that it was all mistake, all nightmare, all something other than Emily choosing dissolution over existence.

The stairs creak overhead, Elias moving through rooms with careful steps that avoid the boards that groan loudest. Vincent tracks his movement by sound: the zip of luggage closing, the soft thud of bags being set by doors, the pause outside Emily's room before continuing past without entering. When Elias appears in the kitchen doorway, his suit hangs crooked on his frame, jacket and pants that fit perfectly a week ago now looking borrowed, like he's wearing someone else's clothes. His hands tremble as he adjusts his cuffs, a gesture toward normalcy that fails when his fingers won't stop shaking.

"We should leave before lunch tomorrow," Elias says to the room, to no one, his voice thin and careful. "It's a long drive. I'd like to get to Missoula before sundown."

No one responds. Clare's fingers tighten on the rosary. Angela pours another cup of coffee. Through the window, Ryan remains motionless on the steps.

Vincent thinks of Jonah Kells, whose absence creates its own presence in the house. No one speaks his name, but occasionally eyes drift toward the windows, toward the fields where he might have walked, toward the spaces he occupied with his gruff wisdom and terrible knowledge. The fungus took him along with Emily, pulled him into its mass, dissolved him into nothing. No body to bury, no grave to visit, just absence that tastes of failure and old coats that dripped with prophecy.

The afternoon sun makes everything too sharp, too defined, after weeks of living in gray suggestion. Vincent sits beside Mira in the yard, their backs against the old oak that somehow survived the fungal corruption, its bark rough and real and wonderfully ordinary beneath his palms. The grass around them has begun to dry, no longer the perpetual wetness that soaked through everything, though patches of darker green mark where the moisture lingered longest, where the earth still remembers being drowned.

The clean air feels alien in his lungs, too thin, too simple. His body keeps expecting resistance, keeps preparing for the thick taste of spores and decay, finding only salt and grass and the faint sweetness of flowers that might actually be flowers instead of fungal blooms. Beside him, Mira breathes with the same careful rhythm, as if they're both learning how to exist in atmosphere that doesn't want to consume them.

Their hands find each other without discussion, fingers interlocking with the desperate familiarity they developed in the mill, in the fog, in all the spaces where touch became anchor against dissolution. The silence stretches between them, not comfortable but bearable only because of this connection, because skin against skin confirms they both survived, both remain, both exist in this afternoon that shouldn't feel so strange but does.

Mira's face carries exhaustion in every line, shadows beneath her eyes that speak of nights without sleep, of vigils held in places that might or might not have been physical. Her dark hair falls loose around her shoulders, no longer damp with fog but dry and catching light in ways that make her look older and younger simultaneously, like she's aged years in days but also returned to something more essentially herself.

Vincent watches a cloud drift across the sky, white and temporary and beautifully meaningless, before finding words for what he needs to ask. "At St. Dymphna's." The church's name feels heavy on his tongue, weighted with significance he doesn't fully understand. "When Clare went there. You were with her."

Mira's fingers don't tighten in his, don't pull away, just maintain their steady pressure. She watches the same cloud, or maybe something beyond it, her dark eyes tracking movement Vincent can't perceive. The silence that follows isn't avoidance but consideration, the careful space of someone deciding how much truth to share.

"But you were also with me," Vincent continues when she doesn't respond, the words coming out flat, factual, refusing to make it accusation or demand. "At the mill. Your hand in mine. I felt you there, know you were there. But Clare saw you at the church. Prayed with you."

The oak creaks above them, branches moving in wind that feels too normal, too much like wind should feel instead of the directed currents that carried fog and worse. A leaf falls, brown and ordinary, landing on Mira's knee. She picks it up, turns it between her fingers, studying its veins and edges like they might contain answers.

"I don't know how." The words emerge simple, without defensiveness or elaborate explanation. Mira continues turning the leaf, her voice maintaining that steady tone she uses when discussing things that exist beyond normal understanding. "It's just something that happens sometimes. I'm here, but I'm also there. Not choosing it, not controlling it. Just being in two places when one isn't enough."

Vincent accepts this without question, without pressing for logic that doesn't exist. After everything they've witnessed, Mira's bilocation feels almost mundane, just another impossible thing in a world that's revealed itself full of impossibilities. He thinks of her hand in his at the mill, that doubled warmth he felt, like someone else's presence reinforcing hers. Maybe she's never fully in one place, always partially elsewhere, partially everywhere.

"During the funeral." Vincent shifts the conversation toward safer ground, though nothing feels truly safe anymore. "The people moved differently. Like they remembered how to walk without being pulled toward something."

Mira nods, the leaf still turning in her fingers. "They stood where they wanted to stand. Looked where they wanted to look. Mrs. Morrison cried actual tears instead of just water running from her eyes." Her voice carries quiet observation, noting the return of humanity to Marrowick's infected population. "The children fidgeted during the service. Small rebellions, but real ones."

Vincent remembers the cemetery, the way people arranged themselves by choice rather than compulsion, the fog pulling back as they lowered Emily's empty coffin into the ground. The priest's voice carrying clear across the gathering, not muffled or swallowed but reaching ears that could actually hear. Ryan standing at the grave's edge, his hands fisted at his sides but his body his own, not tilting toward the mill, not drawn by invisible threads.

"The town feels different," Vincent says, though different doesn't capture the hollow quality of Marrowick now. "Like something got scooped out and hasn't been refilled yet."

"Defeated," Mira offers, and the word settles between them with perfect accuracy. Not destroyed but defeated, still standing but without whatever animating force made it more than buildings and streets. The fungus took something from Marrowick when it died, some essential quality that might have been corrupted but was still vital, still part of what made the town exist as more than geography.

They sit in silence as afternoon deepens, their hands still linked, watching shadows grow longer across the yard. Somewhere in the house, Clare maintains her vigil at the table. Ryan watches the road. Elias packs and repacks bags that are already ready as Angela helps him. And here in the yard, Vincent and Mira exist in the strange peace of aftermath, of survival that doesn't feel like victory, of continuing when continuation itself becomes the only available form of resistance.

The first stars emerge tentative as memory, points of light that Vincent hasn't seen since arriving in Marrowick. They appear one by one through the clearing sky, faint punctures in deepening blue that prove something exists beyond the fog's former domain. The evening air carries a chill that feels honest, natural cold instead of the wet suffocation they've grown accustomed to, making Vincent pull his jacket closer though the discomfort feels almost welcome, evidence of a world returning to its proper state.

Clare pushes through the front door with movements that suggest enormous effort, as if the simple act of standing requires all her remaining strength. She stops at the porch's edge, her black dress hanging shapeless in the still air, and tilts her face toward the emerging stars. Her mouth opens, closes, opens again, and finally releases a single word that barely disturbs the quiet: "Emily."

The name hangs between earth and sky, a test more than a call, as if Clare needs to confirm the word still has meaning, still refers to something that once existed even if it exists no longer. Vincent watches her lips shape the syllables again, silent this time, practicing the geometry of a name that belongs to absence now, to the space where a daughter used to be.

Ryan's silhouette hasn't moved from the porch steps since afternoon, his body rigid as sculpture against the fading light. His mother's whisper doesn't turn his head, doesn't shift his attention from the road that leads toward the mill's wreckage. He might not have heard, or might be choosing not to hear, maintaining his vigil for a return that everyone knows won't come but no one has the cruelty to tell him to abandon.

Vincent and Mira remain in their spot by the oak, close enough to witness but maintaining the distance grief requires. Their joined hands rest on the grass between them, fingers still interlocked but loosely now, the desperate grip of survival relaxing into something gentler. They exist in the periphery of the family's sorrow, present but unobtrusive, like furniture that's necessary but shouldn't draw attention.

"Tomorrow," Mira says, the word soft enough it might be meant only for herself. But Vincent hears it, understands the weight it carries. Tomorrow they leave Marrowick. Soon they return to Duswood. Tomorrow they try to resume lives that will never quite fit the same way, like clothes that have been stretched by wearing and can't return to their original shape.

"The car's ready." Vincent's response lacks energy, states fact without enthusiasm or dread. "Elias arranged everything." The hotel reservations, the route, the long drive back to Michigan through states that won't understand what they've survived, what they've lost, what they've prevented or failed to prevent.

Mira's thumb moves against his hand, a gesture that might be agreement or might be acknowledgment that words have been spoken, conversation attempted, even if neither of them has the strength for more. They've talked around leaving all day without discussing what it means, without acknowledging that Marrowick will continue existing after they're gone, hollowed and defeated but still present, still marking the place where Emily and Jonah disappeared into something larger and hungrier than human understanding.

"Clare says she wants us to stay," Mira says, though want might be the wrong word for how Clare clings to the routines of her house and the last place she saw her daughter, even if what she saw wasn't really Emily anymore. "But Elias says we can't. Says it's time."

Time for what, Vincent doesn't ask. Time to accept. Time to move forward. Time to pretend that life continues after fundamental laws have been broken, after learning that love can be weaponized, that connection can become consumption, that the people you fail to save don't always die but sometimes choose their own dissolution.

Through the front window, yellow light spills onto the porch, warm and ordinary. Inside, Vincent can see the dining room table, cleared of Emily's perfectly folded linens, holding nothing now but a single candle Clare lit after the funeral. The flame wavers in drafts that find their way through old walls, bending far to one side, nearly guttering, before straightening again with stubborn persistence.

The candle burns lower as they watch, wax pooling at its base, but the flame itself refuses extinction. It flickers, dims, seems about to die, then finds new strength from somewhere, rising higher, burning steadier. Not the aggressive blaze of St. Dymphna's candles fighting back darkness, just ordinary fire doing what fire does, consuming fuel, producing light, marking time's passage with patient certainty.

The stars multiply overhead, filling the sky with their

distant light, and Vincent thinks about distance, about the space between stars, between people, between who they were before Marrowick and who they'll be after. The evening deepens around them, cold and clear and empty of fog, and tomorrow feels both too close and impossibly far away, a destination they'll reach without traveling, a return to lives that wait for them like clothes that no longer fit, like homes that will never quite feel like shelter again.

COMING SOON: ROOT SLEEP (BOOK 3)

Root Sleep - As of November 2025, Root Sleep is in post-production. Tentative release in January 2026. Look for updates on Instagram and in my newsletter.

ABOUT THE AUTHOR

N.B. Cross writes quiet horror and dark fiction rooted in small towns, haunted landscapes, and the shadows that live between memory and grief. His short story collection, *Static Between the Trees*, introduced readers to his blend of atmosphere and unease. His first novel, Hollow Stone, began the story of Duswood, a small town haunted by grief and silence. Quiet Bloom is the second book in the Stonebound Trilogy, deepening the mystery as the horror spreads to the fog-choked coast of Marrowick.

Learn more at nbcrossauthor.com and join the Signals from the Static newsletter for behind-the-scenes notes, new stories, and early updates.

Follow at instagram.com/n.b.cross/

ALSO BY N.B. CROSS

Static Between the Trees (short story collection)

Hollow Stone (Stonebound Book 1)